*Dylan walked into his room, only to find
steam billowing from the bathroom*

He turned the corner to investigate...and discovered a woman he'd never seen in his entire life taking a shower, the curtain thrown all the way open.

Dylan's mouth went dry.

Mere feet away from him, a very tall, very...well-developed woman stood under the oscillating spray. Water clung to rounded breasts, then cascaded over dusky, erect nipples to slide down a wonderfully toned stomach. He swallowed hard, powerless to stop his gaze from venturing farther.

He dug his fingers into his palms, vaguely aware of the way they suddenly itched. He was suddenly tempted to join her and explore every inch of flawless skin the water touched. Finally, sanity set back in and he brought his gaze up to her face.

She was watching him.

"Imagine that. My own personal Peeping Tom." A smile flittered across her lips. "You don't mind locking the door on the way out, do you, Tom?" Her voice fell to a husky murmur. "I mean, after you've looked your fill, that is..."

Blaze™

Dear Reader,

Our favorite books have always been ones that focus on emotionally mature, innately sexy and wonderfully bold characters who test the boundaries both in and out of the bedroom. That's why we jumped at the chance to write for the new Blaze series. And soon afterward, we found our characters, Dylan and Grace, jumping all over each other!

In *You Sexy Thing!*, sex therapist Dylan Fairbanks has faced his share of opponents, but Dr. Grace Mattias gets him hot under the collar—and other places—when he's pitted against her time and again while on a promotional book tour. High on flirting, provocative behavior and obeying the spark of attraction, Grace's beliefs conflict with Dylan's more traditional ideology that unanimity between the brain and the body is the key to sexual health. Only, his own brain goes on a permanent sabbatical when Grace decides to try out her theories on *him*....

We hope you enjoy Dylan and Grace's sizzling journey. And we'd love to hear what you think of our first Blaze novel. Write to us at P.O. Box 12271, Toledo, OH 43612, or visit us on the Web at www.toricarrington.com. And be sure to check out www.tryblaze.com.

Happy (and hot) reading,

Lori & Tony Karayianni aka *Tori Carrington*

Books by Tori Carrington

HARLEQUIN TEMPTATION
740—LICENSE TO THRILL
776—THE P.I. WHO LOVED HER
789—FOR HER EYES ONLY
823—YOU ONLY LOVE ONCE
837—NEVER SAY NEVER AGAIN

YOU SEXY THING!

Tori Carrington

HARLEQUIN®

TORONTO • NEW YORK • LONDON
AMSTERDAM • PARIS • SYDNEY • HAMBURG
STOCKHOLM • ATHENS • TOKYO • MILAN • MADRID
PRAGUE • WARSAW • BUDAPEST • AUCKLAND

This one's for all of you who like your books hot!
And for our editor, Brenda Chin, and senior editor and
editorial coordinator, Birgit Davis-Todd. Continued thanks
for giving us the perfect forum to write the books we love.
And for encouraging us to surprise even ourselves!

ISBN 0-373-79019-8

YOU SEXY THING!

1

New York City

"GEE, THANKS, BUD, you're a regular Donald Trump."

Dylan Fairbanks folded back the magazine he was reading and frowned at the hygienically challenged cabby. Did that mean he had tipped the driver too much or too little? Hard to tell. That was the problem with New Yorkers. Their sarcasm cut both ways. He shrugged, deciding a two-dollar tip was more than generous. Especially considering that they'd left his stomach—and his notes for today's appearance—somewhere on the Queensboro Bridge. The autumn breeze had snatched the notes out of his hand and carried them through the half-open window. Unfortunately, the breeze had left behind the stench he'd been trying to clear out in the first place.

A valet opened the door and Dylan climbed out, looking over the fifth hotel he was scheduled to stay at in as many days. It was certainly larger than the one he'd stayed at in Harrisburg, Pennsylvania, the night before. Good. He could use the basic creature comforts like a laptop connection and virtual anonymity to catch up on his correspondence and see to work that he'd fallen criminally behind on since leaving San Francisco last week.

But first he had to find his publisher's PR rep, Tanja Berry. She had disappeared sometime last night with little more than a brief note saying she'd meet him here this morning. He scanned the people bustling in and out of the revolving brass-framed door, wondering exactly when she had planned to meet him. Since no one sported her purple-tipped short black hair, he guessed it wasn't now.

Where was she? He glanced at his watch. She had better show up soon or else they'd never make it to the radio station in time for his interview.

"Dr. Fairbanks?"

Dylan freed his overstuffed suitcase from the revolving monster that doubled as a door then grimaced at a uniformed young man with bad acne. "It depends on what you want."

The guy looked puzzled, Dylan's halfhearted attempt at humor skimming right over his head.

He sighed. "Yeah, that would be me." A prospect that usually left him pretty satisfied with himself and his life, but right now made him want to trade his doctorate for a teamsters membership card.

"You're already checked in, sir." The concierge-in-training handed him a room key, then wrestled him for his one suitcase. "It's Room 1715. Miss, um, Berry suggested you go on up. She's already there."

"Very good." He tugged on the handle of his suitcase, battling the youth for control. "And I can see to this. Thank you." He finally gained possession and nearly fell over backward for his effort.

Miss Berry had likely already given the kid a generous tip for scouting him out. He wasn't about to pay him any more. He brushed away the pang of guilt and told himself he was being savvy. But the simple truth was that he had grown up with very little money of his own, and now that he had money, he was hesitant to part ways with it. You never knew what the future held. And over the course of the promotional tour he was coming to think he was in the wrong business. He was convinced hotel employees made more per annum than he did. He headed for the glass-encased elevators. This was one less entry he'd have to make on his expense sheet. And that was always a plus.

Dylan punched the up button next to the elevators and stood back to wait. And wait. And wait. He ran his hand over his face. Only five days into his three-week promotional book tour and he wanted to change his name and move to someplace where nobody knew his name. Where no one called him "the world's greatest sex expert." Where people didn't know he'd written a book, much less two—the latest one bearing the misleading title *Reaching New Heights—Advice on How to Obtain Ultimate Sexual Pleasure.* Having men sidle up to him at book signings to ask what tips he could give them to drive the opposite sex wild—wink-wink—had lost its patina long ago. And so had the women of all ages and socioeconomic backgrounds who slipped him hotel room keys that he immediately threw into the wastebasket he always kept under the signing table.

If his "fans" had bothered to look beyond the racy cover copy, they would have already had the answers to their bawdy questions. No, he couldn't give anyone tips on how to drive women wild. However, if they were looking to satisfy their spouses, then maybe he could give them advice. As for the hotel keys…well, anyone who'd actually read his bio would know that he had been celibate by choice since his divorce four years ago. Any woman who openly propositioned him, no matter how lovely or innocent looking, immediately forfeited a spot on his very short list of prospects for "the next and last Mrs. Fairbanks." In fact, the list was so short it held only one person.

Speaking of which…

He released the handle of his suitcase then fumbled in his inside jacket pocket for his cell phone. A glance at his watch told him it was not only too early to reach Diana at work on the West Coast, but that he was running seriously late. If this damn elevator—

Ding.

Sighing, he slipped his cell phone back into his pocket and stepped inside the empty, moving fishbowl that served as an elevator. Staring at the unmarked plastic key, he tried to remember the room number. Seventeen-fifteen. He punched the button for the seventeenth floor, only vaguely noticing that the button for the sixteenth was already lit though the elevator was empty. He stepped to the glass and watched as the lobby grew farther and farther away. People milled around the large open area as he grasped his cell phone again. He hit a pre-programmed number then glanced at the magazine he still held, listening to the line ring.

Sex Doctor Grace Mattias Leads the Way into a Brave New Sexual Frontier.

Dylan stared at the headline. " 'Brave new sexual frontier,' my narrow behind." It looked like she was recycling the same old line of BS carried over from the sixties. The left sidebar held a cartoon of a redhead in a tight, short dress holding condoms in one hand, a monstrous vibrator in her other. His gaze drifted to the other page. The caricature there—presumably of him—showed a dark-haired guy holding his hands in front of his crotch with a horrified expression on his face like some male virgin from the Regency period. What the caricature didn't say, the headline did. Doctor Fairbanks Declares Monogamous Marriage Only Path to Sexual Fulfillment.

If he had known the features editor had planned to pit him against someone else, much less this apparently graceless Grace Mattias, he never would have agreed to the interview. Sure, his message was there. Couched between below-the-belt jabs at his conservatism and purposely provocative counterpoints provided by Mattias. Not exactly his most stellar appearance.

The line stopped ringing. "Hello—"

"Diana. I'm glad I caught you. I've—"

"You've reached the residence of Diana Evans..."

Dylan stared at the phone then grimaced. He'd gotten her answering machine enough times in the past two days, he should have been ready for the deceptive pause between Diana's greeting and her regrets. But he'd been fooled every time. Which made him feel like an even bigger fool.

Pressing the disconnect key, he distantly wondered where she was so early in the morning. It was only five in the morning in San Francisco. Much too early to have left for her job as junior partner at Coulter, Connor and Caplain, Attorneys-at-Law. He'd been hoping to make contact with her to share the decision he'd made before leaving for his trip. Well, not *share* it share it. He wanted to arrange for her to meet him in Miami later next week. It was late enough in the year for the north to be chilly and he'd thought balmy Florida would be the perfect place for him to propose to her.

He frowned, looking down at his naked ring finger. Sometimes he swore he could still make out the tan line where his last wedding ring had been. His imagination, of course. It had to be, because he hadn't worn the ring for four years. And then it had only been for a meager four months.

Well, okay, maybe he'd kept it on for a year. He'd been so shocked when Julie had filed divorce papers he hadn't thought to take the blasted thing off for at least eight months. It had taken his mother's threat to sandblast the sucker off in his sleep to make him twist the simple gold band down the length of his finger. Of course his mother, Sharon—who preferred to be called Moonbeam—had objected to the visual symbol of possession—even during the short time he and Julie had been married. She'd had her own wedding rings melted down to a charm in the shape of an eagle over thirty years ago, shortly after she and his father had married. She wore it on a clinking bracelet that bore other mutilated remnants of what she called her "formal, materialistic life."

Dylan didn't even want to think about what his father had done with his ring. Especially since his latest interest included body piercings.

Thirty-six years of marriage and his parents still acted like flower children left over from some long-forgotten era. Hell, he hadn't even introduced Diana to them yet. A niggling part of him still thought his parents had played a role in Julie's sudden defection. It was awfully coincidental that five days after he and Julie had gone for an overnight visit to El Rancho, his parents' communelike spread in northern California, she'd packed her bags and left.

He absently rubbed the back of his neck. He couldn't really

blame his parents for what had clearly been his fault. No
matter how tempting. Or how easy. He and he alone had been
responsible for that fiasco. He'd let his libido dictate a lifetime
decision, one that was better made over time. Like the amount
of time he'd taken to develop his relationship with Diana.

Sure, he'd known the moment he met Diana sixteen months
ago that she was the perfect matrimonial choice. For one
thing, she was the complete opposite of Julie. In place of
Julie's wild brunette good looks Diana was sleekly blond.
Where Julie had preferred tight-fitting primary colors, Diana
chose loose-fitting earth tones. Where Julie had wanted to run
off and get married in Vegas within hours of their first meeting, Diana seemed to prefer to allow him to take his time to
make decisions, never breathing a word about matrimony unless he broached the subject.

Dylan straightened. This time when he uttered the words
"till death do us part," he intended to see them through to
the utter end.

Of course it would help if he could actually get Diana on
the line.

The elevator doors behind him finally slid open. Grasping
the handle of his suitcase, he exited, then followed the arrows
toward room 1715…no, 1615. There. He slid his card key in,
waited for the red light to turn green, then turned the handle.
Nothing.

Damn. What else could possibly go wrong on this trip?

He tried again more slowly. Then again, more rapidly. The
door refused to give.

He stepped back in exasperation. The bellboy obviously
had given him the wrong card.

He stared down the long hall that would take him back to
the elevator, then down at his watch. He was really running
late. The faint sound of Latino music caught his attention. He
spotted a maid's cart a couple of doors down. Without thinking twice, he started toward it, reaching for the cash in his
pocket. He wondered how much it would take to get the maid
to let him into his own room.

Surprisingly, it didn't take much doing. The young woman opened the door for him, then actually held her hand up and said something in Spanish. She walked away without taking his money.

Dylan slowly tucked the cash back into his pocket. *I'll be damned.* Maybe his day was starting to look up.

He stepped into the room to find steam billowing from the bathroom on his left. Probably as-immodest-as-they-came Tanja was catching a quick shower before the interview. He turned the corner, intent on knocking on the door and reminding her of the time, only to find the door wide-open. And a woman he'd never seen in his entire life taking a shower, the curtain thrown all the way open.

Dylan went completely, utterly, speechlessly still.

Mere feet away from him, a very…tall…very…well-developed woman stood under the oscillating spray. Water clung to perfectly rounded breasts then cascaded over dusky, erect nipples, to slide down a wonderfully toned stomach. He swallowed hard, powerless to stop his gaze from venturing even further. Crystalline droplets clung to the red-gold, curly thatch of hair between her slender thighs.

Dylan dug his fingers into his palms, vaguely aware of the way they suddenly itched. To his surprise, he found himself jealous of the water. He wanted to be the one to explore every inch of flawless skin the water touched.

His mind finally kicking back into gear, he brought his gaze up to her face.

She was watching him.

"Imagine that. My own personal Peeping Tom." A smile flitted across her lips. "You don't mind locking the door on your way back out, do you, Tom? I mean, after you've looked your fill."

Dylan felt his skin grow hotter than the steam coating him. "I can't believe… I have no idea… I am so very sorry. I must have the wrong room."

He somehow backtracked his way to the hall, his feet moving though he didn't recall sending them the order to do just that. He stood staring at the room that looked like any other as the automatic locking door slowly began closing. What in the hell had just happened? A scant second before the door could close completely, he stuck a hand out to stop it, then reached in to tug his suitcase out.

He collapsed against the door and closed his eyes, dragging in deep breaths to even out the hammering of his heartbeat.

He supposed this was the way kids felt after they walked in on their parents having sex for the first time.

He groaned at the comparison, then moved away from the door, as if just touching it was somehow…immoral.

He'd made an honest mistake. That's all. He'd gotten into the elevator. Got distracted thinking about the lack of sex in his life. He swallowed again. No, no, the limbo status of his life. Then got out on the floor that had already been pressed before he even entered the damn thing.

He'd never been so embarrassed…so humiliated in his entire life.

Well, okay, there was that one incident when he was twelve when his mother had stripped him of his swim trunks in the pool, trying to teach him the finer points of nudism. But this ranked a very, very close second.

GRACIE MATTIAS TUCKED a thick white towel around her body then padded quickly toward the door. A cautious glance around and down the hall outside told her that her uninvited guest was long gone.

She closed the door then stared at the locks. There was the automatic one. The double bolt. The security chain. One by one she locked and checked all of them, not surprised that her fingers were trembling. It wasn't every day that one got surprised in the shower like that. She realized the logic of her statement, and the unlikely chance that it would happen again in this lifetime, then sighed and undid all the locks again. She forced herself to turn and stalk into the living area of the sumptuous suite. She refused to live her life in fear of what might happen. Or spend every spare moment looking over her shoulder for lurking degenerates. Or check the back seat every time she got into her car. For heaven's sake, she counseled people on how to overcome such emotional fears. She couldn't begin to cater to them herself.

She swiveled on her heel, then secured every damn lock again.

There was fearless and there was stupid. And no matter how adorably dumbfounded the man was who had turned her normal shower experience into something to remember, the simple fact was she didn't know him from Jack the Ripper.

She stepped back into the living area, picked up the phone and dialed a room number.

"Very funny, Rick," she said when her personal assistant answered. Suddenly she wondered why he had a room three floors away from her. Shouldn't he be next door? Ready to protect her honor should some Peeping Tom burst into her room for an eyeful while she was in the shower?

She grimaced. Give her a minute and her subconscious would recreate the infamous shower scene from *Psycho*. She really needed to get a grip.

Something thudded on the other end of the line. "What's funny?" he said.

Gracie sank into the king-size mattress and switched the receiver to her other ear. She'd chosen her assistant for his organizational skills, not for his sense of humor. It didn't hurt that he was five years younger than she was and could double for Leonardo DiCaprio. Of course she'd have to nip his comedic tendencies in the bud right now if she was to remain sane during the next two weeks of her promotional tour. "I know I said I was getting bored with this trip. But did you have to send me a Peeping Tom to liven things up? Certainly even you are more imaginative than that."

Rick's long-suffering sigh sounded over the line. "Grace, what are you blathering on about now? Peeping Tom? You're sixteen floors up. Unless you're talking about someone looking at you through binoculars from the building across the street—"

"I'm talking about the guy who just walked into my room while I was taking a shower."

"Aah."

"So you did have something to do with it," she said with relief, picking up a copy of her book, which lay on the bed next to her.

"Nope."

"Rick, I'm going to hang up now."

"I think you're losing it, Dr. Mattias."

"You're just catching on now? Rick, I lost it way back when you were still calling your penis a pee-pee."

His laugh tickled her ear. "You know, this sex-talk stuff is taking some getting used to."

"This from someone who hears it every day. Anyway, we're not anywhere near indulging in sex talk, Rick. I merely called an important part of your anatomy by its proper name. I could ask you what you call it." Grace fanned her thumb against the three hundred and some pages of her hardcover book. Sometimes it was difficult to believe that she had had the discipline to sit down and write such a tome on human sexuality. Other times, she remembered every single word in there and flushed, horrified that she'd actually said one thing or another.

As long as the media never found out she was a fraud.

Well, she wasn't really a fraud. Exactly. It was just that all of her advice was based on 812 case studies rather than personal experience. Which was as it should be. Still, she couldn't help thinking that putting her theories into practice would have allowed her a more…intimate insight into what she was suggesting others do with their love lives.

She flipped the book over to gaze at the back of the dust jacket. She hadn't wanted to include a picture of herself. But there one was. Funny, the woman smiling into the camera appeared *very* sexually experienced.

She tossed the book onto the floor then curled her toes around the edges.

Another muffled sound filtered through the telephone line,

reminding her that she was still talking to her assistant. "Rick, what are you doing?"

"Would you believe me if I said your Peeping Tom just paid me a visit?"

"Nope."

"Didn't think so." He chuckled, though somehow Grace got the distinct impression it wasn't meant for her.

Crossing her legs, she switched the receiver to her other ear. "Are you messing around on company time, Rick?" she asked curiously.

She realized she knew very little about her assistant's private life. Not that she wanted to, mind you. But it suddenly struck her as odd that he would have one. And so soon after their arrival in New York.

She glanced over her shoulder, toward the monumental view out her window, and wondered what life would be like if she had someone in her room with her right now. Preferably a tall, dark and sexy someone who could fool around with her while she was on the phone. Take a long, breathtaking walk with through Central Park. Go see a Broadway play with. Someone to sip cappuccino with at one of those cozy coffeehouses all over the place.

A shiver shimmied down her spine, reminding her just how long it was since she'd been with someone.

Her stomach growled, reminding her she hadn't had breakfast.

Let's see, a tall, dark and nameless man, or her kitchen with all her shiny appliances and her refrigerator full of food? She twisted her lips. Tough call. Then again, there was no plausible reason she couldn't have both....

"Has there been a time I haven't been there for you, Gracie?" Rick said, offering up a non-answer sort of answer that made her smile. "Look, how serious was this incident? Do you want me to contact security and report the guy? Have them change your key card code?"

Her fingers tightened around the receiver. "No, I really don't want to go through all the hassle. My mind may be

telling me I just survived a close call with death, but my gut
says the poor jerk just got the wrong room. Anyway, reporting
the incident will only distract me from the interview.''

"Speaking of which, I hope this call means you're ready,
because my phone message light is blinking. It's probably the
car the station sent to pick us up.''

Grace yelped and jumped up. She wasn't anywhere near
ready. She eyed the daring, bright pink number she and Rick
had settled on for the outrageous radio talk-show host, then
lifted a hand to her still wet hair. "See you downstairs in
five.''

More like twenty, but he didn't have to know that.

"You're LATE.'' The junior producer of WDRT's morning
radio show descended on Dylan and Tanja like a swooping
crow complete with curved nose and clipboard. Through
speakers set up in every corner, a clip of seemingly unending
commercials poured over the airwaves. Dylan felt hands on
his shoulders. He tensed.

"Sheesh, Doc, I'm just trying to take your coat,'' Tanja
said.

"Oh.'' He allowed her to tug the tan overcoat down the
length of his arms, then grasped the new set of notes he'd put
together in the cab on the way over.

Tanja leaned closer, one of the spiked, purple tips of her
hair nearly taking out an eyeball. She lowered her voice. "Are
you okay? You're wound up tighter than a seventeen-year-
old virgin on prom night.''

He grimaced. "Thanks for the comparison, Tanja.''

The instant he'd met the young PR rep his publisher had
sent to accompany him on his tour, he was convinced his
editor had gone out of his way to make sure he found someone the total opposite of Dylan's character. Dylan could see
Charlie Hasseldorf getting quite a chuckle out of the situation.
Then Dylan had landed in New York and discovered that here,
nearly every professional Tanja's age...well, looked like
Tanja.

The producer clapped his hands impatiently. "Look, I don't have time for any prep so you're just going to have to play it by ear, Doc. The other doc's already in there."

"Other doctor?" Dylan choked, looking at Tanja.

She shrugged and smiled, but it was hard for her to look innocent when she appeared to have just stepped out of a tattoo parlor. "I haven't a clue."

"Well, isn't it your job to find out?"

"We don't have time for this now." The producer fairly shoved him toward the door. "After you, Dr. Fairbanks."

Dylan righted himself. What other doctor? And why hadn't he been told of this beforehand so he could adequately prepare? By now he was used to having his theories challenged by local whackos, but at least he'd been able to do a bit of research before he actually faced the smirking individuals he guessed were chosen more for their disbeliefs than their beliefs.

He was led down a long white hall with various doors leading off it. Dylan straightened his suit jacket and eyed the jeans the other guy was wearing. Perhaps he should have taken Tanja's advice and dressed down for the occasion. It didn't matter that it was radio and the listeners couldn't see him, Tanja had told him. The shock jock could see him. And absolutely nobody wore suits to radio shows.

"Just seat yourself to the right," the producer said, opening a glass door. "Headphones will be on the counter in front of you."

The first thing Dylan spotted in the dimly lit room was a camera.

Damn.

Obviously Tanja had also forgotten to tell him they were being filmed.

He grasped the producer's sleeve before he could vanish along with the PR rep. "Is this being televised?"

"Haven't you seen the show before, Dr. Fairbanks?"

Dylan frowned. "Seen? I thought this was a radio show."

"It is. But snippets of celebrity interviews are put together for a nightly half hour show on a cable access channel. Yours will probably air in a week or two, depending on our schedule.''

Dylan stiffened. He didn't like the way he came across on the small screen. An image of that magazine caricature came to mind. He immediately unclasped his hands where they rested in front of his groin.

For Pete's sake, it was an entertainment show. Certainly he could handle it. Anyway, it was too late to back out now.

He stepped into the room, bringing into view the radio host, his blond head bent over something an assistant held out to him. Then he spotted the table he was supposed to seat himself at. Eyes focused on the padded headphones, he seated himself then slid them over his head, his gaze constantly flitting back to the camera perched in the corner like an all-seeing, critical beast.

"Hi," a female voice spoke into his ears. "I've heard a lot about you, but I don't believe we've actually met."

Dylan's eyebrows popped up as he listened to the low, positively humming voice. He glanced toward a glass enclosure, but the brunette inside—the show's co-host, he guessed—appeared engrossed in her notes and knocking back coffee.

"I'm Gracie Mattias."

An odd, swirling sensation began in the pit of his stomach.

"Here. I'm right next to you. The other side."

Dylan swiveled to his right. Indeed, she was right next to him. And the odd sensation in his stomach pulled into a complicated, inexplicable knot.

The cartoon rendition of her he'd seen in the magazine earlier did absolutely no justice to Dr. Grace Mattias, sex therapist, live and in the flesh. Flesh being the operative word. Generously endowed, alluring flesh. And hair. Fiery, coppery red hair that curled all over the place. He couldn't fathom why, but he thought of her hair wet. Probably because he had showers on the brain since his unfortunate encounter earlier. Or maybe because when wet the red mass would likely skim down her back to tickle the dimples just above her bottom. And she would indeed have dimples. Decadent, deep indentations that would perfectly complement her perfect body and would beg to be explored by a man's tongue.

Dylan swallowed...hard.

Then he silently berated himself for such a completely physical reaction to the woman sitting next to him. His adversary. His opposite in every way.

He didn't know what was with him. It wasn't as if he hadn't seen an attractive woman before, much less an attractive female colleague. But attractive didn't begin to cover Grace Mattias. In fact, nothing much seemed to be covering Grace Mattias. His gaze slid over the hot-pink clingy material of her deep-veed jacket, down, down, to where her skirt barely skimmed the tops of her delicious thighs. Legs that could rival a model's went on and on until he found himself staring at the highest, strappiest sandals he'd ever seen in his life.

Catching himself, he snapped his gaze back to her face. Her pink, pink lips pursed as she gave him the same thorough once-over. "Actually, I think we have met, Dr. Fairbanks."

Dylan managed to shake his head, not trusting himself to speak for fear it would come out sounding like a preadolescent squeak.

She tapped a pink-tipped fingernail against her full, luscious mouth. "Uh-huh. In fact, I'm sure of it." She smiled, revealing nicely ridged teeth that hadn't fallen prey to a dentist's sander. "Though I believe I know you as Tom."

Dylan chuckled, relaxing a bit. "Now I know we haven't met before. I'd never have misrepresented myself as someone else...." Even as he said the words, a low alarm went off in a part of his brain that still worked.

Her smile widened as she folded her arms under her breasts, causing them to pop up even further. "Yes. As in Peeping Tom," she finished.

Oh, shit.

It couldn't be.

It wasn't possible he'd blundered into another situation

with the same woman twice in one day. The law of averages completely went against such an improbability.

Yet here he was. Staring at the water nymph from the shower earlier that morning.

2

DYLAN WATCHED as Grace Mattias pulled her hair back, revealing the lightly freckled, even planes of her face. "Picture me without makeup...and clothes."

He closed his eyes tightly and uttered a pungent curse.

"Dr. Fairbanks?" A male voice said into his ear phones. "The FCC frowns on the use of such language."

He grimaced and forced himself to face forward, well away from the provocative woman next to him and toward the radio host. How bad could it get? This was a morning show, right? Certainly there were guidelines the show had to follow. "Are we on the air?"

"Not yet." This time it was the radio host who spoke. And Dylan didn't like the width of his predatory grin. "But we will be in three, two, one...welcome back everybody. This is Baxter Berning on WDRT and you're listening to America's most popular syndicated talk show. Boy, are you ever in store for a tasty treat today. If you've just tuned in, don't worry about what you've missed. If you've stuck around, then you're about to hit pay dirt. I'd like to begin this segment by introducing two of the foremost experts in the area of *sex*." He drew out the word with suggestive flair then picked up a book Dylan didn't recognize because it wasn't his own. Baxter introduced Grace. Then he homed in on Dylan, ignoring the copy of his book at his elbow as he leaned forward.

Bad news. Whenever they overlooked his book, it meant they were about to go off on a tangent, outside the list of acceptable interview questions Tanja had provided the producer. Worse news.

"Now let's see if I can get this straight, Dr. Fairbanks. Am I to gather from your conversation with Gracie—can I call you Gracie?"

The redhead next to him nodded, causing all that red hair to shimmer under a warm spotlight. Then she leaned closer to her mic, almost as if about to kiss it, and said, "You can call me anything you'd like, Baxter. Just don't call me late for bed."

Dylan cringed. *This* was a doctor? He didn't know any doctors who spoke like that. Okay, there were his parents, but for all intents and purposes, they weren't *real* doctors anymore.

The host reacted. "Ooo. For my listeners, I'd like to point out that Gracie is every bit the sex kitten she sounds like. This is one interview you'll want to check out when it airs on TV." He leaned forward. "Anyway, back to you Dr. Fairbanks."

"Call me Dylan, please," he said, uncomfortably tugging on the lapels of his jacket.

"Right. Anyway, am I correct in assuming that you, um, played Peeping Tom to Gracie's sexy victim this morning?"

Oh, God. It was one thing to have suffered through the unfortunate event in the first place. To be humiliated before a national audience was altogether different. "Not by design, I assure you," he said, then cleared the high-pitched panic from his voice. "It was a simple misunderstanding. I mistook Dr. Mattias's hotel room for my own, and by innocent accident let myself into her room."

"I was in the shower," Grace clarified.

Dylan jerked to gape at her. She didn't have to share that. He cringed and prayed Diana wasn't listening to the show in San Francisco.

"Uh-huh. I've heard of wanting to get a peek at the competition, Doc, but this is fantastic." The host sat back, dragging his mic with him. "So tell us, does the female sex doc look as good out of her clothes as in?"

Dylan's collar felt like a tightening noose as he slanted another gaze Grace's way. *Oh, boy, did she,* his own body responded. But to Baxter he said, "I'm afraid I didn't get a good look."

"Didn't get a good look," the host repeated. "Now that's the biggest load I've ever heard. Are you human, man? I mean, just look at her. That's a piece even the Pope would look twice at. You can't tell me you didn't take advantage of the prime opportunity and devour that tight little body with your eyes."

"If that was a compliment, thank you, Baxter." Grace's voice practically purred in Dylan's ears.

He hit his chin on the mic. "I'll be the first to admit that Dr. Mattias is…attractive."

"Trust me, you're not the first, and you won't be the last, Doc."

Grace laughed, a throaty sound that made the swirling in Dylan's stomach slink lower. "I'm afraid you're making Dylan uncomfortable, Bax. If you'd read his book, and believe me, I have, then you'd know that he doesn't buy into the whole chemistry theory. He believes the human anatomy was designed solely for reproduction purposes and that only within the confines of a monogamous relationship—"

"Marriage," Dylan corrected, regaining his bearings, and unendingly grateful his colleague had shifted the conversation back to solid ground. If they stuck to their books and medical terminology, he'd be fine.

She smiled at him. "All right, then, marriage. As I was saying, Dr. Dylan believes only within the bonds of marriage should sexual, um, attraction be explored."

The host's gaze bore into Dylan. "Does that mean you're still a virgin, Doc?"

He nearly choked. "No. No, of course not."

The shock jock snapped his fingers in front of his microphone. "Then you're one of those, oh, what's the term they're throwing around like yesterday's paper? I got it. A born-again virgin. Are you a born-again virgin, then?"

Dylan hated the term, though by the host's definition, he

suspected his situation fit within the wide parameters. "No comment."

"Come on, Doc, just look at her. Are you telling me that you don't just totally want to bang her brains out? Whip out ol' George and get down to introductions? For crying out loud, Gracie is a walking wet dream."

Explicit images flashed through Dylan's mind. Visions of Grace standing under the shower stream, the water sluicing over her womanly curves, her nipples hard and begging for attention, her thighs warm and wet with an altogether different moisture.

Get it together, Dylan. Now was not the time or the place to explore his most untoward thoughts of the woman next to him.

He cleared his throat. "Don't get me wrong. As I point out in Chapter Four of my latest book, *Reaching New Heights— Advice on How to Obtain Ultimate Sexual Pleasure,* attraction between a man and a woman plays an important role when they first meet. But it's a mere pebble in the foundation of a solid, fulfilling relationship."

The host made a face, obviously not getting the response he wanted. He opened Grace's book and flipped through the pages. "Seems yours and the sex doctor's beliefs are completely contrary then." He grinned at Grace. "It says here that you suggest your patients go out on sexual safaris."

"Some patients," Grace said, straightening her headphones, then fluffing all that red hair back around them. "Those without a dark, painful sexual past who are merely in need of finding themselves…sexually. An awakening of sorts, if you will."

Sexual safari? Dylan thought. It was only when the voices in his headphones went silent that he realized he'd made the remark aloud.

"You were saying?" the host asked.

Yeah, he was saying. Dylan sat up a little straighter, speaking into the mic at an angle as he looked at Grace. "Define sexual safari, Dr. Mattias."

"I'm crushed you haven't read my book," she said, giving him a playfully sexy little pout that made that...feeling slide even lower. "A sexual safari is where I recommend the patient respond to basic, fundamental human need. No asset-probing, spouse-hunting, car-perusing behavior allowed. Rather, the patient is encouraged to act on urges society has taught us to ignore or suppress in the name of pseudomorality and human decency." She smiled. "In essence, I tell these particular patients to act with their hearts rather than their heads."

The host emitted a low whistle. "Baby, let me go get my camouflage underwear and oil my elephant gun."

Dylan ignored him, instead locking gazes with the woman next to him. "So you counsel your patients to have one-night stands. Promote promiscuity. Is that what you're saying, Dr. Mattias?"

"No. I encourage these particular patients to cut loose at least once in their lives so there are no relationship-ruining 'what ifs' and 'what could have beens' later on in life. I counsel them to connect with their sexual selves, learn what pleases them without the heavy complications serious relationships entail. You know, the whole, 'will he think I'm too fat,' 'am I pleasing her' scenario. If you set out to please yourself and yourself alone, then you're in a much better position to know what pleases others, either in that relationship, or in the one that will stand the test of 'until death do you part.' And even you have to admit, Dr. Dylan, that sexual satisfaction is an important element in any healthy marriage."

"Yes, but *only* within the bonds of matrimony. As for the other, growing sexually aware of yourself, there are better, more...principled ways to go about achieving that goal. And abstinence, or delaying acting on that purely physical, animal attraction makes for an even sweeter, more satisfying experience, wouldn't you agree...Gracie?"

The host fanned himself with Grace's book. "And tell me, Dr. Hottie, do you go...man-hunting often?"

For a long moment Grace held Dylan's gaze as if she was

unable to look away. He noticed the lick of pure, undiluted sensuality in the velvety brown depths of her eyes. The telling dilation of her pupils. Finally she smiled, then slowly looked toward their host. "I think I'll follow my colleague's lead and answer a demure 'no comment.'"

"Oh, don't go coy on me now, baby," Baxter crowed. "We have a caller on line four. John, you're on. Do you have a question you'd like to ask one of our guests?"

"Am I on the air?"

"Yes, sir, you are. Shoot away."

"Okay, um…I'm having a problem and I was, you know, hoping one or both of your guests might be able to help me with it."

The host sighed heavily into the mic. "John, if it takes you this long to get to the point, no wonder you're having problems."

Dylan leaned toward his own mic. "Go ahead, John."

"Yes, well, um, my wife and I have been married for five years now and…,"

A long silence ensued.

"And," the host prompted.

"And, well, I'm lucky if we have sex once a month. There, I said it. What can I do about it?"

Dylan opened his mouth to ask for more details, but Gracie's voice, sounding infinitely less like a porn star's and more like a professional, filled his ears. "Were you two sexually active before you were married, John?"

Dylan grimaced. "With all due respect, Dr. Mattias, I don't see what that's got to do with anything. The fact is that they are married, and they're currently experiencing…marital difficulties."

The host laughed. "Yeah, I'd say not getting any is a marital difficulty."

Grace looked at him, a flash of something he couldn't identify lighting her eyes. "I wasn't going to suggest that the couple regress back to the time before their marriage, Dr. Dylan. I was merely trying to ascertain whether or not they'd found themselves individually, sexually, before they took their business in front of a priest or a pastor or a rabbi.'' She turned her head away from him. "John, do you and your wife have any kids?''

"Um, no.''

"So there's no reason you can't turn your entire house into a sexual playground then, is there?''

"Sexual playground?''

"Yes, John. This is what I suggest you do. First of all, you'll want to talk to your wife. Find out what her secret fantasy is. If she hasn't shared it with you in the five years you've been married, this may take some time. But once you do find out, act on it. Transform your house to reflect this fantasy. Cater to her every whim. Let her know that her emotional and sexual happiness mean as much to you as your own desire to, in our honorable host's words, get some.''

Chuckles filled Dylan's ears as he sat back, grudgingly impressed with the advice, though her immediate rejection of his own opinion stung like a son of a bitch. While he wouldn't have suggested the construction of a "playground," sexual communication was always important, making her basic advice sound.

Baxter came back, "Sounds like good advice to me. Thanks for calling, John. And good luck with the old lady.'' There was a tiny click. "We're going to break for a minute or two to let the sex doctor's advice sink in. We'll be right back to ask our guests where they stand on masturbation. You won't want to miss that. I sure don't.''

The sound of commercials filtered through the headphones and Dylan followed everyone's lead in taking his off. The host, so tuned in to him and Grace only moments before, was conversing with the producer, leading him to believe his entire interplay with Grace was for entertainment purposes only.

"So where *do* you stand on the topic of masturbation, Dr. Dylan?''

He shifted to find Grace Mattias crossing her long, long legs and smiling at him suggestively.

Despite his best intentions, Dylan couldn't help grinning at her. He pushed the microphone away to make sure this little encounter wasn't used for ammunition when the commercials were over. "Oh, beyond a doubt, it leads to blindness."

Her instant laughter was spontaneous, warm and contagious. He laughed along with her, his muscles relaxing at the release of some of the tension between them. But he recognized that a whole different kind of tension had just shot up a notch.

"You probably already know where I stand, anyway, seeing as you read my book."

She nodded. "So long as it's not used instead of sex, your marital partner doesn't know about your extracurricular activities and it doesn't involve sex toys, you're all for it."

"In moderation," he added.

"And with the ultimate amount of discretion."

"Very important."

"So you don't think the act of, um, watching...your significant other bring herself to climax can be...sexual stimulating?"

Dylan stared at her. An image of one amazingly sexy and gloriously naked Gracie Mattias stretched across a king-size bed, her thighs open, her engorged womanhood clearly in view, flashed across his mind. Her pink-tipped fingers first cupped her breasts, plucking at her erect nipples, then slid down the toned length of her stomach, toward—

He shook his head, banishing the erotic thought from his mind. "I think masturbation is an intimate matter best kept between one's hands...and oneself."

"Okay, guys, we're back in ten seconds," the producer said, indicating their headphones.

Dylan carefully readied himself and repositioned the mic in front of his mouth, wondering if he'd be able to even think of the word *masturbation* again without connecting it to one wildly sexy Gracie Mattias.

GRACIE STEPPED OUTSIDE and took a deep, satisfying breath of the polluted New York City air. The smell of car exhaust mingled with the scents emanating from a nearby diner and the crisp scent of fallen leaves. If she tried hard enough, she imagined she could make out the slight tang of the ocean not far away.

A drop of water landed on her upturned forehead. Another on her chin. She opened her eyes to realize that it wasn't the ocean she smelled, but an impending rainstorm. Ah, an unseasonably warm autumn day in New York City. In a matter of seconds, it would probably start pouring. But she couldn't bring herself to care. She felt…electrified somehow. So vividly alive. Her skin tingled with excitement. She was gloriously aware of every sweet nuance that made her human. The feel of her breasts pressing against the thin tank top under her jacket, the skirt hugging her hips and bottom, made her feel every inch a woman.

The downpour began.

She hailed a taxi then climbed in, laughing when she found herself soaked straight through.

She shrugged out of her jacket, told the driver which hotel, then settled back in the seat. "Take the scenic route through the park. I've always loved the park."

"Lady, do you know what kind of traffic we're going to run into this time of day?"

She smiled at him in the rearview mirror. "Yeah."

Right now she couldn't care less if it took her two hours to get back to her hotel room. Rick was out running errands for her, the radio talk-show host had asked her for her phone number and she'd just experienced one of the more stimulating challenges of her life in the shape of one super-sexy Dr. Dylan Fairbanks.

An image of Dr. Dylan crowded out all other thought and she smiled. Just thinking about him made her hungry for an unnamable something. She didn't try to name the feeling. She didn't want to. Not yet. She wanted to enjoy the curious warmth spreading through her belly and settling between her tingling thighs.

She stuck her hand into her purse and fished out an extra-large packet of peanuts, compliments of the hotel. While the salty morsels couldn't hope to satisfy her recently awakened hunger, they could at least satisfy her stomach.

She absently crunched on the nuts. Professionally speaking, she couldn't have asked for a better setup. Rick had agreed, telling her postinterview that her choice of attire had worked wonders on the host, distracting him even while she drove each of her points home with a solid rubber mallet. No, she hadn't expected Dr. Fairbanks to be there. But given his expression when he first spotted her sitting next to him, she guessed that he hadn't, either. And when she realized he'd been the one to accidentally walk in on her in the shower that morning...well, suddenly this tour wasn't half as boring as it had been.

Of course, a few of her racier comments later on in the show would have singed her mother's eyebrows. Had her mother been listening. Which Gracie doubted. But Dylan's choked reactions somehow had been more satisfying.

She couldn't have asked for a better way to prove her theories than going nose-to-nose with one of the country's premier masters of sexual inhibition.

A delicious shiver began just below her earlobes and traveled down to her toes. She stretched her feet out as far as they could go, then reached into her monster bag and fished out Dr. Dylan's book. Nowhere to be found was a photo of him. Only a very brief bio outlining his professional experience. Which was impressive indeed. She had expected him to be a fiftyish, balding, overweight guy in glasses who got into spouting off about morality because he didn't have a chance in hell of leading a more interesting life. But the real Dr. Dylan Fairbanks...well, he had turned out to be sexier than sin.

She remembered the way he had looked at her. Both this morning at the hotel, then at the station when they had indulged in off-air conversation. Something about him seemed to sizzle. He had an almost visible red aura that tempted her closer, made her want to see if all his professional doctrines could be put to better use with sexual expertise.

Her chewing slowed.

Was he a hypocrite? She'd run into her share of alpha males who preached to her about values with their mouths, while seeking her leg under the table with their hands. Behavior that always earned the offending male a meeting with the sharp prongs of her fork. She stuffed the book back into her bag next to a copy of her own. She didn't think Dr. Dylan was that type. To the contrary, he appeared to adamantly believe every last word he'd written in his sexually repressed book. She leaned her head against the seat and stared up at the skyscrapers through the back window. Looking at the rain coming down that way seemed somehow surreal, magical.

Her cell phone chirped in her purse. She let it ring.

"Hey, lady, you gonna get that or what?"

"I was thinking or what." Despite her response, she brushed the salt from her hands, then fished the noisy piece of plastic out. Rick, the display read. She punched the talk button. "I'm paying an arm and leg for a taxi drive through the park, Rick. This had better be good."

"You should have told me you wanted to see the city. I could have gotten you on one of those Grayline Tours, or whatever they're called. Anyway, this is good. More than good. I just got a call from the radio station. You're not going to believe this. The number of callers was through the roof. Among the highest they've ever received."

She slipped her shoes off, indulging in a wide smile. "Really?"

He laughed. "All that education and that's the best you can do? You disappoint me, Dr. Mattias."

"Hey, I'm enjoying the moment."

"As well you should. I, of course, took the liberty of passing on the news to your publisher. They're very happy."

"Sure they are. More money for them."

"More money for you."

Grace's smile slipped. The rain clouds soaking the city

seemed to descend from the skies and settle around her shoulders.

Money had dictated so much of her life. Which were the best schools for her to attend? What latest designer was the most fashionable? Whose children were the best to be seen with? Her parents had tried to drill into her from a young age that money and success were all that mattered in life. She had spent much of that same life determined to prove them wrong. She'd dyed her hair green when she was eleven. Hung around with the "out" crowd. Majored in courses designed to make her mother's lips disappear with disapproval.

She was well into her teens before she realized she was behaving like a spoiled little rich girl. Worse, she was committing a sin as bad as her parents' by practicing reverse discrimination.

Since then, she had striven to base her judgments solely on the individual or the situation, not the balance of his or her bank account.

And she'd discovered that her major in human sexuality was something she enjoyed purely for the sake of enjoyment. Not because her parents choked whenever she discussed her studies at the dinner table.

She cleared her throat. "This isn't about money, Rick. It never was."

A heartbeat of a silence. "Then increase my salary. I won't mind."

She laughed and ran her toes along the sensitive bottom of her other foot.

"Enjoy your ride through the park, Gracie."

"I fully intend to."

She pressed the disconnect button and started to slip the phone back into her bag. Then she changed her mind and dialed her mother's number. A glance at her watch told her it was past eleven. After brunch with the church ladies. Before lunch at whatever auxiliary meeting.

"Mattias residence."

"*Hōla,* Consuela. It's Grace. Is Mom around terrorizing the place?"

A soft giggle, then, "Just this morning she sez to me, 'Consuela, I found wrinkle in bedspread. Completely unacceptable behavior. From now on make beds twice.'"

"Sounds like Mom all right." All too much like Mom. A woman with a formidable education who had traded a career for her husband and daughter…and counting wrinkles in bedspreads. Gracie had never needed to look beyond her own mother for the reasons why she never wanted to marry. Her identity was too high a price to pay for a pair of warm feet to cuddle up to in bed at night. She'd always told herself she'd get a dog if she felt the need for constant companionship. Her parents' marriage was proof positive that men asked for too much and gave up too little. It was enough to pick up her own socks. She didn't want to have to pick up a husband's, as well.

She leaned back and smiled, watching the vivid colors of autumn in Central Park sweep by as Consuela filled her in on a punctuation-challenged litany of her mother's recent complaints. All of them nitpicky issues that probably would never have entered her mind if she looked beyond her house and husband and had a career of her own.

Consuela finally sighed, indicating she'd vented as much as she was going to that day. "You want you should talk to her?"

Gracie hesitated then bit her bottom lip. Not because she didn't want to talk to her mother. But because the view outside her window was absolutely breathtaking. Only in New York could you blink your eyes like Samantha on *Bewitched* and move from city chic to abundant nature so quickly. She sighed. "Yeah, put her on. I haven't done my bad deed for the day yet. I figure making her late for lunch should do it."

Consuela told her to hold the line.

Grace trailed a finger down the steamed inside of the taxi window. Once, when she'd been home for spring break in her second year of college, she'd had the temerity to ask her mother if she'd ever achieved an orgasm. Despite her ongoing attempts to shock both her parents to the point of sputtering, she'd asked the question out of curiosity. Her parents had never seemed to share a physical closeness. They spent more time apart than together. And when they were together, they seemed occupied talking about which party to attend and who they should be seen with. The only time Gracie saw her mother actually touch her father was when she was picking invisible lint off his jacket before they left for social events. Even then, she did it in such a way so that no more than her fingertips brushed the material. When Gracie's course material had concentrated on sexual frigidity, it was only natural that Gracie thought of her mother. Only natural that Gracie would want to apply her recently acquired knowledge to everyday life.

Her mother's answer to the orgasm question had been the only time Grace had been slapped.

"Good heavens, Consuela, can't you even see to the simple task of asking who it is?" Gracie heard her mother's voice come over the line, followed by, "Hello?"

"Hi, Mom."

"Gracie!" A fumbling of the phone. "Consuela, it's Gracie."

Gracie didn't want to cause any more trouble for the good-humored housekeeper by pointing out to her mother that Consuela and she had already spoken, but it took mammoth effort.

"Hi, darling. What a surprise it is hearing from you. You're never up this early."

"I'm working, Mom. I'm on that promotional tour, remember? I did a radio interview this morning in New York."

"Oh! Yes, of course. I must have forgotten."

Gracie tucked her chin into her chest and bit her lip. She wasn't sure if her mother actually did forget half the details of her only child's life, or whether she preferred to ignore them.

"So are you nervous? No, pretend I didn't ask that. I don't

think I've ever seen you nervous. Besides, you have that radio show you do every week. Why would you be nervous?''

"Actually, Mom, this was a different format, so I was a bit nervous. It's over though, so I'm feeling pretty pleased with myself." Gracie turned her head, watching as a young mother fastened the hood of a child's raincoat. She smiled wistfully. Had her mother ever stood out in the middle of a downpour completely unprotected to make sure she had *her* coat fastened securely? Not that she could remember. Sounded like something she'd have the nanny or housekeeper see to.

She blindly reached again into her monster purse. Bypassing the bag of peanuts, she instead slid out a copy of her book. "Have you received the book yet?"

"The book…oh, right! I'm sure we have. In fact, I'm positive that we have. It must be around here somewhere. Why just this morning I'm sure I saw Consuela sneaking a peek between the covers."

Ah, the self-protective reversion to "we" that her mother fell back on when she couldn't quite face things on her own. Gracie wondered exactly who "we" encompassed. Her mother and her father? The entire household? Or the entire city of Baltimore? Gracie slowly ran her finger over the raised lettering, wondering at the hypersensitivity of her fingertip. "And you? Have you read it, Mom?"

A pause. Then a sigh. "No, dear, I'm afraid I haven't. And I don't think I will, either, if it's all the same to you."

"It isn't all the same to me, Mom. I sent that copy especially for you. Not Dad. Not Consuela. It…" She sat up then straightened her skirt. An impossible task given its shortness. "It would mean a lot to me, Mom. I'd really like your input."

"Don't be ridiculous, Grace. What good would my input do now? You couldn't possibly change anything."

"I don't want to change anything. I just want you to read it. Can you do that for me?" Grace leaned her forehead against the glass, then rolled the window down and took a deep breath of the cool, damp air. Finally she laughed, then said, "Never mind, Mom. I wouldn't want to make you do anything you're uncomfortable with."

"That's my girl. I knew you'd come around if we talked about it, dear."

But we haven't talked about it. I've talked, you've stone-walled. Just another day in the life and times of Grace and Priscilla Mattias.

At any rate, she supposed she should be grateful she hadn't gotten the usual "Grace, your biological clock's ticking…there's only a small number of suitable men out there and they're all being snatched up by other women…are you ever going to settle down and give me grandkids" speech that punctuated most of her conversations with her mother.

"If it makes any difference, I'm glad your interview went well, Grace. And I'm happy that things are going the way…well, the way that you want them."

What went unsaid was that "things" weren't going the way her mother wanted them. "Thanks, Mom. I appreciate you saying that." She leaned back into the seat and grabbed for her peanuts. Things *were* going just the way she wanted them. Her first book was taking off. She had her new bayside condo in Baltimore that was now being renovated. And she was enjoying every moment of making her own decisions without someone constantly breathing down her neck and asking her just what in the hell she thought she was doing.

She smiled to herself. Yes, she was very happy with her life, indeed. She popped a few peanuts into her mouth. "So tell me, Mom. Which problem do you hope to throw money at during lunch today?"

3

CHOPPED LIVER. That's what he felt like after his bout with Dr. Gracie Mattias, pure and simple and bloody raw. Dylan cast a glance around the lobby. Tanja wasn't even around for him to vent at. She'd abandoned him outside the radio station, claiming she had family in the area and had scheduled to meet a friend for lunch, did he mind? He'd wanted to tell her yes, he did mind, but hadn't. He was afraid he'd sound too... demanding? Unbending? Whiny?

He cringed at the last description, realizing that's exactly what he was doing. He was whining. Just like a five-year-old who had his bike stolen, training wheels and all.

It was ridiculous, really. Overall the interview had gone well. Toward the end he had even begun to enjoy himself, giving as good as he got when it came to trading digs with the sex doctor.

Jesus, had he really just thought of her as the sex doctor? If so, what did that make him? The anti-sex doctor?

He didn't want to begin to analyze that bizarre train of thought.

Dylan poked at the elevator button again, somehow managing a half-assed smile in the general direction of a young couple who had just stepped in from the rain to stand next to him. Their cheerful, attentive-to-each-other disposition made his disposition even darker.

"This is the first day of the rest of our lives."

Dylan grimaced, then nodded at the young woman to show he had heard.

"We just got married." The man looped his arms around

the woman and tugged her closer. "This is the first day of our honeymoon."

"Congratulations." Dylan forced a close-mouthed smile then turned back toward the elevator.

Kissing noises sounded beside him. He rubbed the back of his neck, wondering where the stairs were, and whether he was up to climbing seventeen floors. "Uh," he began, interrupting the couple from their amorous pursuits. "A word of warning. When the elevator stops, you may want to make sure it's actually on the floor you want."

The couple looked at him, then each other, sporting quizzical expressions he had been sorely tempted to bestow on a few of his more…interesting patients. Like the one who got into wearing women's silk stockings under his Brooks Brothers business suits when he appeared in Superior Court.

He cleared his throat. "I found out the hard way that they don't always do that. The elevators. You know, stop on the floor you want. Creates a bit of a…mess." Although he really couldn't call what had happened this morning a mess. An unfortunate mishap, maybe. A wild accident. But definitely not a mess. Not when a man got to take a peek at a woman of Gracie Mattias's caliber.

"Um, thanks."

"Don't mention it."

Finally, a ding. The elevator doors opened. Dylan stepped in and to the back, automatically making room for the couple. He reached around them and pushed the button for his floor.

"Hold that elevator!"

Dylan clenched his jaw and covertly reached around the couple to punch the close button. All he wanted was to get back to his room, shrug out of his damp clothes, then review his schedule for the next two weeks. Make a list of things to have Tanja see to. First and foremost, making sure that he knew exactly who he was going to be up against in coming interviews.

"Thanks." A breathless someone stuck her hand between the closing doors, then slid in between them.

Dylan stood a little straighter, willing the doors to close before someone else could delay his ascension to his room and sweet peace.

"It's you."

Dylan jerked to stare at the late arrival. And nearly dropped to his knees. Which wouldn't have been an inappropriate response given the woman he was staring at. He hadn't noticed at the radio station, but Dr. Grace Mattias was tall. Nearly as tall as he was at six foot. A goddess. No, no, Galatea in the Pygmalion tale. Galatea, the statue Pygmalion had crafted of the perfect mate. Aphrodite had taken pity on the poor guy and brought the statue to life because of Pygmalion's deep love for the inanimate object. That's who Grace reminded him of. Even more with her damp hair curving against the skin of her cheeks and neck. Tiny droplets plopped against her soaked white tank, drawing his gaze to the hardened tips of her breasts.

Heat, sure and swift, swept through his groin and he fought the urge to groan aloud. Gracie Mattias wasn't destined for wife and motherhood as Galatea had been. No, she was put on earth solely to torture men like him with her oozing sensuality and provocative ways.

She cocked her head slightly to the side and gave him a hesitant smile, as though trying to analyze what was going on in his head. He'd be better off remembering that Gracie was completely capable of doing just that. He immediately snapped straighter.

"Don't look so shocked," she said. "I think we've already, um, established that we're staying at the same hotel."

The couple with their arms wrapped around each other looked their way. "In separate rooms," Dylan pointed out.

"Of course in separate rooms. We don't even know each other."

Dylan grimaced. "From the sound of it, that's not necessarily something that would stop you."

"Ooo, that was a low blow, Dr. Dylan. We're not on the radio show anymore. You can put the jabs away now."

He dipped his chin and managed a wry grin. "Sorry. That was kind of a cheap shot, wasn't it?"

"Bargain basement."

He slanted her a gaze from the corner of his eye. She seemed completely unconcerned with her disheveled appearance. This was at odds with her carefully put together front for the radio host. She didn't make apologies and utter some inane comment about how she must look. She didn't move to get a hairbrush from the depths of the huge handbag slung over her shoulder. And she didn't try to repair her makeup. He wondered exactly how long she had been out in the rain.

He took a deep breath, pulling in a subtle, tangy scent that hovered somewhere between juicy, overripe oranges and tart, green apples. Her shampoo, maybe. Though it wasn't beyond the realm of possibility that she, herself, naturally smelled like the succulent fruit.

"Excuse me, do you mind if I take a look?"

Dylan blinked at the young woman standing in front of him. The bride was gesturing toward the window behind him that overlooked the vast lobby as they moved upward.

"Sorry. Sure, go ahead."

She did. And took her new husband with her.

Dylan stood ramrod straight in front of the closed elevator doors. Gracie joined him.

"Newlyweds," he said quietly.

"Ah."

A dull thump sounded from behind him. Dylan looked over his shoulder to find that the newlyweds had apparently taken in enough of the view and were now taking in each other. His eyes widened as the woman practically climbed up on the man. The man's hand skimmed her side then cupped her behind the knee. In a smooth move, he lifted her leg then thrust his body against her softness.

Dylan jerked back to face the elevator doors.

"Exhibitionists," Gracie whispered.

He looked at her blankly. "Rude."

She tossed her head back and laughed. "Come on, Dr. Dylan, I should think that since they're married almost anything should go in your book.''

He jabbed a thumb over his shoulder. "Nowhere did I write that this was acceptable behavior."

Gracie's deep, deep brown eyes held amusement. "I meant figuratively, not literally."

"Oh."

She held up a finger. "Speaking of which." She began rummaging through her bulging bag, then tugged something out with a little resistance. "Here."

He stared at the book she held as if he was afraid it might bite. Seeing as it was her book, he wasn't taking any chances.

"I had one left over from the stack my publisher sent to the station. Go on, take it."

He did.

"I figure that you were caught at a bit of a disadvantage this morning. You know, having not reviewed my theories and all."

He held up the magazine tucked under his arm still opened to the page focusing on her. "I wasn't as uninformed as you think."

"Oh my God! Can I see that? How did you get a hold of a copy so quickly? Rick, that's my assistant, hasn't said a word about its release."

Dylan reluctantly let the magazine go. He stood silently wishing the elevator would get to his floor already as Gracie silently read the piece. He tensed at her little bursts of laughter, trying to ignore the low moans coming from the couple behind them. Then she flipped the magazine over to where he was featured. Dylan gave in to the urge to work his finger inside his overnight collar.

"Says here you're married."

"Divorced."

"Oh, baby," the bride moaned.

Dylan noticed that Gracie sneaked a glance at the couple, her brows jumping high on her forehead. She turned forward again, color touching her cheeks. Dylan didn't even want to think of what it would take to shock the shocking sex doctor. She leaned closer to him, giving him another whiff of her fruity scent. "Um, I wouldn't look back there if I were you."

"I wasn't planning to."

The elevator finally drew to a stop. *There is a God.* The doors slid open and Dylan immediately began to step out. Away from the groping newlyweds. Far, far away from the enticing Dr. Mattias.

Gracie slapped the magazine against his chest. "This is how you got yourself in trouble the last time. This is my stop, remember?" Her smile held mischief and amusement as she got out then held the doors open with her hand. "Would you like to know what my recommended course for therapy would be for you, Dr. Dylan?"

His gaze drifted to where her breasts pressed against the flimsy material of her tank, the lace of her bra clearly visible beneath the damp fabric.

"I mean, given what I know about you so far, which isn't a whole lot outside of your book."

He jerked his gaze back to her face. "I'm not sure I want to hear this."

"Good, because I'm going to tell you anyway." She flipped her wet hair over a mostly bare shoulder. "What you need is a nice, traditional wild turn in the sack. And I'd recommend you see to it posthaste."

Dylan nearly choked on whatever response he would have made as she waggled her fingers at him then sashayed down the hall. And sashay was the word for it. Finally the doors slid shut. He closed his eyes and swallowed as an article of clothing he didn't even want to try to identify landed next to his left foot, no doubt compliments of the couple behind him.

WILD TURN IN THE SACK, INDEED. Dylan set about the nerve-calming, erotic-image-banishing task of unpacking his solitary suitcase. Something he would have had a chance to do earlier had he not accidentally interrupted Gracie Mattias's shower that morning. Something he would be doing efficiently now if not for her inflammatory words. With quick, irritated movements, he rehung his blue shirt next to his navy slacks, well away from his tan jacket. Not that it mattered. He was scheduled to be in New York for only another day anyway. Tomorrow afternoon he was scheduled for a brief interview with a reporter from a top psychology magazine, then he was flying to St. Louis.

He decisively closed the closet doors then sat down to take off his shoes. Only then did he grow aware of his semiaroused state. He closed his eyes, determined to ignore the physical messages his body was sending him. He stripped out of his damp clothes and put on the hotel robe. There. He felt better already.

His sexual reaction to Gracie didn't surprise him. He was only human after all. And she was one hundred percent female in heat. It's how he acted on that basic, fundamental response that differentiated him from a mindless animal. Humans, in general, had the ability to make conscious decisions. While many still subscribed to the ''I couldn't help myself, it was an accident'' philosophy when it came to extramarital affairs, the argument had never held much water for him. A man could always help himself. There was nothing accidental about falling into bed with a woman. In fact, whenever one of his patients tried using the excuse on him, he usually came back with something along the lines of ''Right. So what you're telling me is that you just tripped and fell right into her vagina.''

He carefully hung his suit on the towel warmer in the bathroom, smoothed out the wrinkles, then walked back into the other room. He sat down at the desk, eyed his laptop, the phone, then settled his gaze on Gracie's book. *Sex is Not a Four-Letter Word—Smashing Sexual Conventions.* The title was spelled across a glossy white cover in pink and gold raised lettering. He pushed it aside and picked up the telephone receiver instead. Maybe he'd be able to get through to Diana.

A brief knock sounded at the door, then Tanja breezed right in. "Can you believe this rain? Isn't it awesome?"

"My words, exactly." Dylan grimaced at her. "You know you might want to think twice about just walking in here like that. You never know when you might catch me…in various stages of undress."

"I should be so lucky." She stopped in the middle of the room, hands on slender hips, even the purple spikes of her hair seeming to radiate energy. "Come on, Doc, you're not the type to walk around your own apartment in your birthday suit, so there's no real danger there, is there?"

"Coulter, Connor and Caplain, Attorneys-at-Law."

Dylan stopped glowering at Tanja then asked to be put through to Diana. He drummed his fingers against the desktop, then slid Gracie's book into the drawer before the PR rep could spot it. Four rings, then he was put through to Diana's voice mail.

Tanja pried the receiver from his hand and soundly hung it up. "You can call whoever that was back when we get to Chicago."

"Hey! I was just about to leave the number where I could be contacted."

"It's changing so what's the point." She swung the closet doors open, eyed the contents, then took out his suitcase and launched it toward the bed. Moments later, his clothes followed.

"What do you mean Chicago? We're supposed to be going to St. Louis next. And that's not until tomorrow."

"Change in plans."

"Change in plans?" He caught another launch of his neatly pressed clothes and tried to save them further wrinkling. "Don't I have a say in that?"

Tanja stared at him, tapping her black-painted nail against her lips. "Nope." She chose a couple of items from the pile and thrust them against his chest. "Get dressed. Our plane leaves in an hour."

"What about the interview tomorrow?"

"Small-time."

Feeling stupid, he turned to follow her thorough and completely shameless invasion of his privacy. "What's in Chicago?"

Tanja stopped hooking his toiletries into his bag and grinned at him. "Only the most popular televised talk show in the country."

"I thought that was Rosie."

"Yeah, but Rosie wouldn't give us the entire hour." She stuffed the shaving bag into his arms. "With one condition."

He frowned, clutching his things for dear life. "What condition?"

"That you share the spotlight with one very controversial Dr. Grace Mattias."

For the second time in an hour, Dylan found himself sputtering for a response. "No way…not a chance in hell…over my dead body…" The objections tumbled from his mouth one right after the other, having little or no impact on Tanja as she put his laptop away.

"Come on, Dylan, you guys made quite the team this morning. Everyone loved you. You pulled in some of the highest ratings the show has ever seen."

His brows shot up. "We did?" He'd never gotten high ratings in any of his promotional efforts before. Hell, he hadn't been able to give away his first book, and it had never gone to a second printing. The thought that he may have reached not just someone but a wide range of someones today…well, that was what this was all about, wasn't it? It might mean a turning of the tides. Instead of days filled juggling patients with teaching, he could reach a nationwide audience. Command impressive fees for speaking appearances. Prove once and for all that his parents were wrong and he was right.

Tanja smiled at him and added his briefcase to his overloaded arms. "You did." She turned him around, then patted his bottom. "Now get a move on, Doc. We've got a plane to catch."

4

Chicago

A *KITCHEN.*

Well, maybe not a kitchen, but definitely a kitchenette. One of those kinds that you could barely move around in but held all the basic necessities, like a new microwave, an old stove and an empty refrigerator. Gracie was vaguely aware of the door closing after the bellboy as she stood staring at the cramped space immediately to the left in the enormous Chicago hotel room. She'd come across a place like this once before, in Fort Lauderdale. Likely this wing used to be an apartment complex that had been converted to a hotel. A quick glance around the spacious living-dining area, and the bedroom and bath to the right, fueled her speculation.

The strap to her laptop-carrying case slid off her shoulder. She allowed the case to drop slowly to the floor, enraptured with her new find. She hadn't had grains of salt under her fingernails since she began this crazy promotional tour. She opened and closed cabinet doors, peered into the empty but cold refrigerator, eyed the limited number of pots and pans, all with a ridiculous grin on her face. Someone watching might have thought she'd unearthed Atlantis instead of a chipped old stove, but she was beyond caring. She'd been in dire straits ever since she and Rick had caught dinner at a poor excuse for a Thai restaurant last night in New York and she had itched to get back into the restaurant kitchen to show the clueless Greek owner how it should be done. Instead, Rick had guided her out of there before she irreversibly embarrassed someone. Like herself.

Gracie ran her hand across the clean counter then straightened the miniature coffeemaker. Okay, so the place didn't even come close to resembling her own state-of-the-art kitchen in Baltimore, but it was workable. Truth be told, she'd done a lot with much less in her first apartment, right after she'd graduated from college. Back when she had been determined to strike out on her own, pull her own weight and ignore the checks from her father's accountant that piled up, unopened, on the scratched desk near the door that bore at least three dead bolts and countless chains and security devices. She'd never been prouder than when she'd made that little one-room place home. And she'd learned the finer points of making do with what one had. A trying but immensely gratifying experience. Especially when all her hard work had landed her a spot with a midlevel psychiatric practice before branching out on her own four years later.

She leaned against the wall and tapped a finger against her lips. A list. She had to make a list of what she needed from the store. The essentials were here. She wouldn't have to invest in salt and pepper or sugar. The hotel had provided coffee and a small selection of teas, though she always traveled with her own supply ordered specially from Arizona.

What should she make? Something simple, requiring the fewest ingredients. But something that would fill the small place with a delectable aroma and would go with a good bottle of red wine. No, white. Fish. She was in Chicago, wasn't she? Surely they would have a good selection of fish. Waking up to the smell of fish would remind her of home if not endear her to her neighbors.

A brief call to the concierge gave her directions to a small family-owned grocer a couple of blocks away. She hung up the phone on his offer to have an order placed on her behalf, then grabbed her purse and headed for the elevators.

A small cowbell above the advertisement-covered door announced her arrival at the grocer. No larger than the hotel room she had just left, the neat grocer had a good selection nonetheless. And plenty of fresh produce. As she happily made her selections, she allowed her mind to wander at will. Although only after five p.m. central time, darkness enveloped the street, weaving a web of billowed intimacy Gracie embraced. Chicago's climate was similar to New York's, albeit windier, earning the architecturally rich city its name, but it had an altogether different atmosphere. The unique, laid-back flavor of the mid-west was laced throughout despite the city's valiant efforts to shrug it off. And the people weren't as cynical, the lapping waves of Lake Michigan against the coast seeming to lull them into a feeling of peace.

"Can I see the trout, please? Yes, that one. To the left." Grace accepted the paper-protected fish from the woman behind the counter and examined the clear condition of the eyes and the pinkness of the gills. She stared down into the open mouth, the sight comically reminding her of Dr. Dylan Fairbanks's reaction when she'd told him he needed to get laid.

She handed the fish back. "I'll take it."

She added the item to her basket and turned toward the produce section. While Dr. Dylan's facial expression had resembled that of the trout, she had the distinct impression that he was anything but a cold fish. Something elemental lurked in his green eyes. A maturity, an intensity, an innate sexuality that made it difficult to meet his gaze head-on initially, yet held you captive thereafter. An intriguing paradox that reminded her how her skin had tingled after their meeting at the radio station. How verbally sparring with him had made her wonder what going a couple of rounds with him in bed might be like.

He *was* a sex therapist, so she didn't doubt he'd know all the exciting little details. But there was a difference between knowing and practicing. And she suspected that Dr. Dylan would put into practice everything he'd learned.

A shiver shimmied down the length of her spine, making her feel suddenly warm in her light raincoat.

Absently adding a couple of lemons to her basket, she

moved on to pick through lettuce. An idea danced along the fringes of her thoughts and she unsuccessfully tried to grasp it. She envisioned her book. No, no, it didn't have anything to do with her mother's refusal to read it. She made a face, banishing the image of Priscilla's tight-lipped face before it could spring roots. She moved to the tomatoes, testing them and adding a couple to her groceries. Rick? Did it have anything to do with her assistant and his mysterious company that morning in his New York hotel room? No, that wasn't it, either. Although the idea of a couple struggling against twisted sheets did ring a distant bell. Either that, or someone else had just entered the grocery store.

She edged along peppers and mushrooms then came to a halt before a large display of cucumbers. She slowly picked one up.

The bell rang louder. And along with it came a vivid image of Dr. Dylan Fairbanks's grinning face when they'd discussed masturbation.

Stumbling right in on the heels of the image was her sheer terror when the radio shock jock had asked Dr. Dylan whether or not he was a born-again virgin. She'd barely registered his response, so afraid that the host would shine that "virginal" light on her. Thankfully, he hadn't. But that did nothing to assuage her longstanding fear that someday, someone *would* ask her the question, despite her carefully made-up appearance of being one hundred percent hot tamale who practiced the very advice she preached. And then where would she be? Not that she was a virgin by any stretch of the imagination. But she wasn't what she pretended to be, either.

Leading up to the promotional tour, she'd been petrified of being fingered for a fraud. Her theory on the need for sexual safaris was the greatest of her unpracticed advice. She remembered seeing an interview once with a marriage counselor who had never been married. The host had virtually thrown the psychologist's advice right out the window, despite her years of backbreaking field research. Of course it had been one of those late-night, openly televised forums where the host made a point of going for the cheap shots. But the fact remained that if her limited sexual experience were to come to light, her hope of getting her word out would be little more than a car left abandoned at the side of the road with its hood up.

She absently ran the pad of her thumb over the prickly exterior of the cucumber, the innocuous movement sending a thrill of awareness over her skin. There was no denying that she was attracted to Dr. Dylan, though she firmly limited her attraction to him to physical attributes. What other reasons were there for being attracted to him? She didn't know him. She knew some of his stuffy opinions, but that was a far cry from knowing the full man.

Who wouldn't be attracted to him physically? He was tall, enigmatic, handsome as all get-out, and downright sexy.

And the concept of a sexual safari with him posed a decadently intriguing challenge, indeed....

She stood stock-still for a full minute, staring blindly at the cucumber she still held, her mind growing sluggish as it put two and two together. Then everything snapped together. Her heart did an erratic flip in her chest as she tripped straight over the path her subconscious had been trying to lead her down for the past few minutes.

That was it! She needed to put on her safari gear and bag one sexy prey in the shape of Dr. Dylan Fairbanks. Mussing some bed sheets with him would put an end to her feelings of being a fraud.

The earth began rotating again, and along with it a show of thigh-quivering mental images. A bare, sculpted torso. Strong, hair-covered legs. Ragged breathing. Soft, needy cries. Slick, sweat-covered skin. A pulse-throbbing erection pressed against soft flesh, preparing to enter.

Gracie's breath caught as she swallowed against the saliva gathering at the back of her throat. She shakily patted her hair. Okay, the prospect of sleeping with Dylan clearly wasn't offensive. She gave a feeble laugh. Who was she kidding? She was practically wetting herself just thinking about it.

Trying to get a grip on herself, she considered that sleeping with Dr. Dylan could have some drawbacks. After all, he wasn't a nameless, handsome face picked out at random in a neutral gaming zone.

She put back the cucumber she held and picked up one of the larger ones.

She would get the once-in-a-lifetime chance to prove beyond a shadow of a doubt that Dr. Dylan Fairbanks and his ancient, out-of-whack philosophies were way off base.

She added the cucumber to her basket, and couldn't help noticing the suddenly rubbery condition of her knees, and the anticipatory searing heat that rushed through her bloodstream.

Yes. Hunting Dr. Dylan was exactly what she needed to do…

DYLAN OPENED THE DOOR to the small grocer's, grimacing at the sound of the cowbell announcing his arrival. Right now he just wanted to blend in with the background. Carve out a little privacy so he could start thinking straight again. Not that the hokey cowbell prevented that. Rather the bright yellow V-necked sweater and olive-green cargo pants he had on pretty much ruled out blending in with the background.

He tugged at the too-snug shirt material, telling himself for the fifth time since leaving the hotel that he should have left his suit on. But after the soaking it had taken in New York, then the wrinkling on the plane, he wasn't sure it was salvageable, much less wearable. The morning's mishaps had slid into a day full of disasters—the latest debacle being the loss of his luggage—and he had little choice but to allow Tanja to go shopping for him. Why didn't it surprise him that the PR rep had completely ignored his express instructions to find something suitable, something he would buy for himself and instead bought him a temporary wardrobe more suited for a teenager than a responsible adult?

He felt like a…break-dancer.

He cringed. Boy, he'd just dated himself there, hadn't he? In all honesty, he had no idea what a kid on the cutting edge of fashion was called nowadays. And he'd had no idea what to do when Tanja had given him a tart little wave and disappeared on him...again.

At least one thing was going in his favor. The instant he'd discovered the kitchen in his hotel room, he found the perfect opportunity to temporarily place his budget and himself on a diet. Though it had been years since he'd had to worry about money, and weight had never been a problem, waste was something he'd never been very good at. A habit that stemmed directly from his parents.

Finally freeing a pint-size cart from the one it was attached to, he turned the corner and promptly bumped into an older gentleman. He was rerouting a path around him when he realized the guy was eyeing the prophylactics section. He did a double take, not wanting to see the man who was old enough to be his grandfather read the back of a package that touted the words "colored," "ribbed."

"Sorry," Dylan said under his breath, and headed down the next aisle.

He reminded himself that his foul mood wasn't the result of what he'd just seen—although it hadn't helped any. His foul mood had gotten worse when he'd taken his seat on the plane to Chicago and found himself sitting across the aisle and one row back from one Miss Hottie. A woman who not only hadn't seemed to notice him, but kept crossing her long, long legs in a way that had been...well, downright distracting. He hadn't checked, but he was certain he had a bruise from where the businessman sitting next to him kept elbowing him in order to get a better look.

He checked the price for a box of shredded wheat, frowned, then put the box back. He pushed the crippled cart down the aisle, idly wondering what the sex doctor had on tap for tonight. And who those plans included.

He slowed in front of the frozen food section. Only two freezers, but the essentials for the single professional on the move were all there. And a good deal more affordable than the box of cereal he'd just placed back on the shelf. Not that he didn't have money. But given the way he was raised…well, he wanted to be frugal. On occasion that meant forgoing his favorite cereal for a cheap TV dinner.

He reached in and grabbed the brand on sale and tossed it into his cart, telling himself he'd only succumb to buying it if nothing else popped out at him.

He resumed warring with the uncooperative cart. It didn't help matters that every time he moved, the metal thingies on the side pockets of the unfamiliar pants clinked. He glanced down, wondering how much damage he would do if he just ripped them off. Who wanted to make so much noise? A young woman with a small boy watched him as he passed. He managed a polite smile. Just barely. He wished something else would hurry up and grab his attention before he gave up and went back to the hotel to nuke the frozen dinner.

He had turned the corner to the produce section when something grabbed his attention all right. More accurately, *someone*.

He tried to pull the cart to a halt, only to have the front wheels fight him and end up crashing against a display for canned beans. Dylan hardly noticed. Despite the fact that Grace Mattias had her back turned to him, there was no mistaking all that red hair. Did the woman always dress like that when going to the market? While he couldn't make out much of her legs, he'd recognize those shoes anywhere. And her white raincoat was cinched tightly at the waist, emphasizing her trim figure.

He glanced around, trying to determine if she was alone. Judging by the basket she carried, and the absence of any hovering, panting male, he surmised she probably was.

Though why he should care, he didn't want to begin to explore. Lord knows, he was the last man who wanted to be hovering or panting over a woman like Gracie.

Still, he found himself watching her as she picked up a pear, running her fingertips along the odd-shaped fruit, then lifting it to her nose. He swallowed hard at the thorough, thoughtful inspection, then opened his mouth, as if about to take a bite of the fruit she held himself. He caught himself and snapped his teeth together. She put the pear back on the display, then began to turn. Dylan quickly pretended interest in the items next to him. *Peaches.* Figured.

There was no reason to think Grace would recognize him. Hell, *he* didn't even recognize him. He couldn't have looked more different from this morning had he tried. Which, of course, he hadn't. But maybe Tanja's bad taste had its advantages. The last thing he wanted was to engage in conversation with Gracie Mattias so soon. It was bad enough he'd have to appear with her tomorrow after what she'd said to him before leaving the elevator in New York. To have her see him here, alone…well, he could only imagine what she'd have to say about *that*.

"Why, if it isn't the world's most prominent sex expert."

Dylan nearly crushed the overripe peach in his hand at the sound of Gracie's voice. He fought the desire to play it off, glance around as if to question who she was talking to. But the way she'd addressed him left no doubt to whom she was speaking. And pretending otherwise would only make him look…more desperate.

He turned his head, managing surprise. Which wasn't difficult because a scene from an Al Pacino movie suddenly sprang to mind. Pacino had met the heroine-slash-suspected-serial-killer at a small market just like this one. She'd also been wearing a raincoat…and had nothing on underneath it.

Something warm and wet dripped between his fingers. He glanced down to find he'd pulverized the peach.

To his chagrin, Grace's smile widened. "Don't tell me. You have a kitchen, too."

"Kitchen?" he repeated dumbly, reaching for a handkerchief that wasn't there. What good were so many pockets if they didn't hold anything?

She handed him a paper towel she'd torn from an overhead holder. "Yes. My hotel room has a kitchen. Well, a kitchenette really, and I decided to cook. I naturally assumed that was the reason you were here as well. We must be in the same…hotel. Again. Which only makes sense if the show's putting us up."

She made a production of looking into his cart. Which made the fact that the only item in there was a frozen dinner that much worse.

"Sense. Yes." Dylan wondered if sleep was going to be anywhere on his itinerary of things to do now that he knew Gracie would be showering…er, sleeping under the same roof.

She straightened, shifting her full basket from one hand to the other. "You know, since you're obviously eating alone—" she gestured toward the cart "—and I have plans to…eat alone, why don't we eat alone together?" Her smile had the strangest effect on him. "I'll even let you get the wine. After all, it's not like either of us has to drive home or anything."

"Wine…"

It suddenly slammed into him that Gracie Mattias was actually inviting him to her place, her room, for dinner.

It also occurred to him that she was coming on to him stronger than Limburger cheese.

But why would she be coming on to him? Yes, there had been a certain provocative quality about their conversations thus far, but they'd seemed harmless enough. And when she'd suggested in the elevator that he needed a wild turn in the sack, she hadn't indicated she saw herself as a player in that particular scenario.

She reached around him to sample the peaches, giving him an undiluted whiff of her subtle perfume. He found himself fighting a groan.

"Um, I don't think that would be a very good idea."

She turned her head to glance at him, putting her enticing mouth mere inches away from his. "What wouldn't?"

He gestured helplessly, his words lost somewhere between his chest and his mouth. "The peaches," he said finally. "They're never as good as when they're in season."

Well, that didn't make much sense. He'd meant to say he

didn't think it would be a good idea if they had dinner together. Alone. In one or the other of their hotel rooms.

He stood straighter. And why wouldn't it be a good idea? Because Gracie was wildly attractive? Certainly even he was adult enough to keep his libido in check during something as innocent as dinner. He hadn't been looking forward to spending the night alone. Over the past five days, he'd had his fill of alone. He could do with a little company. And if there was one thing he'd learned, it was that keeping company with Gracie Mattias was anything but boring.

Wasn't this what he had signed on for when he'd decided to write his latest book? To sway people to his way of thinking? What better method to do that than by having dinner with his leading adversary? He'd certainly had his share of tough sells. She couldn't be any tougher than those he'd encountered thus far. He'd tried to prove Gracie wrong on the public front. Perhaps a more private one would do the trick.

"My place," he said, giving her a room number. "You bring the food, and I'll supply the wine."

"Isn't it usually the other way around?"

He gave her a grin of his own. "Yes, well, I got the impression that you don't like to do anything the old-fashioned way, Dr. Mattias."

"Then your powers of observation are better than I thought." She nodded. "Okay. But that means you have to supply dessert."

Dylan's stomach dropped to his groin. The way she said the word made him think all sorts of decadent thoughts that included—but certainly weren't limited to—licking whipped cream off sexy Gracie's mouth...and other more sensitive places.

Maybe this wasn't such a good idea....

Grace began walking away. "See you in an hour, Dr. Dylan. Oh, and make that white wine, will you?"

DYLAN TORE OPEN the package of assorted cookies, cursing when they flung to the far corners of the counter, everywhere but on the plate he had put out to hold them. Cookies and milk, he'd decided, was as wholesome a dessert as ever there was. Gracie didn't have to know it had taken him longer to chose the dessert than it had to find a decent bottle of wine. Anything involving strawberries, sticky chocolate, or that had a smooth consistency, he'd instantly ruled out. Day-old, crunchy cookies were the only thing that had fit the bill.

He piled the cookies onto a plate then angled into the dining area. He'd set the small table a little earlier but now stood staring at it. The whole setting looked somehow too intimate, too...suggestive. Too much like a scene for seduction.

Wrong.

He'd agreed to this little meeting solely to try to bring her around to his way of thinking. Placing the cookies on the table, he decided the overhead light wasn't bright enough. He circled around the room, flicking on every lamp in the place, then flicked on the television and tuned in CNN. A quick trip into the kitchen found the wine he'd been letting breathe on the table resting instead on the counter. After he'd propped his briefcase along with his laptop onto the dining table next to the place settings, he stood back. There. Everything looked more casual. More businesslike. More like the last thing on his mind was sampling Gracie Mattias instead of her food.

He grimaced and rubbed his stubble-covered chin. If that was the last thing on his mind, then why did it spring forth so quickly?

The phone rang on the table in the corner, breaking his thought cleanly in two. He glanced at his watch, then stepped to pluck up the receiver.

"Dylan, it's Tanja."

He frowned, wondering at the sound of pulsating music in the background. "She lives." And apparently better than he did, if the music was any indication.

"Look, I just got a call from your editor. Is your cell phone switched on?"

Dylan glanced toward his briefcase where the instrument in

question lay silent on top of some papers. "I don't think I turned it on after the flight. Why?"

"Because that Diana you've been trying to contact has been trying to call you, that's why."

"Oh, shit." Dylan glanced again at the time. He firmly told himself that he hadn't forgotten Diana. After all the day's disasters, and last-minute change in plans, he'd just been...distracted, that's all. And his state of mind had absolutely nothing to do with Grace Mattias. At least not on a personal level. His interest in her was strictly professional.

The sound of a brass horn through the receiver nearly deafened him. "Tanja, where are you?"

"At a jazz joint, of course. Have you never been to Chicago before, Dylan?"

Oh, he'd been to Chicago. Several times. But he'd never even thought about going to a jazz joint.

He found the idea strangely appealing now.

He raked his hand through his hair. "Shouldn't you be preparing for tomorrow? Seeing as all this sprang up at the last minute—"

"Everything's taken care of, Dylan. Leave it to me."

He grimaced. He'd left more to her than he should have and look where that had gotten him. Holed up in a Chicago hotel room in clothes that made him want to turn on rap music. "Tell me why I'm not reassured."

"Because you're a control freak, that's why." Her laugh took some of the sting out of her words. "Have a good night, Doc. I'll see you in the morning."

Dylan began to tell her not to hang up, but couldn't get the words out before the dial tone buzzed in his ear. Slowly he replaced the receiver in its cradle. A jazz joint? Any hardworking PR person would be mapping out a list of approved questions for tomorrow's host to ask. Working on a briefing strategy so that he would come away from the interview looking his best. Oh, but not his PR rep. Tanja was too busy hanging out at a jazz joint to do something as tedious as her job.

Stepping to the dining table, he took his cell phone from his briefcase. He had, indeed, neglected to turn it back on after the flight. He pressed the auto dial for Diana's number in San Francisco at the same time a knock sounded at the front door. Listening to the line ring, he pulled open the door to find Gracie standing in the hall smiling at him.

"Room service," she said, breezing past him into the room.

Clutching the phone to his ear, he turned to watch her walk by. Her form-fitting white tank top skimmed over generous breasts. And her very short skirt fit across her pert little bottom.

Dylan nearly dropped the cell phone when it stopped ringing. "Hello."

"Hi—"

"You've reached the residence of…"

He yanked the phone away from his ear and stared at it. He'd fallen for it again. Turning from where Grace watched him curiously, he finished listening to Diana's directives, then left a brief message outlining where he was and where she could get a hold of him. When he glanced back at the table, he found Grace had unpacked the food she'd brought along and sat inelegantly munching on a chunk of fresh French bread. "Phone tag, huh?"

Dylan stepped to the table and tossed his cell phone back into his open briefcase. "Yeah."

She tucked her long, curly red hair behind her ear and smiled up at him. "Always fun."

Dylan's gaze was still plastered to her ear and the hair she had tucked behind it. Diana's hair was blond and short and neat. Gracie's was red, curly and…wild. Still, he'd never stared at Diana's hair this way. "Yeah…fun."

She didn't seem to notice his inattention and her smile took on a decidedly teasing quality. "Hope it's not anything important."

"Huh?"

She gestured toward the phone he'd put down. "The call."

"Oh. No. Not really." Just the rest of his life, that's all.

"Well, come and get it while it's hot."

Dylan nearly swallowed his tongue whole. "Huh?" he finally managed to squeeze out after much, too much, time had gone by.

She laughed. An unspeakably sexy sound that would be right at home at that jazz joint Tanja was at. "The food. It's best if eaten hot."

"Ah." He sat down, trying to hide the reduction of his vocabulary down to sounds rather than words. That proved one of the points he made in his book. "Steer well away from women who leave you tongue-tied. It's during those encounters that you begin thinking with parts of your body not related to your brain." He nearly laughed aloud.

Gracie speared a piece of fish and slid it into her mouth. After swallowing, she asked, "Are you going to share the joke? Or am I the joke?"

"It's nothing. Just thinking about what someone said. Not related to you, I assure you." He found himself putting his paper napkin in his lap and stopped himself. "This looks good."

As a single male who didn't often make the effort for himself, he appreciated a nicely prepared meal. And this one was indeed well prepared. The items were so well put together, had he not seen the fish and vegetables in her basket at the market he would have suspected she'd ordered it in. He squinted at her. Which, of course, was still a possibility.

He then realized he'd forgotten the wine in the kitchen. Excusing himself, he went to retrieve it. She apparently recognized the vintage and she hummed with appreciation. He filled her glass, then his own, then reseated himself.

After her ceaseless repartee earlier in the day, her sudden silence proved unnerving to him. So much so that when she reached across him for the bread by his arm, he nearly jumped out of his cargo pants.

She laughed quietly. "Boy, you're wound up, aren't you?"

He rubbed the back of his neck. "It's been a long day."

"I don't know. I've had worse."

He'd had, too, but he thought it best to leave the conversation there lest she discover his behavior had nothing to do with the day and more to do with her nearness.

He watched her fork a sprig of asparagus then nibble on the end. The fish in his mouth turned to sandpaper and he was suddenly incapable of swallowing it.

Sure sign number one that his interest in her was taking a seriously wrong turn.

He forced his gaze back to his plate, wishing he'd turned up the sound on the television. The silence that stretched between them left too much room for thought. And chased away every last argument he'd hoped to make tonight.

Gracie's appearance wasn't helping matters much. Though he suspected that no matter what she was wearing, Gracie Mattias would ooze enough sex appeal to start World War III. That appeal wound its way around him, cocooning him in some sort of sensual haze that almost made him dizzy.

She quietly cleared her throat. A sound that should have been normal, but was somehow low and suggestive coming from her. Almost like a feline purr. "So, Dr. Dylan, how long has it been for you?"

He nearly choked on his wine. "Pardon me?"

Grace motioned toward the food on the table. "How long has it been since you've had a home-cooked meal?" Her brown eyes sparkled. "Why? What did you think I meant?"

He decided to come straight out with it. He might feel dumb, but he was a little sick of playing it. "Sex."

He was satisfied by her sudden coughing fit. He handed her her water glass. When that didn't seem to work, he gave her a soft, then a harder thump on the back. She finally spat out into her napkin whatever was lodged in her throat. "Gad, talk about bad table manners. Martha Stewart would be crushed." She fanned her reddened cheeks with one hand, took a drink of water with her other. She smiled. "Thanks."

"Don't mention it." The incident should have served as a bucket of ice-cold water to his libido, but instead the heat generated from the brief, innocuous touch of his hand to her back was nearly stinging in intensity. "I do have to question the timing of the…episode, however." He gave her a teasing grin.

She cautiously tested another bite of food. "You mean what kind of sex therapist in her right mind would choke at the mention of the word *sex?*"

He nodded. "Something like that."

"Let's just say I didn't expect the word to come from your mouth, Dr. Dylan."

"Just Dylan. Please."

"I'll try. But you have to admit, Dr. Dylan does have a certain ring to it." She sat back, wineglass in hand, and openly pondered him. "So how long has it been?" She smiled. "And this time I do mean sex."

Four years, six months and twenty-five days, his subconscious offered silently. An answer he had been proud of only a short time ago. A fact he wanted to change posthaste when sitting next to Grace.

"Touché," he said. He wasn't about to share the very personal details of his sex life with her. To do so would only invite further temptation. Hell, just looking at her made him remember how exciting it was to trap a woman's moan in her throat by covering her mouth with his. Brought vividly to mind the sweet arch of a woman's back as she strained to get closer. Filled his nose with the musky smell of a woman's heated sex.

His chest tightened and he suddenly couldn't get enough air.

Sure sign number two of his growing attraction toward her.

He found himself on the verge of groaning and fought to refocus on the meal. He was surprised to find the food on his plate nearly gone. Funny, he could barely recall having eaten a single bite of it.

"Is that the type of question you advise your patients to ask?" he said, counseling himself to work through his uncomfortable condition. Find common ground, stand firmly on it, and maybe he just might get around to making at least one point tonight. "The sex thing?"

She tucked her hair behind her ear again. "Depends on the patient. You?"

"Never."

"Never?" The arch of her brow fascinated him. "Oh, wait. Yes, I remember. Sex shouldn't even enter the equation conversation-wise until well after the third date, right? Chapter One, Section Four, if I'm not mistaken."

"Chapter Two, Section One, but I'm flattered."

Her smile made him wonder if she'd purposely quoted the wrong passage. "And in the case of STDs, sexually transmitted diseases? Say genital herpes? Don't you think it's important a person know up front whether or not the person they're dating is in a position to pass on a lifelong disease to them?"

He wiped his mouth with the napkin. "I suppose you suggest they provide a recent HIV test the moment the guy picks the girl up."

"Or when the girl picks the guy up. If they want to have unprotected sex…yes, I do."

He grimaced. "A relationship has to do with more than just sex, Gracie."

"Granted, but you can't ignore that sex does play an important role. If two people aren't sexually compatible, then they may be setting themselves up for a lifetime of misery if they don't find that out up front."

"Ah, a new twist on the process of elimination." He leaned his elbow on the table. "If they build their relationship solely on how good the initial sex is, they're destined to keep that divorce rate right up there at fifty percent."

She began to say something, then snapped her mouth closed. Dylan gazed at her lips, moist from where she'd just sipped her wine. "How's your track record on the STD issue, Dr. Dylan?"

He couldn't have answered her if he'd tried. His throat had just completely closed up.

She held up her hands and gave a small laugh. "Okay. Why don't we just say that on this issue we agree to disagree?"

He nodded. "Good idea."

She leaned forward and resumed eating, apparently happy to continue on as if their exchange had never occurred.

But after long minutes ticked by with no sound other than the suddenly far too intimate sounds of her eating, Dylan felt the desire to prod her back to life. Something, anything to snap his acute concentration on her nearness.

Why didn't she say anything more? Prod him to answer her questions about sex and STDs? Make one of her barbed, well-aimed remarks? Tell him he was all wet? Something, anything, to break this surreal spell their silence was putting on him.

"This your first book?" he forced out, the words sounding unnaturally loud in the quiet room.

She sipped her wine, then nodded. "You?"

"Second."

Well, that attempt at jump-starting the conversation had succeeded with flying colors, hadn't it? He knew his inability to speak in coherent sentences was another sign, but he refused to acknowledge it. If he ignored the signs, maybe they would just go away.

Oh, great advice, Doctor.

Gracie's hand on his wrist nearly made him vault from his chair.

Sure sign number four. The rush of desire so strong he swore he had a hard-on.

"Could you pass the wine, please?"

Dylan stared at her for a long moment. Either her pupils were dilated, or he was projecting his own circumstances onto her. "Oh. Sure." He poured her more wine, then topped off his own glass, though it was still full.

She smiled at him. He smiled back, then cleared his throat.

So he'd made a huge mistake in inviting her here. Humongous. Phenomenal. But the meal was almost over. And he hadn't made a fool of himself, or betrayed his beliefs once. Good. Very good.

He hurriedly finished what was on his plate, then wiped his hands on his napkin. "Well, that was certainly enjoyable. Thanks so much for bringing it."

There was that laugh again. He'd have to make a note to himself: never make Gracie Mattias laugh.

"But we haven't even had dessert yet," she said.

Every last damn image he'd had of her since seeing her in the shower that morning slid provocatively through his mind. And in every single one she was naked, hot and needy.

"Do you have milk?"

She could have been speaking a foreign language for all the sense he made out of her words.

"For the cookies."

He practically leaped from the chair. "Oh. Yes. I'll...go get it."

In the privacy of the kitchen, he propped his hands against the counter and took huge, silent, calming breaths. *Get it together, man. She's only a woman. Just like any other woman.*

Who was he kidding? She was temptation incarnate.

A year or two ago he'd had a married male patient who had been hopelessly attracted to a next-door neighbor. His advice to him was to envision a matronly aunt whenever he crossed paths with her.

Dylan tried to envision his old Aunt Reggie, who had always seemed ancient to him, wore support socks with her flowered housecoats, and always smelled like cabbage.

He closed his eyes, realizing the imagery wasn't working. Funny, he couldn't remember if his advice had worked for his patient, either. Shortly after that session, the guy had never come back.

"Do you need some help?"

Dylan turned around in the cramped confines of the kitchen, putting him nearly nose to nose with his own personal temptation.

"Do I ever."

Then he did the very thing he counseled his patients against. The last thing an almost engaged man should even entertain doing. He thrust his hands into all that glorious red hair and brought his mouth down on hers like a man on death row being offered his last meal.

5

SWEET MERCY. Gracie threw her eyes open wide, rendered completely speechless by Dylan's unexpected, all-out fiery assault on her mouth. Halfway through her fish she'd begun to wonder if she had what it took to bag one Dr. Dylan Fairbanks. Aside from his apparent initial awkwardness, he hadn't been the one to end up choking.

She'd used nearly ever weapon in her sexual arsenal. Lingered over her food as though she found it unbearably delicious. Found a reason to touch him by asking him to pass the wine. Crossed and recrossed her legs. Sent him little signals with a flip of her hair here, a slant of a suggestive glance there, not to mention the repeated licking of her lips. And he'd ignored every single last one of them, sitting adjacent from her as cool as you please, completely composed, his integrity intact.

Then there was that damnable silence. It seemed to amplify the sound of her own heartbeat in her ears, her one-sided flirting making her all the hotter for him. With every click of an invisible clock, she'd wanted him more and more, until she was afraid she was going to shove his laptop to the floor and crawl across their plates to kiss him.

Oh, God but he had an incredible mouth.

Gracie returned his assault with equal fervor, pulling at his firm lips, nipping at his tongue, and delving her own tongue deep into his mouth. She felt like a hungry child who had been denied an edible gift then found it waiting for her on her bed pillow. Her lips molded so perfectly against his that she thought for a ridiculous moment that they had been made to kiss his. Far from the awkwardness usually experienced during first kisses, this one shot way beyond fumbled positioning, teeth knocking and tongue sparring. They shared something that made her thighs quiver. It was almost as if she'd been kissing him all of her life. Well, maybe not all of her life, but certainly a helluva lot longer than a half minute. And she thought she wouldn't be able to get enough of him even if she took a deep breath and inhaled him whole.

She curled her fingers in his sweater. She'd been ready to pack it all in when he hadn't even glanced at the cleavage she'd worked so hard to display during dinner. Not once. And he'd appeared in such a hurry to get her out of there, she was sure the last thing on his mind had been her.

Then she'd stepped into the kitchen and he was on her like a Velcro suit.

She felt his hand on her outer thigh and whimpered, his skin seeming to brand hers with fire. She tugged him closer by his sweater, his hand skimming over her flesh, setting nerve endings aflame in its wake. He curved his fingers over her silk-covered bottom and gave a squeeze so torturously possessive she shuddered. As she tugged, he pulled, bringing her softness against his hard arousal. Gracie's breathing grew so ragged she was afraid there wasn't enough air in the room to satisfy her need for the necessary element. She shoved her hands deep into his back pockets and squeezed his tight rear end, wanting to feel him even closer.

He tugged his mouth from hers and trailed a hot, wet path to her ear. "God, I've been itching to touch you since I saw you in that damn shower this morning all naked and lathered up."

His words sent a shiver skittering along the surface of her skin, leaving her tiny hairs standing on end. Tugging on the hem of his sweater, she bunched the soft fabric in her hands and shoved it up as she slid down. With fingers she couldn't seem to move fast enough, she popped the snap to his pants and drew the zipper down, immensely satisfied with his quick indrawn breath. His hands tightened in her hair, apparently torn between wanting to push her away and yank her closer but settling for just touching her.

A tug on the open material and his erection sprang free from both his pants and briefs. She laughed. "My, my. Careful there…you could put an eye out with that thing."

He groaned and before she could get a chance to fit her lips around the tip of his erection he yanked her back to her feet with one hand, tugged his pants back up with his other. "Do that and I'll finish before we even get a chance to begin."

Then his mouth was on hers again, his hot hand on her bare thigh, and all thought of protest instantly scattered to the corners of her mind. He slid his hand from beneath her sinfully short skirt and grasped her hips, turning her until she was against the counter, then lifting her on top of it. Her quiet laugh told of her surprise, but it didn't stop her from spreading her legs and wantonly yanking him between them. When the hard length of him nestled against her swollen folds through her panties, she nearly cried out in exquisite pleasure.

She'd known the sexy doc would be good, but for God's sake, they hadn't really even done anything yet and she was a tongue flick away from orgasm. He bent to her right breast, forcing her to grope for a supporting grip against the counter behind her. Her fingers touched something and she glanced to see that it was a cookie. She pushed it out of the way, arching her back as he fastened his mouth over her engorged nipple right through the material of her tank and bra.

Dear God…

Her womb contracted so violently she nearly catapulted from the counter. Sensing her crisis, Dylan ground against her, his hold tightening, his mouth breathing hot air through her tank and onto her damp nipple. Gracie heard a low, gut-tightening moan fill the room and realized only distantly that it was her own as she succumbed to the delicious shivers racking her body.

Dylan pulled his mouth from her breast and lay his head

against her shoulder. "Oh, God, if I don't take you now, Gracie, I swear I'm going to burst."

She began impatiently pushing his pants out of the way. "So take me."

He caught her wrists in his hands, his green eyes intense. "I can't."

Her heart dipped low in her stomach then rebounded to lodge in her thick throat. "What?"

"I...I don't have anything to protect you, damn it."

She nearly collapsed in a mixture of relief and unbearable pleasure. Freeing one of her wrists from his, she dipped her fingers into the vee of her tank, sliding out a brightly colored foil packet. His brows drew slightly, almost comically, together as he looked from her to it, and she knew that protection hadn't been the only thing stopping him from taking things between them all the way. But she'd be damned if she was going to let him wriggle out of it now.

She slid her legs around his waist, pulling him tightly against her. "Now...where were we?"

She slanted her mouth against his, feeling all powerful when, after a brief hesitation, he groaned and kissed her back with double the intensity he had earlier.

She wasn't sure if it was him or her, but somehow they managed not only to free her of her panties, but him of his pants, and finally he was cradled between her legs, his hot, throbbing, latex-covered erection sandwiched between her slick, swollen flesh. The coolness of the tile under her bottom, and his heat between her legs, snatched away her breath. When he fit the tip of his arousal into her opening, she was certain she'd never be able to breathe again.

After the mad upward spiral of her desire and her climax only moments before, she thought herself more than ready for him. But the hesitant stretching of her muscles told her it was better if they took it slow.

Until he slid himself in to the hilt, filling her in one long stroke, making her shiver.

She could no longer hold herself upright. She collapsed

back onto her hands as she tightened her legs around his waist, bracing her hips for his next delicious stroke. Then his next.

Every cell of Gracie's body felt brilliantly, vividly alive. The tiny hair on her arms and at the back of her neck stood up on end, her legs ached, and her muscles contracted, trying to pull him in farther even as he withdrew to thrust into her again. She moved her hips to grind against him, barely aware of his throwing his head back and groaning at the unexpected move. Then he snapped upright, a needy expression contorting his handsome face. A lock of hair fell over his right brow as he grasped her hips and thrust into her harder...faster, chasing every coherent thought straight from Gracie's mind. Driving her insane with desire.

Her breath coming in rapid gasps, she felt him tense, sensing him on the verge of climax. She tilted her hips forward more, taking him deeper, biting hard on her bottom lip as his fingers bit into the flesh of her thighs. She couldn't help noticing how magnificent it was, to view a man as delectably attractive as Dr. Dylan Fairbanks in the throes of pleasure. His entire body tensed, the veins in his neck stood out in stark release, his teeth were clenched tightly together as he gave himself over to emotions he had no control over.

Finally he collapsed, his temple against hers, his arms shaking as he propped his hands against the counter mere millimeters away from hers, his thumbs covering hers.

She swallowed hard, fighting to catch her breath. Amazingly, she could still feel him filling her. Completely erect. She was just about to shimmy her hips, to let him know she was up for more if he was, when the shrill ring of the phone in the other room tore through the thick film of intimacy weaving them together.

For long moments, Gracie questioned whether or not he even heard the ringing. She smiled and rubbed her temple against his. "It could be the concierge telling us the hotel is on fire."

She heard him swallow, only then realizing he had yet to look at her.

"I wish it was the concierge. But I'm afraid it's someone else. Somebody I don't think I really want to talk to just now."

Gracie's grip against the counter slipped as he pulled away. Before she could ease her feet to the floor, he was already buttoning his pants and heading toward the kitchen door. He stopped, turned, then ran his hand through his tousled hair. "Don't…um, go anywhere. Stay right here. In the kitchen."

Gracie smiled at his obviously agitated demeanor, reluctant to shrug off the astounding feelings they'd just shared even as she put herself back together. Ignoring his directive, she rounded the corner into the main room, watching as Dylan paced, the receiver held closely to his ear.

"I've been trying to contact you for three straight days," he said, an edge to his voice she wondered would be there if not for her. "I see. Sure." He caught sight of where Gracie stood smiling after him and completely froze, his eyes larger than the dinner plates they had just eaten from. "Can you hold on a minute? No, no, don't hang up. Lord knows when I'll be able to get you on the line again."

He dropped the receiver to his side, his palm covering the mouthpiece. "Sorry, I have to take this call."

Gracie shrugged, as if to indicate that he should go ahead. Then the serious, weighty way he stared at her slowly began to sink in. He had to take the call and wanted to do so without her presence.

"Oh."

She reached down and put her shoes back on as he stood in the same, unmoving position.

Was the person on the other end of the line a woman? His ex-wife? Girlfriend? She didn't know. And tried to ignore her curiosity to find out.

She stood straight, glancing toward the table.

"I'll have the maid take care of that," he told her.

She flicked her gaze back to his face. "All right." She

tugged at the straps of her tank, as if she could somehow make them conceal her better. "Well, I guess I'll see you tomorrow then."

She pretended to ignore his grimace as she gathered what little was left of the pride he'd just shot to hell around her feet and headed for the door. "Sweet dreams," she called out, waggling her fingers in a teasing way before the barrier clicked closed.

She leaned against the door and swallowed.

Wow…

What in the hell had just happened in there? She wasn't completely sure. What was worse was that she wasn't sure she wanted to find out.

What she did know was that her nerve endings sang a tune full of life and energy. That her thigh muscles ached just the tiniest bit. And that her womanhood throbbed with a sensation she wasn't sure she had experienced before.

She also knew that she just had been dropped like yesterday's newspaper.

Well, not dropped, exactly. How could you be dropped if you'd never been picked up? She'd set out to have a sexual tryst with one handsome Dr. Dylan Fairbanks, and she'd accomplished that task. In spades. What she hadn't been prepared for was what came afterward. How…abruptly it would end.

She twisted her lips. She certainly hadn't expected any long-term commitment. In fact, she'd been against that scenario from the outset. This had been her shot at her own personal sexual safari. And, oh boy, cutting loose sure did have its benefits. She'd never felt so uninhibited, sexy, wild. She supposed Dylan's own aversion to such…provocative behavior merely added another edgy dimension to the entire encounter. There had been something…challenging and dangerous about enticing Dr. Dylan to step from his conservative restraints and give himself over to temptation. And knowing that she had been the one to make him do it was doubly intriguing.

Still, something flitted along the outskirts of her immediate thoughts to tease her, taunt her, dare her to name it. This was ridiculous really. She and Dylan were grown adults, secure in their own identities, established in their respective careers and lives. Add to that that they'd just shared some incredible sex, and well, they had it all. Didn't they?

Of course they did.

The sound of Dylan's muted voice drifted through the wood as he continued talking to whoever was on the phone. Pushing from the door, Gracie stuck her chin out and moved toward the elevator and her own room where she could take notes on her experience and compare it to the case studies she had used in her book.

DYLAN SAT FROZEN on the couch, the telephone receiver dangling from his hand. He stared at it, unable to recall why he was holding it. Then his broken conversation with Diana came back to him in bits and pieces. Lame segments that still didn't make sense because his ears were roaring and his body felt as if he were covered in lava.

He glanced toward the door. The same door Grace Mattias had just walked out of minutes before. His mind went completely blank, making him forget about Diana and the phone call all over again. The shrill beep-beep indicating that the receiver was off the hook nearly catapulted him from the cushion.

It took him three tries before he fit the shrieking instrument into its cradle.

What in the hell had just happened? One minute he'd been a glass of milk and a cookie away from showing Grace the door. The next he was showing her something else entirely. A side of himself that he hadn't seen in a long, long time.

Had he really shoved her onto the counter, pushed her skirt up and had at her like a teen having a go at the stacked baby-sitter?

Dylan dropped his head into his hands and groaned. Loudly.

What had he been thinking? He grit his teeth. Obviously he hadn't been thinking. At least not with any part of his body that mattered.

For God's sake, he was a civilized male who not only knew civilized behavior, he wrote about it.

Bits of fragmented memories taunted him. How many times when an adulterer patient told him "it just happened" had he loftily responded with "oh, you just happened to trip and fall into her vagina."

Only in his case, he hadn't fallen into Gracie's slick, tight flesh…he'd thrust into it again and again.

He threw himself back on the sofa and groaned.

Of course, he and Diana weren't married. But that didn't alleviate his guilt. In his mind, he was just as dirty as those two-timing slouches he used to chastise. What did it matter that he and Diana hadn't even had sex yet? That's what made his relationship with her special. He'd made a conscious decision to wait. To pursue his commitment to her with total and complete chivalry. To prove that men did not live by sex alone. That they were driven by more than their sex drive. Capable of celibacy until their wedding night.

How had one hour alone with Gracie Mattias shot the past four years to hell?

Pulling away the pillow he had crammed down over his face, he glanced at the front of his pants. Despite everything, he got rock hard all over again just thinking about her.

He pushed off of the sofa, put a call in to the concierge to arrange for color- and style-specific clothes be delivered to him, then headed for the shower.

Only his actions refused to allow him freedom from his tormented thoughts. He remembered the way Gracie's face had fallen when he'd essentially booted her out of the room. Until that moment he never would have thought Gracie capable of that expression. In that one instant she looked like spurned teenager and hurt lover all rolled up into one.

Of course, that expression had lasted only an instant, after which she'd smiled the familiar sassy smile of hers and waggled her fingers at him as she said goodbye. But the fact remained, he had seen the expression. It hit him like a fist to the gut.

He switched the water in the shower to ice-cold, then stepped into it, clothes and all. His breath whooshed from his lungs and every thought rushed from his mind other than to force himself to stand under the punishing spray until every last sign of arousal vanished. And until he could figure out what he was going to do to right this wrong.

Which, despite the frigid cold, took a full three minutes.

Gasping for air, and shivering, he finally switched the stream off and stripped out of his clothes. First thing he needed to do was apologize to Grace. While she had been an equal and willing participant in the evening's events, he still felt the need to apologize for his behavior. He'd been an animal, a greedy horny toad. He'd thought nothing of shoving her skirt up her smooth thighs and taking his pleasure, with absolutely no thought of her and her needs. Hell, he hadn't even made a stab at foreplay. He didn't even know if she'd gotten any enjoyment out of the experience.

Not that he intended to remedy it if she hadn't. Oh no. From here on out, rule number one was to stay as far away from Miss Hottie Grace Mattias as possible. And never, ever be in the same room alone with her again.

Just because he'd fallen off the horse didn't mean he couldn't get right back on it again. What had happened tonight was no more than a missed hurdle. A momentary blip on the screen. A crack on the sidewalk of his path. There was no reason to think he couldn't continue right on as though it had never happened.

Except, of course, that he needed to tell Diana.

He cringed, thinking the cold shower hadn't been necessary at all. The mere prospect of divulging what had happened between him and Gracie to Diana was enough to chase every hot, seductive thought from his mind.

But tell her, he would. Honesty was always the best policy. He only wished he knew when that moment would come.

He'd been so distracted during their brief conversation, he'd completely forgotten the reason he'd wanted to talk to her. To invite her down to Miami where he planned to propose.

Shrugging into the hotel robe, he made his way into the other room to begin the long process of cleaning up the mess, both on the table and of his life.

6

IT WASN'T POSSIBLE that he looked even better today than he had yesterday.

That was the only thought that sprang forth and refused to budge from Gracie's mind when she bumped into Dylan Fairbanks in the syndicated television talk show's green room, which wasn't green at all, but purple. Overwhelmingly purple, from the walls to the carpet and everything in between. Even the appetizers set out on a tray seemed to have a purple tinge to them.

"Want to take a guess as to the host's favorite color?" her assistant Rick asked, giving her one of his lopsided smiles.

Gracie pried her gaze away from Dylan and absently considered the finger food. "Oh, I don't know...green?"

When Rick didn't respond with a laugh or other wisecrack, she looked at him.

"What is it?" she asked, suddenly alarmed.

"Nothing. It's just that I think you're looking a little green right about now."

"Very funny." Gracie felt like whacking him in the arm. But he looked good in his nifty new suit and she didn't want to wrinkle it. She returned her attention to the food.

No, no crackers. They tended to gravitate straight to her front teeth. Something crunchy. Ah, a carrot! As usual, she got up late this morning—awakened by a phone call from Rick—and hadn't had time to even make herself a cup of tea much less breakfast. It was just as well, because the lingering scent of the fish she'd cooked the night before had robbed her of her appetite.

"If I didn't know better, I'd say you're nervous."

Unfortunately Rick appeared to know her better than she was comfortable with. Hmm…maybe she should advertise for a new assistant when she got back to Baltimore. She sighed, knowing she'd never do that. Rick was the best assistant a woman could ask for. Like a wife, minus the emotional debris. "But you do know better."

His grin made a comeback. "Yep." He glanced at the open notepad he held. "Do you want to go over the format again?"

She shook her head. "No. I think I have it straight. I go one-on-one with the host first. Then Dr. Dy—Fairbanks gets his shot. Then the host will put us together for the remaining half hour."

He turned the page. "And remember, the host is pretty conservative."

Giving in to temptation, she popped a piece of cheese into her mouth, careful to chew with only her back teeth. "With an audience that's majority female." She waved off his warning. "Don't worry, I already have a strategy all worked out."

"The 'feminine mystique' angle?"

She hummed. "God, is this cheese good or am I just enormously hungry?"

"You're enormously hungry."

She swallowed and smiled at him wryly. "Oh, before I forget, my answering service took three calls last night—"

Rick closed his notepad. "The Decateurs had a bad episode with the body oil you recommended, a possible referral from Dr. Moss and an inquiry from a potential new patient. Got them."

She wagged a finger at him. "I knew there was a reason I keep you around."

He feigned shock. "You mean beyond my dashing good looks?"

She laughed. "I'm more of the tall, dark and handsome type myself."

Movement caught her attention from the corner of her eye as she popped another cheese square into her mouth. Speaking of tall, dark and handsome, a particular one in question was bearing down on her.

"Excuse me a moment, won't you." Dylan urgently grasped her arm, pulling her away from where she had been talking to Rick. She gaped at him, nearly tottering off her heels.

"I need to speak to you," he said quietly.

Gracie tried to ignore where his touch felt like pure fire against her skin as she straightened her skirt and quickly tried to finish chewing her cheese. She swallowed hard. "You can speak to me all you want. On the show in five minutes."

"Now."

Something inside Gracie rankled. She glanced to where Rick was looking on with a raised brow from one side of the room, while Dylan's publicity rep peeked around the show's producer from the other side. The purple streaks in the PR rep's hair went nicely with the decor, Gracie thought wryly.

She looked back at Dylan. Well, not directly at him, at him, but at a mole on his forehead, near the edge of his right brow. A particularly delectable looking mole. "So talk."

He suddenly looked altogether agitated, making her feel the same. Until she figured out what he was about to do. She finally met his gaze straight on, refusing to acknowledge the sexy green of his eyes. "Oh, no, don't tell me you're about to apologize, Dylan."

His instant stiffening told her that's exactly what he was about to do. "Why not?"

"Because that would be the worst possible thing you could do right now, that's why not." She lowered her voice. Was it her imagination, or were Rick and Tanja covertly edging their way closer? "I don't know, Dylan. There might be some in need of your apology, but I'm not one of them. We're adults, right?"

"And what we did last night was purely adult," he said before she could continue.

"And completely consensual. I have absolutely no regrets. If you do...well, I don't want to know about them." She crossed her arms under her breasts. Today she had on a royal-navy suit and white silk blouse, in recognition of the daytime televised venue, but her skirt was still short short, her heels high high. "I may be a psychologist, but I'm not about to let you ease your mind by confessing all to me. I'm not interested in what happened beyond I had a damn good time. That's it. Got it?"

"You had a good time?"

Her stomach dipped at the surprise in his voice. "I think I said 'damn' good time." She uncrossed her arms at the admission and pretended to pick lint from the sleeve of her jacket. Only when she had her emotions back under control did she dare meet his gaze again. She smiled. "Do I strike you as the doormat type, Dylan? The type who would have sex merely to satisfy someone else?"

He stood for a long moment, apparently not breathing if his resulting whoosh of an exhale was any indication. "No."

She tried not to notice how relieved he looked, and how much she wished she could plaster her mouth right on top of his. "And I don't think you are either."

"Me? Oh, no. No, of course not."

She bit discreetly on her bottom lip. "Then last night was all about fundamental urges and spontaneous combustion. Two adults having consensual sex, pure and simple. There's no reason for either of us to apologize. At least not to each other."

"It's not going to happen again," he said. More like blurted.

"I wasn't planning on it."

He suddenly frowned. "Why not?"

She couldn't help laughing. She'd been about to say last night hadn't been planned, either. But she couldn't say that, could she? Because she had set out to seduce him. If only she had planned down the line a little further, things might have looked better right now.

She sighed, all trace of amusement gone. "Look, Dylan, last night I had a great time, all right? But let's face it. You and I...well, we'd end up maiming each other if left in a room alone together for prolonged periods of time. That doesn't bode well for either a relationship, or a serial case of one-night stands, does it?''

He looked genuinely perplexed. "Relationship? One-night stands?" He scratched the area over his ear, drawing her attention to his well-shaped hand and long fingers. She remembered all too vividly what his hand had felt like molded around her breasts.

The fabric of her blouse and jacket seemed to rasp against her hardening nipples and she caught herself licking her lips in anticipation of something that couldn't be again. Or could it?

Dylan's face went completely white. "I'm engaged."

No, it most definitely couldn't.

Gracie nearly choked. "Did you just say you were engaged?"

He averted his gaze, his hand moving from his ear to the back of his neck. "I meant to say something last night...that's why what happened shouldn't have...and it's for that reason I need to apologize."

"You're engaged?" she found herself repeating again, and wished it were physically possible to kick herself in the rear. Well, she supposed it was possible, but not in the way she needed to be kicked. One good boot that would send her flying was in order. Something that equaled the virtual punch she had just taken to the stomach.

Okay, Gracie, you can handle this. You even address this scenario in your book, remember?

While that was the case, and her advice to any unsuspecting women—or men—was to get as far away from the cheating slime as fast as possible, to have it happen to her...well, that was different. Wasn't it?

She took a deep, even breath. Control. She needed to regain control over this situation.

"Gracie?"

She nearly hit the ceiling at the sound of Rick's voice so close to her back. She turned.

"It's time."

Gracie gave Dylan one last smile, deciding to overlook the thoughtful expression on his face at what she had probably just given away.

"Well, I guess you do need to do some apologizing. As I said however, it's not to me."

Good. That was good. Right? She'd handled herself like the pro she was. Cool, calm and collected. Even managed to score a couple of points, if she was a good judge.

But as the show's producer led her out of the room first, she thought it would take the jaws of life to extricate her nails from the palms of her hands.

He's engaged.

She didn't really understand the enormity of her upset. Her heart literally felt as if one of those hokey medicine men had slipped his hand into her chest and was taking great pleasure in squeezing the life from the all-important organ.

Okay, so maybe she didn't feel as blasé as she'd pretended about what had happened in Dylan's kitchen last night. Maybe the fact that she had spent half the night scribbling notes that didn't always make any sense was a good indicator. When she'd finally drifted off to sleep, her dreams had been filled with images of him gripped between her thighs, his face contorted in pleasure. But she was pretty confident that Dylan's abrupt dismissal of her was more to blame for her reaction than any delusions of attraction that went beyond sex. Pride was a funny thing. It made people do stupid things. She was confident that pride was behind her sleeplessness and her continued sexual interest in the sexy sex doctor. No woman liked to be forgotten so quickly, even if she never intended a relationship to go beyond the one-night-stand stage. In a shadowy, unexplored corner of her mind, she liked to think the man in question was questioning whether he'd ever be the same again, and whether he'd ever find another woman to better the experience. Panting after her, so to speak.

The woman in question certainly never expected to find out the man not only wasn't panting after her, but that he planned to marry someone else.

"Stop talking in the third person, Gracie," she murmured to herself as she straightened her skirt.

The producer she followed through the mazelike, narrow hallways to the soundstage gave her a strange look, then turned back around.

In the end, however, did it really matter if he was engaged or not? At least he wasn't married.

The line of reasoning wasn't working.

Okay, then, since she'd certainly had no plans to pursue a relationship after last night, because she'd genuinely been in the dark as to Dylan's…lack of freedom, and the fact that the fiancée was unknown to her, she hadn't really broken any of her own rules. Had she?

Note to self: write an addendum to include in reprints of my book. When indulging in sexual safaris, make sure you and the prey in question never cross paths again.

There! That was it. The reason why her own personal sexual safari was a bust. She hadn't stopped to consider the impact to her and Dylan's professional relationship. Well, that was easily remedied, because after this show there was absolutely no reason to expect their paths to cross again anytime soon. Indeed, given his disclosure, never would be a good estimation of when that would happen again.

"Take the seat to the left," the producer instructed.

Gracie did as she was told.

She sat still as a microphone was strategically placed on her lapel. She frowned. Why was she labeling last night a bust? It might be a lot of things, but a failure was not one of them. She had been highly successful in bagging her prey. She'd gotten exactly what she wanted. Sex on the kitchen counter with one sexy Dylan Fairbanks.

But if she had been so successful, why had she wanted to press her mouth against that adorable mole at the corner of Dylan's brow just now? And why was she sitting in front of a live audience of two hundred, on a soundstage, picking her brain over what had happened with Dylan. Rather than focusing on what she would say to the popular host?

The producer handed her a copy of her book and a crowd warmer stepped out to address everyone. She cleared her throat and focused her attention on the young woman, thinking it just as well that she didn't have time to answer the questions she had just posed to herself, because she wasn't sure she would like the answers.

DYLAN TUGGED at his too tight tie, a tie that had been perfectly adjusted a mere hour ago but now threatened to choke him. Checking the number on the door, making doubly sure he was on the right floor, he gained access to his hotel room and slammed the door after himself.

Dog food. That's what one sexy, frustrating Dr. Gracie Mattias had just made of his life and his philosophies on national TV. And not even the choice brand, either. The generic stuff. The kind that made you want to heave the instant you opened the can.

He absently rubbed the back of his neck and dropped into a dining room chair, his laptop open in front of him. He knew what the generic variety smelled like because he'd had a dog once. A mutt of questionable pedigree from a local animal shelter. It had been a gift from his mother, Moonbeam, when he'd finally scrounged enough cash together to move off the El Rancho compound and into his own apartment in San Fran.

"It'll help keep you human," she told him, the pup tucked under her arm as she stood outside his apartment. An apartment he'd been in for a mere twenty-four hours. He'd battled between closing the door on her and making room in his book-laden arms so he could take the panting canine. He'd wanted to stage a protest that would put to shame those his parents were well-known for...then she'd given him that smile. That one he'd never been able to argue with.

He punched at the button that would boot his laptop. Human. Right. The mangy mutt had set out to make his life a living hell from the get-go. He'd begun with his furniture, scratching and gnawing the scant secondhand pieces during the day while Dylan was away at Stanford teaching basic psych. The destruction continued on into the night, when often were the times he'd been awakened by rancid doggie breath. He recalled midnight trips to the bathroom interrupted by strategically placed doggie mines.

Finally, after everything in the apartment bore evidence of his canine roommate—destroyed or otherwise deemed unusable—Dylan had feigned a long-scheduled trip for a seminar in Chicago and dumped the mutt at his parents'. There the unfondly named Killer had stayed.

The hound was at least ten years old now. Amazing. There were times when he entered his trendy house in Pacific Heights and tensed, waiting for a secret attack from the twenty-pound beast. Strange, because Killer had never sunk his teeth into a single piece of Dylan's rich brown swanky Italian leather furniture. Regardless, Dylan swore he could make out battle scars around his ankles.

Not unlike the battle scars he wore after today's bout with Gracie Mattias on the syndicated TV show.

He cringed, the memory bringing him full circle to the dog food the frustratingly sexy sex doc had made out of his arguments on self-restraint in front of a nationwide audience.

He ignored that after last night he was probably the last person to be speaking on the merits of self-restraint. Especially to Grace Mattias, who had spent that same night shooting every last inch of his self-restraint to bits, then following it up by incinerating the remaining fragments on today's show.

He covered his face with his hands, all too easily conjuring up the image of her sitting across from him, choosing to cross her long, long legs at the exact moment he opened his mouth to respond to one of her loaded remarks. But it was one exchange in particular that made him groan aloud even now.

Interrupting the host of the show, Gracie had leaned forward and asked, "Tell me, Dr. Fairbanks, would you have me and everyone else believe that you haven't given in to your most basic, fundamental urges since your own admitted vow of celibacy?''

Feeling as though Gracie had just placed her hands around his neck and commenced choking him, he'd looked to the host for help. But she appeared as interested in the answer to the loaded question as Gracie was.

He'd cleared his throat, silently reciting ten of the many dead-sure, giveaway signs of lying as he considered his answer. He wasn't overly concerned about how far Grace intended to take the topic, though he supposed in retrospect he should have been. To flat out lie wasn't the way he operated. ''Dr. Mattias, as a psychotherapist, you're familiar with the advice given to patients trying to break self-defeating behavior, are you not? For the sake of argument, let's say we're talking about a smoker.''

''Ah, burning. Good analogy.''

Actually, it was the best he could come up with and it sucked dead toads, but he'd needed to put out the fire before his entire professional—and personal—life went up in smoke. ''So tell me, Doctor, what do you say to a patient who has gone without a cigarette for four solid years, then one day lights up?''

''To explore the interesting things you might do with a cigar?'' she'd said with a suggestive smile.

He'd winced but ignored her aside. ''Do you shrug your shoulders and tell him he might as well take up smoking again? No. You encourage him to crack the whip and get right back up on that wagon, don't you?''

''Well, so long as it involves a whip...''

Thankfully the host chose that moment to jump in, expressing an interest in discussing the various sex toys Dr. Mattias would suggest a couple use to make their love lives more interesting, then broke for commercial.

He'd survived with all his body parts intact. Just barely.

For the past ten minutes he'd sat in front of his running laptop without really seeing it. He clicked open a couple files, not wanting to mull over something that had been bothering him ever since that exchange. A question weightier than the exchange itself.

More specifically, why Gracie hadn't revealed that he…she…they….

Oh, for God's sake, he couldn't even think the word.

"We had hot, wild, irresponsible sex," he said between clenched teeth.

He poked agitatedly at the keyboard until he'd spat out every possible adjective he could type to describe his feelings about his own behavior, then leaned back in the chair and rubbed his thumbs over his closed eyelids.

Well, why hadn't she?

It stood to reason that she had nothing to lose and everything to gain by letting that ferocious cat out of the bag. Especially after he'd virtually blurted that he was engaged. Well, not officially engaged yet, but he soon would be. Still, strangely, she'd held the bag closed and out of sight…except, of course, when he'd heard the sucker growling during her one and only reference to his celibacy. Or, more accurately, the breaking of that celibacy.

Then, of course, there was the whole issue of faithfulness she could have delved into but hadn't.

"It doesn't make any sense."

He snapped his eyes open, realizing he'd said the words aloud, emphasizing just how significant it was.

He realized that it just might be a question that would forever go unanswered.

"Thank God."

The predominant thought that had seen him through the remainder of the show was that at its end he and one inexplicably sexy Gracie Mattias would never have to cross paths again. In fact, he was so anxious to hurry that prospect along, he'd made it a point after the live show to hightail it out of there, relying on Tanja's considerable talents as she led the way through the backstage maze then out the door and into the chauffeured Lincoln at a near run.

Last night was an aberration. A one-time mistake. A nightmare he had the choice to wake up from. And he was doing exactly that. From here on out he was back to being the guy with whom he was familiar. The one he knew. The man he looked at in the mirror every morning confident that he was living his life exactly the way he intended. The guy who planned to marry Diana Evans.

From now on there would be no tart-mouthed sex doc to mince his philosophies into dog food. No long legs and provocative behavior to tempt him. No kitchen counters and overactive libido.

He glanced at his watch. He had an hour to get ready for his afternoon flight. The last thing he wanted was to be late and have Tanja trek in here and do his packing for him.

Shutting off his laptop, he slid it back into its carrying case, then turned toward the bedroom. Not that he had much to pack, just what he had on, the few clothes he'd ordered and a few toiletries he'd bought downstairs. The clothes from last night he'd thrown in the garbage and was pleased to see the maid had taken them away.

He stepped into the bedroom and stopped. On top of his bed was his luggage. The same luggage the airline had lost the day before.

He grinned.

In more ways than one, things were definitely looking up.

7

HOT. SO INCREDIBLY HOT. It only went with the territory that she should get the one room in the Houston hotel whose air conditioner was on the fritz.

Careful not to mar her freshly painted nails, Gracie bent over to consider the locking gadgets on her balcony door. She was seven floors up for God's sake, what kind of security risk could there possibly be? You'd have to be a rock climber or a sky diver in order to gain access to the tiny sitting area much less break into the room itself. Maneuvering some kind of slide mechanism, releasing the bar on the floor, then flipping the ordinary lock, she pulled. A speaker in the corner of her room broadcast an earsplitting siren. She squealed.

A woman's voice sounded over the system. "Security alert. Security alert. It has been determined that the breach action is noncautionary. Sorry for the inconvenience."

Gracie quickly closed the door and leaned against it, staring at the speaker. Had she done that? All she'd wanted was a breath of fresh air, not the onset of World War III.

The telephone rang. Her gaze slid to the instrument, then back to the screeching speaker.

"Hello?"

Silence. Or at least what she thought was silence. Who could tell with all the racket?

She covered her other ear and tried again. "Hello? This is the occupant of Room 6732. If this is security, please shut that damn siren off."

"Gracie?"

She slapped her hand to her head. "Mom. How did you

find me here?'' Sure, her mother had her cell phone number, but half the time the instrument sat in her bag switched to off. Who needed emergency sexual advice? Her opinion was that her cell phone was strictly for the convenience of her calling others. If there was some sort of emergency, Rick's phone was on twenty-four/seven.

Which is probably where her mother got the number.

"Is everyone all right?" she asked, realizing that this just might be a family emergency.

"Everyone's fine on this end, dear. What is that infernal noise? Have you gotten yourself into trouble again?"

Gracie stalked to the corner of the room and examined the speaker, searching for some sort of shut-off switch. "No, Mom, I haven't gotten myself into trouble…again." She rolled her eyes heavenward. One time. One lousy time when she was sixteen she got pulled into the police station for making out in the back seat with her teenage boyfriend and her mother made it sound like an everyday occurrence. "It's the room's emergency system. I'm trying to shut it off now."

"Well, it doesn't sound like you're doing a very good job of it. Just what type of hotel are you staying at? Has there been a raid?"

"Raid?" Gracie couldn't help her bark of laughter. "No, Mom, I don't think your run-of-the-mill prostitutes could afford this place." Still, having Priscilla think the alarm was the result of some sort of drug bust was more exciting than the truth that she'd merely tried to gain access to the balcony of her un-air-conditioned room.

"Prostitutes? For God's sake, Grace, who said anything about prostitutes? I was referring to something more of a military nature."

"I'm in Texas, Mom, not a Third World country."

"Same difference."

She rolled her eyes then paced toward the balcony door again, wondering if slipping the locking mechanisms back into place would do the trick. The phone cord stretched across the bed, dumping the contents of her nail polish remover all over the paisley comforter. She groaned in increasing agitation.

"What? What's happening now?" her mother prodded as Gracie swiped at the mess seeping across the spread with the towel she'd wrapped around her wet hair. Of course it only stood to reason that not a single nail escaped contact with the acetone, ruining her manicure with only a half hour to go before her book signing at a local mall.

"Grace Marie, answer me."

"Nothing's happening, Mom. Nothing that a gunshot to the head wouldn't solve."

Giving up, she flopped down on the bed, pushed the acetone-laden towel away and covered her other ear with her hand. "Oh, well, they'll have to turn the alarm off eventually, won't they? So tell me, Mom, how are you doing?"

Priscilla sighed then said, "Not very well, if you want to know the truth."

Anyone else might find her sitting on a stained bedspread in a sweltering hotel room with a squealing alarm going off and simultaneously talking on the phone bizarre. But given the two days since Chicago, strange events were becoming par for the course for Gracie. Only she could have accidentally boarded a plane bound for Vancouver rather than Houston and ended up sitting in an airport for five hours until she could get on the next open flight out. Fate dictated that she be the one to find out the hard way that you really shouldn't be drinking coffee when the pilot warned of severe turbulence ahead. And only she could order a hamburger and fries from room service and get some sort of green wrapped sandwich she wasn't sure she should eat or use as a doorstop.

And only she would be sitting in the middle of the current mess asking her mother what could possibly be wrong in the land of Baltimore suburbia.

God, please don't ever let her turn into her mother.

"Well, you know how I am about…private matters, Gracie. Do you plan to be home soon?"

Private matters? Her mother wanted to talk to her about

private matters? She shook her head, concerned something had jarred loose. Of course, she reminded herself that "private matters" could include almost anything on her mother's list, such as her foot massager had gone postal. "No, Mom, I won't be home soon. I'm on tour, you know, to promote that book I wrote, for at least the next ten days, remember?"

"Oh."

Yes, "oh" about summed it up.

Silence reigned. Well, at least over the phone line. Gracie vaguely registered a pounding on the wall next to her. Obviously her neighbor wasn't as accustomed to such weird occurrences.

She focused again on her mother. "Mom? Look, I'm sure whatever it is can be discussed over the phone." Still, nothing. "You know, you'd be surprised by how many people I counsel over the phone rather than in person. They tend to like the anonymity."

"I'm not one of your...patients, Grace."

She smiled. She knew that would get her. "Good, you're still there."

"Of course I'm still here. I wouldn't hang up without saying goodbye."

She was right there. Gracie couldn't count the times her mother had hung up on her out of frustration or anger. And every time she had warned her in advance. Something along the lines of, "I'm hanging up on you now, Grace. Goodbye," or "I'll talk to you again when you're more reasonable. Goodbye."

She racked her brain trying to come up with a reason to get her to do so now. She didn't have the time for this. Really, she didn't. She needed to be getting ready for her book signing.

"Your father and I haven't...shared a bed in over three months."

Gracie had been in the process of crossing her leg under her. The declaration caught her mid-move and she instead slid onto the floor with a thud. Abruptly the alarm cut off, though an odd ringing kept on in her ears. "What...what did you just say, Mom?"

She wanted to emphasize the word *Mom*. Wanted Priscilla to remember that it was her daughter she was talking to. What happened to the wacky foot massager? *That* she could deal with. She scrunched her eyes closed. She really wasn't sure she wanted to hear this. Which was funny, because she'd taken a wicked sort of pleasure in questioning her mother about her sex life up until now. Mostly because Gracie had known her mother would never respond.

She snapped her eyes open. Well, guess what? Never just came up on deadline.

"You heard me." Priscilla cleared her throat. "Your father and I...haven't shared a bed for—"

"Three months." *Yeah, yeah, I heard you. I was just hoping you would lose your nerve and take the words back.* Say something that sounded similar and play the whole thing off. Like "shared a beer," or "pared a bear," something, anything but what she'd just said.

"Uh-huh." Oh, but that was good. She had virtually just flushed six years of higher education down the toilet, and probably proved her mother's skepticism of her aptitude with that two-syllable response.

Let's see...how exactly did one respond to a question of this nature from their own mother? "Um, you and Dad have always shared the same room. Did one of you move into a guest room?"

Her mother's sigh was both exasperated and exasperating. "Of course not. We're still *sleeping* together. You know, in the same bed."

"Good. That's good. That indicates at least a measure of intimacy."

"How? I turn in at ten. He comes in after midnight after I'm asleep. And when I get up in the morning, he's already gone. We might as well be sleeping in separate beds for all I see of him."

That's exactly how she saw her parents, so why shouldn't that be the reality?

"Gracie?"

"What?" She pushed herself up from the floor and sat on the bed. "Oh, sorry. Just lost in thought there for a moment."

"I tried waiting up for him once."

Seeing as that would have been her next question if this had been a regular patient, Grace nodded. But this wasn't a regular patient. This was her mother, for Pete's sake! She bit hard on her bottom lip to keep herself from saying that this...lull in her parents' love live was quite all right, normal in fact. That it wasn't unheard-of for married couples to go years without sexual intimacy. But that would go completely against her proactive philosophy.

Speaking of which... "Mom, have you read my book yet?"

Silence.

Someone knocked at the door. Gracie tamped down the desire to tell whoever it was that the alarm was off already, and couldn't they see she was dealing with a family crisis, then she looked at her watch. Oh, God! She only had ten minutes to get ready for the book signing!

Another knock. "Gracie?" Rick's voice filtered through the door. "The cab's waiting."

Of course it was. Was it too much to ask to have someone else running late?

"Look, Mom, I'm really, really sorry—" *no, she wasn't* "—but I have to go. I'm already way behind schedule and I'm not even dressed yet."

"But—"

"I'll call you later, okay?"

She began to tug the receiver away from her ear, ignoring her mother's protests, then she pulled it back. "Goodbye."

She returned the receiver to its cradle with more force than necessary and stood staring at the offensive instrument for a long, quiet moment. With any luck, by tonight her mother would have completely forgotten about this rip in parallel worlds and everything would go back to being normal.

Another knock, this time more insistent. "Gracie, I can hear you. Chop-chop, Dr. Hottie, we've got a book signing to do."

She wanted to tell her assistant to go ahead, do it without her. She'd give him complete control over the signing, he could even sign his own name for all she cared. All she wanted to do was crawl into bed, draw the covers over her head and pretend the past twenty minutes hadn't happened.

Instead, she yanked open the door and stared at Rick. "All right, already."

A HALF HOUR LATER Gracie tottered into the bookstore with Rick shaking his head behind her. "One of these days you're going to break your neck, wearing those things."

She glanced back at him, then scanned the huge atrium of the shopping mall behind him. "Well, if I do, it'll be all your fault. If I recall correctly, it was you who took one look at my button-down blazers, which are completely in style by the way, and told me I needed a sexier image. In fact, you were the one who picked out these very shoes."

"Yes, well, I thought you would know how to walk in them."

"Contrary to popular male belief, Rick, women are not born with the innate ability to walk in heels."

"Boy, we're in rare form today, aren't we? What's eating you?"

"Aside from an air-raid siren going off in my room, my thong underwear being wedged in my butt and a phone call from my mother wanting sexual advice…nothing. Everything's just peachy." She lifted a finger. "By the way, make a note. I never want to get married."

She caught his wince, though she couldn't say exactly what he was wincing about. If he could sympathize with the thong bikini thing, she'd prefer not to know about that right now.

She turned around to lead the way to the manager's office

and ran smack dab straight into someone. "I'm sorry. I wasn't watching where I was going."

"No apology necessary. I wasn't paying attention, either."

Gracie stumbled back a couple steps to gape at her anonymous co-bumper. She blinked once. Then twice. Then thought she didn't need to be walking in order to fall off her heels. She stared into the not-so-anonymous shocked face of one far too sexy Dr. Dylan Fairbanks. Her favorite mistake.

But it wasn't until she looked beyond him, to his PR rep Tanja and her cute purple-tipped hair that she knew she wasn't hallucinating. Judging by the way Tanja averted her gaze and smiled in amusement, she also had the sinking sensation that of the four of them, she and Dylan were the only ones who hadn't known about the possibility of their running into each other again.

Dylan regained control over his tongue first. "What are *you* doing here?"

Well, that was certainly a greeting a girl looked forward to after the morning she had just experienced. Especially from a two-timing faithless groom whom she never would have slept with had she known he was engaged. "Well, hello, how are you doing, long time no see to you, too, Dr. Dylan."

Rick cleared his throat and put a hand on her arm. "Dr. Mattias is here for a book signing."

Tanja's exotic dark eyes widened…a little too wide, Gracie thought. "Really? So is Dr. Dy…er Fairbanks."

Rick's grin at the petite, pretty PR rep made Gracie want to fire him. "You don't say?"

"Well, someone had better say something that makes sense and quick," Dylan said, his wide chest puffed out in that way that made Gracie want to plant her hands against it.

Instead, she shifted her briefcase from one of those same itchy hands to the other. "What time is your signing?"

"Two to five."

"Really?" she asked, drawing the word out and slanting a gaze at Rick. "What a coincidence. So is mine."

Rick cleared his throat. "Sorry, Grace, I meant to tell you, but there just wasn't time. The store manager caught the TV show the other day, and when she heard you two were going to be in town together, she thought it would be a good idea to schedule you together.''

"And how would she know we were both scheduled to be in town?"

Dylan looked at Tanja. "I wasn't even supposed to be in Houston. I was in Dallas for a seminar this morning."

Tanja smiled. "Okay, same state, then. And, um, Rick and I compared schedules the other day in New York."

Gracie covertly rubbed behind her ear, two and two clicking into place a little too neatly. She remembered that day all too well, mostly because that's the morning she had met Dylan...in her shower. She'd called Rick immediately afterward and recalled getting the impression he wasn't alone.

Hmm...why did she suspect that promotional schedules weren't the only things that had passed between the two traitors?

Grace trained her best evil eye on Rick.

"Come on, Grace," Rick said, grimacing. "I told you about the phenomenal response our polling agency pulled on the show. Then there was the radio appearance before then. Even your publisher agreed that scheduling you with Dr. Fairbanks was a good idea."

Tanja piped in, "Dylan's publisher, as well."

Gracie couldn't help noticing that Dylan gave the pretty pixie a glare to equal hers.

She said to Rick, "I'm not upset because I'm scheduled with Dylan. I'm ticked that you didn't tell me before now."

"I didn't..."

Gracie pointed at the sign nearby clearly showcasing the two of them, along with a clipping of a newspaper piece. A piece that had to be days in the planning. "Don't even try it, buster."

Dylan leaned closer to Tanja. "You're fired."

She laughed, then caught herself and cleared her throat. "You can't fire me. I work for the publisher."

He tugged at his tie. "Well, then, you're dismissed."

Gracie rolled her eyes. "Aren't you overreacting just a bit?"

"Overreacting? No, I wouldn't say I'm overreacting. I've just been told that I'm to spend the next three hours with a woman whose belief system goes completely against mine. I'd say my reaction is dead-on."

Oh, yeah, well, those belief systems weren't all that different the other night, were they?

For a second Gracie was afraid she'd said the words aloud given the way everyone was looking at her. Then she realized they were waiting for a regular response from her. She nearly leaned against the display to her right in relief. "Trust me, Dr. Dylan, this isn't going to be a picnic for me, either."

"Is everything all right?"

Dylan looked a breath away from telling the interloper to butt out, but clamped his mouth closed as he apparently noticed her badge identifying her as the manager.

Gracie smiled and extended her hand, giving Rick a quiet aside. "You and me, later." To the manager she said, "Everything's fine. Just a little mix-up is all. It's nice to meet you."

Introductions were made, idle conversation indulged in for the next few minutes as customers navigated around them in the store's entrance. Then they were shown to the back where two armchairs were positioned in front of a mock fireplace. A long table, which she and Dylan were obviously to share, stretched out before them.

Gracie rounded the table from one side, Dylan the other. She didn't know for sure, but she guessed he was going as out of his way to avoid her gaze as she was his. He smacked what looked like a laptop case down on the table; she followed suit with her briefcase. He pulled his chair a little farther to the other side; she did the same with hers.

Rick appeared at her side. "The stockperson is collecting the books from the back now."

Gracie's heart skipped a beat. She grasped his arm before

he could walk away. A completely devious plan was taking shape in her head. "Wait a minute...."

"Uh-oh. I don't know if I like that look."

"After what you just did, I don't particularly care what you like," she said with a generous smile. "Besides, do this and I just might think about forgiving you."

During the past few weeks she'd become very acquainted with the back rooms of bookstores, mostly because the bathroom was located there. While the odd store kept their stock neatly organized, the vast majority of them were lucky to find the day's shipment in the chaos. A glance around the monstrous, busy, shorthanded store told her that this particular one undoubtedly fell into the chaos category. "I don't know what's going on between you and Tanja, but you can't breathe a word of this to her. This is what I want you to do...."

A half hour later, Gracie sat happily greeting readers on her side of the table, signing dozens of copies of her book...while Dylan sat glowering on the other side, the manager repeatedly apologizing for the loss of his books.

"I put them near the door myself, ready to be set out, Dr. Dylan—"

"It's Fairbanks."

"Yes, of course. Sorry. Dr. Fairbanks." Gracie would have felt bad for the poor woman, except that she appeared a veteran of the signing wars and already looked a little put out by Dylan's pouty behavior. "My staff is going through the stock now. I'm sure your books will turn up very soon."

He waved her away.

Gracie handed a signed copy of her book to an elderly woman who needed the help of a cane to walk. "I hope you enjoy it."

"Oh, I'm sure I will, dear."

Gracie's smile froze in place as she thought of this morning. While the reader could have been her mother's mother, the dynamics were the same. *If you don't like the book, whatever you do, please don't call me.*

Dylan leaned closer to her, his clean, fresh aftershave giving him away before he spoke. Gracie nearly jumped out of her skin.

"I'd love to see her expression when she gets to the part about sexual safaris."

Gracie hiked a brow. "What? You don't think the older generation is entitled to a healthy sex life?"

The hardening of his jaw drew her attention to the enticing stretch of flesh. "Of course I do, but what you're prescribing is more liable to give them heart failure."

She leaned closer to whisper into his ear, nearly closing her eyes and enjoying the smell of him. "Ah, but what a way to go, huh?"

His cringe was exactly what she'd been after, but it also chased him back to his own side of the table. A shame, indeed, because she felt much better with him closer.

She smiled as a reader approached the table, glanced Dylan's way, then picked up one of her books. "You'd better be careful, Dylan, or I might think you're jealous."

"Jealous? Of what?" He gestured toward her stacks. "Except, of course, that you have your books and I don't."

Only moments before, Tanja had been handing out flyers promoting Dylan's book, but she seemed to have disappeared. Gracie cracked open the book the reader handed to her then glanced around. Interestingly enough, Rick had vanished as well.

Curiouser and curiouser.

Another reader, another sale made under Dylan's glowering glare.

He got up from his chair. "That's it. I'm going back to check out what's going on."

Gracie held out the signed book to the reader then rose just as quickly. "I'm coming, too."

Dylan pulled up short. She nearly rammed into him from behind. "What for?"

She straightened her skirt. "Why, to help, of course." She flashed him a smile. What she was really trying to prevent was him stumbling across Rick with the goods in hand. "I feel...bad, you know, about my having books and you none."

"Bad. Uh-huh. Tell me why I'm not buying that?"

"Because you're cheap?"

She loved it when his jaw twitched that way.

He turned back toward the stockroom and she followed, covertly looking around for Rick and where he might have stashed the boxes holding Dylan's books. She didn't see anything. Not that she expected to, but one never knew. Before she could blink, she and Dylan were standing in the back room amid stacks upon stacks of towering boxes.

"I have my staff on it right now," Dylan mocked. He looked at her. "Do you see a single staff member?"

She pretended to look when what she was really doing was scoping out Rick. "Um, nope?"

"That sounds more like a question than an answer."

She crossed her arms. "Well, Dylan, the truth is it's hard to tell. The entire Houston Oilers could be hiding out back here and we would be none the wiser."

He grimaced. "Good point." He began weaving through the maze of boxes, nearly toppling a mountain on Gracie where she was on his heels.

"I hope you're insured," she said, awkwardly moving to still them.

He glanced at her over his shoulder. "I am. I think it's under the heading 'in cases of intentional maiming.'"

"Very funny."

"I thought so."

He stopped. This time she was so busy dodging teetering boxes she did walk straight into him. He turned around to steady her when she would have fallen back into a stack of old magazines.

She stared at him, appalled at the gulping sound she made at finding herself so unexpectedly close to him. She could handle anything so long as there was distance between them. But this....

He grinned at her. "A thank-you would be nice."

Gracie stared up into his face, unable to do anything but wonder at the heat of his hands through her jacket. She tried like hell to remind herself that the cad was engaged. Instead, she was curious about why he hadn't let her go yet.

She licked suddenly parched lips, recognizing the sign of anticipation for what it was, and knowing he did, too, if his smoldering gaze was anything to go by. The tightening of his fingers against her flesh told her it was.

He cleared his throat. "We really need to be looking for my books."

She nodded, then blurted, "Why *did* you have sex with me?"

Had she really just said that? Judging by the shocked expression on Dylan's face, she had.

She watched his magnificent throat work and squelched the desire to swallow the hot moisture gathering in her mouth.

If ever there was a time when one was given license to babble, this was definitely it. She licked her lips again and plunged straight in. "It's something I've been meaning to ask you, you know, why you had sex with me when it's obvious you hadn't wanted to, but, gee, it seemed I never got the chance. I mean with you being engaged and all—"

The remainder of her words were sealed off with the same type of breath-stealing, thigh-quivering kiss that had landed them in so much trouble the last time they were alone together. Gracie registered this, but she was helpless to do anything more than welcome it.

Making a low sound in her throat, she melded against him...crushing her chest to his...molding her hands against his tight little rear...butting her pelvis against his...and attacking his mouth with repeated open-lipped kisses like he was a buffet and his mouth the main course. She felt his erection grow between them and hummed in spiraling agreement, at that moment not caring that they were in a public bookstore, that anyone could walk in at any minute, or that the world would judge her a fool for giving herself to an engaged man...again. All she could think about was that she wanted him deep inside her, her slick, hot flesh surrounding him...*now.*

Dylan murmured something against her mouth. She couldn't be sure, but she thought it was something along the lines of "This is crazy. Absolutely, stark, raving mad." Even as he said it, his hands palmed her breasts through the material of her jacket and blouse, kneading the sensitive flesh almost roughly, and his leg found its way between hers, drawing it up until her skirt lifted and the course material of his wool pants rubbed provocatively against her damp silk panties.

Seeking firmer ground, he backed her through an aisle of boxes, his mouth never breaking contact with hers as she restlessly laved him with her tongue. Finally, a wall. But when Gracie reached back to brace herself against a quaking shudder, she knocked over a pile of boxes. Ignoring them and the racket they made, she fumbled for the front of Dylan's slacks to get at the thick erection swelling inside. At the same time, his fingers found the damp center of her panties. She collapsed against him as he dipped those same hot fingers inside and pressed them against her throbbing core.

Somewhere in the back of her mind, she thought that she'd always wanted to do it in a library. Well, okay, this wasn't exactly a library, but it did smell of books, and when you closed your eyes tight enough, it was easy to imagine it was a library. And her eyes were definitely closed.

"Help...me," she whispered, unable to get his belt undone.

When he pulled slightly back, she discovered why she'd had such a hard time. He had a double-locking belt. A double-locking belt, for God's sake. She gave a breathless laugh as he pressed against her, his head against hers as he apparently fought for air.

She'd just about figured out the complicated contraption that was the male equivalent of a chastity belt when he caught her hand firmly in his. She froze, realizing at the same instant that he wasn't pressed against her anymore.

"There they are."

Her heart nearly stopped. "Wh...what?"

He pulled away, staring at a box sandwiched in the middle of others. "My books."

Gracie collapsed against the wall, trying desperately to make sense of his words. When they finally registered, she curled her hands into fists, swearing she'd never go near another engaged man again if he would just forget the damn books and finish what he'd started.

He began levering the box out. She dragged in deep, heaving gasps of air and closed her eyes. Obviously, God wasn't taking special requests today.

"Heads up."

Gracie moved just in time to prevent herself from getting beaned by the boxes that had been resting on Dylan's books. She was just about to open her mouth and make an official demand for either his head or his...erection, when movement on the other side of the cleared half-stack stopped her from uttering a word.

"Tanja," Dylan said.

"Rick," she said.

The couple looked like a mirror image of what she and Dylan had been doing just moments earlier. Rick had a hand up Tanja's trendy black sweater, while Tanja's fingers were tunneled in his hair. You couldn't have wedged a magazine between their hips if you'd used a crowbar.

Gracie supposed she should be thankful the couple hadn't been caught doing it on the box of Dylan's books. But she was more concerned with being caught herself.

She hastened to push herself from the wall, trying to put herself back in order even as Dylan and the young couple did the same. The situation was so absurd, she might have laughed. If only she wasn't feeling so damn horny she could scream.

Rick's quiet chuckle broke the awkward silence. "Looks like we all had the same thing in mind."

Dylan's back snapped upright. "*We* were looking for my books."

Rick's grin appeared not affected at all. "So were we."

Gracie rolled her eyes to stare at the ceiling. "Okay, just so we're all straight on what happened back here, we're all in agreement that we were looking for the books, right?"

"Oh, good, you found them," a fifth voice said.

Gracie nearly hit the ceiling she was staring at when the manager's voice sounded around the corner.

Dylan hoisted up the box. He glanced at Gracie, his usual grimace firmly in place, his dark hair still adorably, sexily tousled. "Yes, we did."

The manager motioned at him. "Dr. Dylan, I'll have to ask you to put that down. It's against company policy for you to handle stock."

"They're my books."

She smiled at him patronizingly. "And I paid for them. Now put them back. I'll have one of my staff come back and collect them for you."

Clearing her throat, Gracie navigated her way around Dylan, being extra careful not to touch him. "I'd suggest you do as she asks. She doesn't look like someone you'd like to mess with."

"She wouldn't be the first."

Gracie caught his meaning and gaped at him. The way he was acting, you'd think she'd been the one who'd molested *him*. Oh, but wasn't that special?

She made a none-too-elegant face at him and left the room.

TEN MINUTES LATER, Gracie was no closer to getting a handle on what had happened back in the storeroom than she had while it was happening. She checked her reflection in her compact again, then slid a covert glance toward Dylan, who was sitting closed-faced, tight-mouthed and still bookless next to her.

She snapped the compact closed. "Good thing you found your books when you did, huh? No telling what might have happened otherwise."

He tugged at his tie. "Nothing would have happened." He

met her gaze squarely. "I would have stopped it before it went too far."

Oh, but he was smug now that all was said and done, wasn't he? "Ah, so that's the reason for the double-locking belt."

She didn't miss his glance at the area in question. "It was a gift," he said.

Gracie let her gaze travel the path his had taken. Her eyes widened at the bulge she saw behind his zipper. Was she crazy, or did he still have a hard-on? Talk about gifts...

She immediately snatched her attention away from dangerous territory. "A gift, huh?" she said, keeping her voice from showing her own state of distraction. "From your fiancée?"

He winced. She took the response as an unqualified yes.

He looked over his shoulder toward the stockroom door. "What's taking so damn long?"

Gracie couldn't stop herself from leaning closer and lowering her voice suggestively. "I don't know. Do you want to go find out?"

He jumped and she withdrew to her own side of the table with a satisfied smile. Oh, Dr. Dylan might pretend he wasn't as on edge as she was, but his giveaway reactions said differently. High and mighty and impervious to her in public, put them in a room alone together—or in a room they thought they were alone in together—and the truth was revealed in all its tongue panting, slacks-bulging glory. It was reassuring to know that the uptight guy had no more control over his hormones than she did.

Gracie accepted a book for signing from a reader, catching a glimpse of a woman approaching Dylan's side of the table. A well-dressed young professional woman around Gracie's age who was blond, built and obviously on the prowl. It was more than just the way her gaze seemed attached to Dylan. It was the way that gaze honed in on him like a starving man at a good old Texas BBQ.

Gracie handed the book to the reader and thanked her, taking more interest than necessary in the woman who sashayed up to Dylan's side of the table as if he wore a sign that said Open for Business.

"Oh, dear, don't tell me you've sold out of your book already?" she said in a slow, measured Southern drawl Gracie openly envied.

Given the ridiculousness of the situation so soon after the stockroom, Gracie laughed. Dylan slid her a scathing look. She held her hands palms up and made a "what?" sign.

The woman seemed not at all affected by Gracie and her reaction. The woman cooed. "I was so looking forward to buying it."

Gracie itched with the desire to grill the woman on the contents of the book and exactly why she was interested in buying it, but she held her tongue. Her own book definitely wouldn't be able to offer the woman anything. She probably not only appeared to know every trick in any book, she presumably thought she had invented them.

Dylan grinned, flashing a wickedly sexy dimple at the woman. He leaned forward and said, "I'm assured more copies will be available in a few moments if you'd care to wait."

More copies? He'd yet to sell one.

Gracie's face heated. Of course no one had to know that the reason for his poor sales rested solely in her lap.

"I'd love to," the woman drawled.

Gracie was thankful that there wasn't another chair in sight. She was convinced the woman would have pulled it up right next to Dylan's.

She accepted a copy of her book from an older gentleman who requested she sign it for his wife. Gracie scolded herself for paying too much attention to the conversation taking place not two feet from her right ear and smiled up to him. She normally asked for the name of the person for whom the gift was intended, but this time said, "Actually, I think it might be a good idea if you read the book yourself. In my experience, I've discovered that women tend to be affronted when given a gift of this nature. You know, as if you're making personal comment on their need for sexual tutelage."

The Southern belle put her hands on the signing table—something she would never have been able to do had Dylan's books been there—and practically leaned across the expanse toward him.

The gentleman she addressed reddened. "My wife is over there. She requested I come over here and get it signed for her."

"Oh." Gracie's smile widened. "Then my apologies, sir." She asked the name, signed the book, then handed it to him. "Still, you might want to give a section or two a look. Chapter Four, I think, might provide a bit of entertainment." She winked at him.

He looked at her as if she were insane. Either that or an oversexed sex therapist. Neither prospect seemed particularly appealing to Gracie as he walked away.

She sighed and flopped back in the chair, nearly groaning when she realized Miss Texas was still chatting up Dylan next to her.

Just look at him. He was lapping up every sugar-coated word like a love-starved puppy. Which got her to thinking…

Seeing as Dylan's latest book was his second, it meant he was a veteran to the promotional trail. She tapped her unpainted fingernail against her lips, thinking, thinking. If that was the case, had the other night been the first time he'd been tempted by the sexual wares of another? Or was he used to being molested by horny women in stockrooms?

Oh, he'd said he was celibate, but was that really the case? Or did he mean he'd only been celibate with his fiancée?

Gracie crossed her arms, suddenly deciding she didn't like the direction of her thoughts. She also decided she didn't like being left out.

She sat up and folded her hands on the table. "Oh, pardon me," she said, interrupting the far too quiet conversation next to her and smiling solicitously at the woman, "but I just adore that necklace you're wearing. Where ever did you find it?"

The woman turned to her and beamed. Gracie's smile turned genuine.

There was only one thing women enjoyed more than staking out a sexual conquest, and that was talking about shopping.

As Gracie listened to the long explanation on how the woman had come across the piece in a little out-of-the-way antique shop in Austin—not a difficult task considering she really did like the necklace—she noticed Dylan's grin had left and he now sat glowering at her instead of the other way around.

Five minutes into the conversation, in which Dylan was relegated to making noncommittal grunts of agreement and smiling congenially, the manager finally rushed to the table followed by two stock boys who immediately spread Dylan's books out in front of him.

His resulting grin made Gracie's tongue swell, threatening to choke off air. God, but he was devastating when he smiled. Completely irresistible.

The woman ended up buying both of their books, then with a little wave, bid them adieu.

Finally Gracie found herself alone with Dylan again. Well, alone as two people could be in a public store, minus a sexually active PR rep and an assistant. This was as good a time as any to find out just how serious his engagement was. And whether or not he routinely climbed on and off the celibacy wagon during promotional junkets like these.

"So," Gracie began, straightening her books. "How's your wife?"

Well, that was certainly one way to open the conversation. She began to question her own faculties until she caught his wince. While not entirely judicious, her query produced the response she was after.

He slanted her a wary glance. "I'm not married. Yet."

"Yes, but you're as good as, right?" she prompted.

He tugged at his collar in a way that made her want to do some tugging of her own. "And what would you know about committed relationships?"

She smiled, deciding to ignore the jab at her principles.

"You mean given what happened in Chicago? Or what just happened in the storeroom? Given both incidents, I'd say I know at least as much as you."

"That was a low blow."

"And you deserved it."

"True."

She looked at him a little more closely. He really did feel bad about all this, didn't he? It wasn't a source of minor agitation. It truly bothered him that he'd been unfaithful. So what did that say about the reason he'd done it? Not just the other night, but a few minutes ago?

Her stomach dipped, then bounced right back up into her throat. Was it possible that he had been so incredibly attracted to her he hadn't been able to help himself? Or had time away from his fiancée and circumstances weakened him to fundamental urges?

She wasn't sure she liked either choice, but still couldn't quite squelch her curiosity to find out. She felt as she had when she was fifteen and in her freshman year of high school. Her parents had insisted on sending her to an exclusive private school away from home and away from her friends. Of course, she'd felt out of place and developed a crush on the first male she crossed paths with. In an all-girl institution, it happened to be her English Lit teacher. There had been something...*dreamy* was the word she used then, about the way he quoted Shakespeare.

By midterm, she had convinced herself that he felt the same way about her. But when she approached him after class one Friday afternoon, she abruptly found out that wasn't the case. She'd felt so humiliated.

She'd been transferred immediately to another classroom and had persuaded herself that the entire school knew of the incident.

Remembering it all now made her shudder. Well, that little visit to the past had certainly helped, hadn't it?

She restacked her books, then moved them again. "You know, seeing as you are engaged, you might consider being a little more…conservative with prowling females from here on out. Just a bit of advice.''

"I wouldn't say you are a prowler.''

She glared at him. "Not me, Einstein. You're just as much to blame as I am in our case. I'm talking about Miss Texas.''

"Miss Tex…oh.'' His dark brows drew together, making him that much more attractive. Then his brows lifted and he sat back. "Oh. You mean…what you're referring to…are you saying that nice young woman at the table just now was coming on to me?''

"Like a steam wrap.''

He looked at her. "I beg to differ. She was just indulging in conversation until my books were available.''

Gracie glanced at the books in question, hoping she wasn't as flushed as she felt. "Conversation…right.''

"Is it so hard to believe that she was just interested in my book?''

"Yes,'' she said bluntly. "It is.''

His laugh was unexpected and sent a shiver skidding down her spine. "Spoken like a true competitor.''

"I'm speaking as a woman. If it's one thing we know how to do, it's spot another woman on the make. And her dance card definitely had your name written all over it.''

"Dance card?''

She waved her hand. "You know what I mean.''

"Uh-huh.'' He sat back and crossed his arms, pulling her gaze to his flat, tight midsection. God, how he had felt squeezed between her thighs. Much better than a pillow any day. "So now you're speaking for all women.''

Gracie made a face at him. "Ask your fiancée. I'm sure she'll tell you the same thing.'' She tucked her hair behind her ear. "Men are always a little slow on the uptake when it comes to women, on the make or otherwise.''

"Is that so?''

She nodded. "It's a known fact.''

"Documented?''

"Very funny.''

He clicked his Mont Blanc pen closed then tossed it to the table. "You know, if I didn't know better I'd think you were the jealous one."

"Jealous? Me? I don't have an envious bone in my body."

"Everyone has a jealous bone or two, Gracie. It's what makes us human."

"Then I'm an alien."

The glimmer of amusement in his green eyes made it impossible to turn away from him.

She cleared her throat, fighting against the heat wave of attraction that swept over her. He was practically a married man, for God's sake. And so long as they weren't alone in a storeroom or anywhere else, she could handle that. Right? "Anyway, you can't tell me you haven't had your share of come-ons during events like these."

"I could say the same of you."

"I've experienced one or two. Not always from males, either. And you avoided my question."

He finally glanced away, releasing her from whatever magical spell he'd put her under with his gaze. "Like you said, I've had my share. Females have come on to you?"

"Uh-huh. And how does your fiancée feel about females coming on to you when you're on the road?"

He winced again.

In fact, she thought, looking at him a little more closely, he winced whenever she referred to the woman he planned to marry. Because he had yet to tell her about the other night? Or were there other reasons responsible for his interesting behavior?

"What's her name?"

"Pardon me?"

"Your fiancée. What's her name? She does have a name, doesn't she? Or does she go around referring to herself as the future Mrs. Dylan Fairbanks?"

There it was again. That wince.

"Okay, you're giving off enough signals here to choke a Texas cow, Dr. Dylan. What gives?" At his look of surprise, she held up her hand. "Wait, don't tell me—you're already married." The prospect made her sit back in her chair and groan aloud. God, she thought the guilt was bad when she found out he was engaged. The idea that she had slept with a married man made her want to throw up.

"Her name is Diana. And no, we're not married," he said.

Gracie whooshed a deep breath, immediately relieved.

"In fact, we're not even officially engaged yet. I, um, was planning on asking her next week."

She stared at him as if he'd just grown another head. "What?"

Her voice raised to a decibel level she hadn't known she could reach. Somewhere between a shout and shriek, it earned them the attention of not only passersby, but also some of the outside mall patrons.

"What what?" Dylan said, startled. "Even you said that I'm as good as married."

"That's when I thought you were already engaged." She stuck her head in his direction. "Do you know what kind of hell I've put myself through these past few days?" She waved her hand to indicate the area behind them. "How…upset I was about what happened back there? Aside from calling myself every name in the trucker's handbook, I considered having the words 'home wrecker' embroidered on my underwear just so I would remember the next time I decided to give in to my baser instincts."

"Come on, Gracie, what's the difference? Engaged… practically engaged…the only difference is a word."

"A very significant word." She started ticking items off on her fingers. "And a wedding date. And a guest list. And a down payment on a house with a white picket fence." She balled her hands into fists and made a strangled sound of frustration.

Gracie barely noticed when Rick came hurrying up from some hidden location in the stacks, concern marring his face. She was too busy trying to reduce Dylan to the puddle of slime that he was.

But Rick would not be ignored. "All right, Gracie, what gives?"

She snapped open her mouth to tell him.

"No, forget about that for a minute. There's something I want to tell you first."

She stared at her assistant, out of the corner of her eye noticing Tanja slink up to stand next to Dylan. She didn't like the looks of this.

Rick cleared his throat. "Um, we all know how both of you reacted when you showed up to find the other here."

Gracie's eyelids narrowed by millimeters. "Uh-huh."

Tanja said, "But after seeing the chemistry we both just witnessed we have to question the sincerity behind that response."

Gracie wished it *were* possible to shoot glare daggers.

"What Tanja means is…" Rick straightened. "Well, after considering the exceptional success of your joint appearances, and consulting with your publishers, we've all decided that it's in everyone's best interest if you are scheduled together for the duration of your tour."

Gracie stared at him for long moments, mouth agape, seconds away from spittle drooling out of the side, convinced her assistant had just gone completely, utterly, loony-bin-material insane. It was all she could do to stop herself from falling off her chair. She turned her head to stare in the same openmouthed way at Dylan and found him making a choking sound and grasping desperately at his tie.

8

DEAR LORD, how was he going to make it through ten more days of this godforsaken promotional tour?

Seven hours had passed since he'd learned he and Gracie would be working together, side by side, for the remainder of the tour. But somehow the news had yet to completely seep through his skull. He hadn't succeeded in getting a grasp on the situation through dinner with Tanja, Gracie and Rick at a Houston steak house that touted traditional barbeque. Gracie had unabashedly licked each of her fingers after clearing a plate full of ribs, making him want to groan with longing. And now sitting in his hotel room, trying to meet the deadline of his weekly newspaper column, he was still grappling with the knowledge that Dr. Hottie would be by his side for days. Even the frustrating questions he chose to respond to—the worst being whether or not oral sex was really sex at all or just foreplay—could not distract him.

All he could think about was Gracie's response to finding out he wasn't engaged. *Yet,* he reminded himself. He wasn't engaged yet. Gracie's response kept getting pushed aside by the wicked image of her gazing at him provocatively as in turn she slipped each of her sauce-covered fingers into her mouth at the restaurant. Neither the picture nor the thought was conducive to getting a good night's sleep or working up a game plan that would see him safely through the next week and a half.

Dylan repositioned the too soft pillows for the third time, then sat back in the bed again, clutching Gracie's book in his hands. Chapter Five—Sexual Safaris. He cringed, then leafed through the other chapters before coming back to five. Cracking the hardcover to hold it open, he glanced at the clock to find it after midnight. He really wished Tanja could have gotten them out to Baltimore tonight rather than having to wait until morning. When he completed an event, spending the night in the city in question seemed…anticlimactic somehow.

"Haven't you had enough climaxes in the past week?" he grumbled under his breath. He winced when his body gave him an unequivocal no.

But his body was completely unreliable without his head guiding his actions. Look at the mess it had gotten him into already. He'd better get a handle on his libido quickly if he held out any hope of making it through the next ten days.

Baltimore was next on the list, Memphis the day after that, then Los Angeles and he would be home in San Francisco for two short days before hitting the road again.

Ticking off his immediate schedule wasn't working. An obvious understatement when an image of Gracie's flushed face filled his mind again. Rather than fighting it this time, though, he settled back against the pillows a little more comfortably and sighed. So long as the thoughts weren't of a sexual nature, he'd be fine. And, oh boy, did she give him loads to think about in other departments.

Had she really given herself that hard a time when she'd thought he was engaged? All indicators pointed that way. Which flew in the face of everything he thought he knew about the outspoken, sexually uninhibited woman.

Maybe she was right. Perhaps men were slow on the uptake when it came to women, despite all the input since the sixties' sexual and cultural revolution. He certainly had not thought the woman he'd been talking to was coming on to him. Then again, he'd missed the signals Gracie had been sending him, as well, perhaps even as far back as the shower scene.

He'd never be able to think, see, or discuss the movie *Psycho* again without seeing Gracie naked in that shower, her supple skin lathered up and inviting.

He grimaced. *Stick to the nonsexual.*

Since the beginning his estimations of Gracie, and his attraction for her, had been way off the mark. Off the mark? Who was he kidding? Hell, they'd landed clear off the charts. It began with overrating his ability to sway her to his way of thinking, and had taken a serious downward spiral when he'd taken her like a wild man on that kitchen counter.

A knock sounded on the wall behind him, followed by a low, unmistakably female moan. On the heels of his previous thought, the sounds were not a good omen.

God, no. Not tonight.

Well, he supposed he should be thankful of at least one thing. He was in no danger of succumbing to his attraction for Gracie tonight. Rick had managed to get Gracie a seat on a flight out to Baltimore tonight. In fact, she'd left for the airport right after dinner. He'd thought it a little odd that Rick had stayed behind, until he explained that Gracie was from Baltimore.

Good. That meant he wouldn't be sleeping under the same roof with her in Maryland, either. Very good.

He cracked open the book in his lap again, though he had never closed it, and tried to concentrate on the words written there.

He did have to give Gracie credit. In his cursory examination of the book, he couldn't help noticing that she'd put together a cohesive piece on her philosophies. Too often psychologists were so wrapped up in their own self-importance they didn't give thought to things like consistency and structure. But from the titling of Gracie's chapters to the bibliography and credits listed in the back of the book, he found hers didn't appear that way at all. In that department, she passed with flying colors.

Another knock on the wall…another moan, this time more pronounced.

Dylan swallowed hard and reached out and switched on the television. CNN. He pressed the volume control, but it refused to go up high enough to drown out the undeniable evidence of a couple having sex coming from the next room. He switched it off and instead turned on the radio. He found a broadcast of National Public Radio's nightly news. There. That was better.

He looked down at the book again, at the chapter dedicated to sexual safaris. And found himself immediately engrossed...and appalled. He quickly finished the section, then paged back to the beginning, unable to believe what he'd just read. Arbitrarily, he took back the points he'd given Gracie for organizational abilities. When combined with the minus points earned on content, one very sexy Dr. Grace Mattias was seriously in the hole.

He clapped the book closed, clutching it tightly with both hands. She certainly wasn't suggesting that the only way a person could find themselves sexually, to learn to be comfortable with their bodies and voicing their wants and their needs, was through anonymous sex, was she? She alluded to the fact that attraction stemmed from emotion, and emotion led to consideration of the other's feelings. But she encouraged the reader to put all that aside and enjoy sex for sex's sake alone.

He also recognized that she had followed her own advice the other night, right before they...well, adjourned their activities to the kitchen.

She'd avoided conversation of a personal nature, keeping questions limited to the professional. After all, as she pointed out in the chapter, the less you know someone, the better.

Of course, he'd veered away from the personal as well, but for survival purposes.

The next giveaway was no discussion of her intentions. Her intent to let things play out naturally and not box herself in should she decide to change her mind at the last minute.

Oh, if only she had changed her mind, he wouldn't be having trouble sleeping now.

Next was the total lack of inhibition.

He knocked the back of his head lightly but effectively against the wall behind him. He could have done without that particular reminder. It brought back not only the memory of her luscious mouth, but the feel of her hands on his erection, her lips poised mere millimeters away. He was convinced that one flick of that naughty tongue would have done him in then and there. Then there was the vision of her with her skirt hiked up around her waist, her panties history, her bare bottom resting on top of that counter, her thighs spread in invitation. Or the way she'd leaned back, shamelessly tilting her hips upward to allow him deeper, mind-blowing penetration, her breasts rocking with each thrust into her slick wetness.

He swallowed hard, agitated to discover that a certain part of his body was growing firmer.

He really had to stop this…this fantasizing. Only it wasn't a fantasy, was it? It was a memory. One he needed to erase but quick before he could even think about moving on in life with Diana.

For long moments he concentrated on the radio broadcast until news on the current situation in the Middle East evened out his breathing and brought him back to a semimanageable state.

What had he been thinking before he'd been so thoroughly interrupted? Oh, yes. Gracie's sexual safari advice.

Step one had been no personal questions. Two, surrendering to the call of nature. Three, complete inhibition. And four…

Four was no postcoital mention of any future contact with the sexual conquest.

He slapped the book closed. Well, that certainly hadn't gone as planned, had it? Not only had they had future contact, but they would continue to see each other throughout the days ahead.

While the prospect both excited and scared the hell out of him, it wasn't what bothered him most about Chapter Five. Oh, no, not by a long shot. What got under his skin and refused to budge were her names for the couple involved in the safari. Words like hunter and prey were sprinkled deliberately throughout, further lending a wild quality to the advice, as well as encouraging anonymity.

And he knew without a doubt that he had ultimately played willing prey to Gracie's very skillful hunter.

Tossing the book to the second double bed, he shut off the light and slid down under the covers. Why did he get the impression his dreams would be filled with jungle images, big guns and soft flesh? He pummeled the pillows into place. And why didn't the prospect bother him more?

As he lay back and closed his eyes, he decided he'd done enough self-analyzing for one night. After all, there was always tomorrow to beat himself up.

THERE WAS NOTHING quite like a crisp autumn sunset on the banks of the Chesapeake to clear a tired mind. And if Gracie's mind was anything, it was definitely tired. Overrun. Plagued with questions that robbed her of appetite and held sleep hostage.

Not that she would starve—she'd never enjoyed a meal more than when devouring those ribs in front of Dylan's hungry stare last night—or die from exhaustion, but the brisk breeze did allow for a new perspective on things. Especially out from under her parents' roof.

She turned toward the mammoth wood-and-glass structure behind her, pushing her ponytail from her face when the wind blew it there. She tucked her chin into the neck of her Irish cable-knit sweater and tucked her hands into her jeans' pockets. She swore she could make out her mother watching her from an upstairs window. But whether it was Priscilla returned from her outing, or the reflection of the wispy clouds dotting the darkening blue sky, she couldn't be sure. She did know that after the strangely normal drink she'd shared with her parents last night in her father's stuffy library, she was waiting for the other shoe to drop.

Never one to do things by halves, with her first advance check from the publisher, she'd bought a condo not too far from her parents' house and decided to completely renovate it. Which made it unlivable during the three weeks the contractor would take. No problem, she'd told herself at the time.

She'd be on tour anyway, and during the two days she would be back in Baltimore, she'd stay in her old room at her parents' house.

What she hadn't factored into that little plan was her mother calling her in Houston wanting to share her sex life.

She clamped her eyes shut. The price one paid for built-in bookshelves.

Not that her mother had said anything to her last night during that drink. Oh, no. Priscilla was more sophisticated than to even let evidence of their personal discussion show in the presence of her husband. But those few minutes Gracie had spent on the phone with her mother proved fateful. Gracie could no longer look at her parents together without thinking about her mother's comment.

Had her parents really not had sex for three months?

Not that you could tell. They seemed the same as ever to her. Her father sat in his chair. Priscilla perched on the arm of that same chair in the beginning, then moved to sit in the chair next to him. They talked of the same old things. Work, weather, politics, not an inflection or hesitation hinting at the concern her mother expressed to her yesterday. Of course, she didn't know their complete sexual history, either. For all she knew, a normal sex life to her mother was a once-in-a-while go at it.

Or her parents very well might have set the sheets on fire every night.

She sighed. Her mother hadn't breathed one word while they were with her father in the library. She'd waited until Gracie was in bed, sheet pulled up to her chin and just nodding off to sleep, to sneak in and startle her.

"Gracie? Gracie? Are you awake?"

For a long moment, Gracie had pretended to be sleeping, but that hadn't stopped her mother. She'd sat on the edge of Gracie's bed, determined to wake her. Then she'd had to listen to the story all over again.

After figuring out that her mother wasn't going to leave her alone until she responded in some definitive way to the quest for advice, she'd said, "Mom, have you ever considered just talking to him?"

Priscilla's appalled expression had been priceless. "Women of my generation don't initiate conversations of that...delicate nature."

Gracie had sighed and said, "Well, maybe it's time you did."

She knew her mother hadn't been happy with her suggestion. And probably discarded it the moment she finally left the room.

At least that's what Gracie preferred to think her mother had done. Imagining her parents discussing the problems that plagued their sex life was not the way to get a good night's sleep.

She cringed and turned back toward the Chesapeake, not liking the direction of her thoughts. In all honesty, she wasn't enjoying much of what she thought about lately. What had life been like before? Before her book and Dylan and her mother's new bizarre attempt at bonding with her? She couldn't remember. But she was sure that it had been...great.

No matter how hard she tried, there was no returning to that idyllic period anytime soon.

A jogger passed her, shouting a hello. She smiled and waved, then walked backward watching the fifty-something man run in the other direction. Oh, what she wouldn't give for a nice refreshing jog right now.

What was she talking about? She couldn't run twenty feet before doubling over in pain with a godawful stitch in her side. She'd accepted long ago that walking was about as close to jogging as she was going to get.

She'd also learned that occupying her mind with mundane thoughts would not solve anything. Before long she'd be right back where she started.

She couldn't stay out here forever. It would be getting dark soon and she would have to return to the house, no matter how much she yearned to check into a local hotel.

Of course the thought would have to occur to her now, after

she'd already essentially checked into her parents' place until tomorrow.

She pushed her hair back again and sighed. Right about now Consuela would be setting the table for dinner, her last chore for the day. Considering that she hadn't eaten anything since the ribs in Houston last night, the prospect of a good meal should appeal to her. But it didn't. Her mind was far too busy turning details over and under, inside and out.

And with Rick in curious cahoots with Tanja, she suddenly had plenty of details to worry over.

Initially she'd been thankful when Rick had scheduled her for an appearance on a local news-entertainment show, simply because it meant she could avoid being alone again with her mother. Only Priscilla had already left the house when Gracie had finally rolled out of bed, running late, as usual. And with Rick meeting her at the television station, he hadn't been around to remind her that Dylan would be appearing with her.

Let's see, she thought, holding her hands out. On one side she weighed her mother...the other, Dylan. It was difficult to decide whom she wanted to be around less.

Of course, he'd appeared as pleased as she was about being together again so soon. Well, at least, until he and the conservative male host quickly figured out that they were of the same mind and bonded. Between the two of them, they'd basically made her look like a sex addict. She made a face. Chalk one up for Dr. Dylan. She'd considered telling Dylan that she suspected the host probably hadn't gotten laid for a good ten years and pointing out the signs that he was latently homosexual but would never acknowledge the closet door much less walk through it.

But she figured she looked bad enough in his eyes without heaping that little bit more on top of it. She couldn't quite figure out why she cared what he thought about her one way or another. Still that teenager feeling abandoned at the private school longing for attention? Or was she stinging after his rejection of her after the kitchen encounter? She smiled at her pun. Encounter. Counter.

She sighed, not even finding her own attempts at humor amusing.

It didn't help matters to know that her mother and her cronies religiously watched the show. Probably made an extra effort today because she was on it. She could see ten perfectly coiffed women her mother's age seated in an elegant living room, sipping tea out of antique cups, gathered around a television set rolled into the room just for the event.

It was just as well that she'd opted out of attending the lecture scheduled for this afternoon at a nearby country club. If she thought the host and her mother's cronies were a tough audience, she could only imagine what she would have faced there.

Besides, Dylan was the one with the teaching background. Just his format. And so *not* hers.

Coward.

Yes, she was. And damned proud of it, too.

Rick hadn't been pleased, which, after his clandestine activities, cheered her. But she'd preferred to spend the afternoon bugging her contractor at her condo than facing a bunch of pinched-faced retirees any day.

In an instant, it seemed, day slid into night. Taking her hands from her pockets, she started trudging the fifty yards or so back to the house in the dark, hoping she wouldn't trip over something and break her neck.

Sneaking in the side door, she took off her shoes and tiptoed upstairs to her room to change. Aside from the sand on her jeans, she had sawdust in her sweater and a smear of something she didn't want to try to identify on her left pant leg. There was one thing her mother hated more than her being late to dinner and that was showing up at the table looking like a ragamuffin, as her mother used to call her when she was younger. Of course her green mohawk deserved something far more severe than ragamuffin, but hey, it was the best her mother had been able to do.

In her bedroom she'd peeled off her clothes and headed for the connecting bath. A quick hot shower later, she rifled through her still-packed suitcase, frowning when she found nothing but dirty clothes. She had planned to put a load in the wash earlier, but had forgotten in her state of hopelessness. Giving up on the idea of the suitcase magically providing her with clean clothes, she turned toward her old closet. Certainly she'd left a few items in there. Whirling open the door, she stood in front of the dated selections. Yikes, had she really worn this stuff? She fingered a denim jacket with her name spelled out in pink sequins, evidence that these…things were indeed hers.

The least hideous item in the bunch was a denim dress she didn't think she'd ever worn simply because her mother had bought it for her. With short sleeves and V neck, it stretched down to just above her knees. Not exactly seasonable, but beggars couldn't be choosers.

"Underwear," she murmured to herself, going through the bureau drawers. The drawers seemed to have every pair of pajamas she'd worn since birth but there was absolutely no sign of underwear.

"Gracie!"

Her hands froze on a pair of blue cloud-covered flannels and she rolled her eyes heavenward. God help her, but her mother's voice had the same impact on her now as it did when she was a kid caught going through her *mother*'s underwear drawer. She hadn't found anything interesting then, and now she wasn't finding anything period.

She shoved the last drawer closed. Well. This was an interesting dilemma now wasn't it? She'd been concerned about showing up at dinner in inappropriate clothing. Now she was facing sitting at the table minus one important piece.

She considered the length of the skirt. Okay, this was doable. So long as she was careful when she sat down, made sure her chair was well under the table, no one would know she wasn't wearing any panties.

"Gracie!" her mother called out from downstairs again. Muttering under her breath, she filled a wicker basket full of her dirty laundry and hurried into the hall.

"Coming!" she yelled, though unnecessarily, because she could already see Priscilla standing at the bottom of the stairs.

Halfway down the stairs it struck Gracie that something was wrong with this picture. She slowed her steps and squinted at her mother's smiling face. Uh-oh. She was smiling. Priscilla never smiled when she had to call Gracie twice for anything.

Oh, no. Please don't make her bring up her little problem *now*. Not when the fresh air from her walk had made her appetite return for the first time since yesterday.

All too soon the steps ran out and she was face-to-face with her suspiciously happy mother. She moved the wicker basket from where she held it strategically in front of her and tucked it under her arm. "Um, Mom, I really don't think now is the greatest time for us to continue our little discussion. Dad's waiting—"

"Discussion?" Priscilla's perfectly arched brows drew together, then flew up high on her forehead as she apparently caught on. "Oh, heavens no! That's not why I was waiting for you."

"Okay," Gracie said, drawing out the word. She couldn't quite bring herself to ask what the reason was. She was too afraid of finding out the answer. Her mother had probably invited to dinner the whole crew of friends who'd likely watched this morning's show with her. No, no wait. She was chafing in her suit to tell her that in the two hours since she'd returned from peeking on the renovations being done at her condo that it had caught fire and burned down.

Gracie bounced slightly, repositioned the basket. Whatever it was, her mother had better spill it soon, because she was getting a wicked draft up her skirt from where the front door was still open.

Priscilla's smile widened. "I have a little surprise for you, Grace."

Gracie barely heard her as she slowly turned her head toward that ominously open door. It was November. Her mother didn't leave the door open in June, much less November.

"Oh, for Pete's sake," Priscilla said with a sigh. "What is taking him so long?"

Him? What did she mean by him? Gracie started shaking her head, hoping against hope that her mother was talking about her father.

But as her mother dashed out the door, then reappeared moments later practically towing the man in question inside, Gracie knew her hopes were in vain.

The wicker basket slipped from her grip and thunked to the polished wood floor as she found herself staring at one very yummy Dr. Dylan Fairbanks.

9

DYLAN SAT STIFFLY at the formal dining room table staring at where Gracie sat completely shell-shocked across from him. She looked as if he'd just appeared out of thin air. Which, of course, he had...with a little bit of Priscilla Mattias's persistence. Persistence? More like mother-handling. The woman had literally dragged him out of the country club, maneuvered him away from his waiting taxi and stuffed him into the front seat of her Lexus. She then proceeded to drive him here, to her house.

A clink of a serving spoon against a dish brought his attention back to the conversation. Gracie's mother said, "It's the funniest thing, really. After catching this morning's show at Adele's—'' she slid a glance at Gracie that puzzled him ''—Colleen invited us all to her country club for the seminar. Her reasoning, and my entire reason for going, of course, was in the hopes that you could somehow redeem yourself, Grace.

"Of course, I had no idea that you had decided to opt out." She took a sip of wine. "Very bad form, by the way. You could have feigned an illness in the family or something."

Gracie rolled her eyes. "A lie your presence would have certainly negated."

"I didn't mean for you to say I was ill."

"No, but you would have immediately made it clear that no one else was, either."

"Not if you had told me in advance." Priscilla frowned. "My, but you're in a mood tonight."

And Dylan didn't doubt that he was the cause of it. Even if he didn't think that way, he would have known the instant

Gracie looked at him, turning the stare she had just bestowed on her mother on him.

"Anyway, where was I?" Priscilla continued. "Oh, yes, the country club…"

Dylan slowly spooned some sort of black rice onto his plate, then handed the serving bowl to the dark, tall, robust man who had been introduced as Dr. Richard Mattias, the most renowned reconstructive surgeon on the Eastern Seaboard. The movement placed Dylan's tie smack dab in the middle of whatever fish was on his plate. He cast a glance around to see if anyone had noticed, but Gracie was busy glaring at her own food, Priscilla was rattling on about it being her first time at the country club, and gee they really should join and Richard was watching his wife with a bemused expression on his handsomely lined face.

Dylan discreetly dabbed at the stain with his linen napkin. He was astounded by the glimpse he was getting into Gracie's life and upbringing. Given her free-thinking philosophies, he'd figured she had come from a lower to middle class background, raised by parents that were by-products of the seventies disco scene. Instead he was surprised to find both Priscilla and Richard ultra-conservatives who probably had never even seen *Saturday Night Fever* and had no idea who John Travolta was.

He really didn't know where he got off making assumptions about anyone, considering his own background. His parents Moonbeam and Frank often commented that they had no idea how they'd produced a kid so thoroughly uncool.

By the same token, he got the definite impression that Gracie's parents thought she was somewhere between a quack and a loose woman.

Which put Gracie's parents and him on the same side, didn't it? Something he would never have imagined possible.

He glanced at her across the table as she said something to her mother, her tone more congenial than exasperated presumably now that the shock of his appearance had worn off a little. He supposed that part of his job was to be an expert on people. But that Gracie proved him wrong so many times…well, it was more than a blow to his ego, it made him rethink his entire approach.

He slowly tuned back into Priscilla. "…so we all ended up sitting in the back, and it struck me that we were all acting like a bunch of schoolgirls—"

Richard's chuckle broke into her narrative. "Cilla, do you plan on getting to the point sometime soon?"

Dylan didn't miss Gracie's surprised glance at her father. Another subtle insight into the life and times of Grace Mattias? Did father and daughter disagree more than they agreed? Given surface appearances, he gathered that they did. Not surprising given Dr. Richard Mattias's traditional surgical position to his only child's determination to set the world free sexually.

That meant that mother had to be the mediator of the three of them. The one who kept the peace. Although Dylan wasn't sure what peace she was keeping, considering the clever verbal jabs she aimed in Gracie's direction every now and again.

He found himself liking all three of them. As far as dysfunctional families went, their differences seemed to bring them together rather than pull them apart. There was a connectedness between them that set off a tiny pang in his stomach.

He hadn't yet taken Diana to meet his parents, even though he'd shared dinner with hers on numerous occasions.

He wondered what Gracie would say on that topic, then reminded himself that he didn't want to know.

"Well," Priscilla said, sighing and draping her napkin across her lap. "The long and the short of it is that Dylan's visiting our fair and delightful city from out of town and when I discovered he didn't have any pressing plans for the night, I invited him here."

Dylan nearly choked on his wine. The room fell silent and he pardoned himself, claiming the liquid had gone down the wrong pipe.

He met Gracie's watchful gaze. "She really was quite persuasive."

Was that a playful light in her brown eyes? Yes, he believed it was.

Richard chuckled. "Trust me. Gracie and I understand just how persuasive Cilla can be."

Gracie smiled. "Oh, yes. When Mom gets her teeth into someone, er, something, she doesn't let go."

Dylan laughed, glad to see Priscilla was taking all this really well. More than likely she was used to the playful ribbing.

"Yes, well, not everyone has a daughter as stubbornly set against marriage as you, Grace. Someone has to watch out after you," Priscilla said.

For the second time in as many minutes, Dylan nearly choked again, this time without the aid of beverage or food. When the coughing fit went on, Richard rounded the table and gave him a hearty pat on the back. "Good God, boy, are you all right?"

Dylan nodded, then picked up his glass of water, making sure Gracie's dad didn't decide he was in need of another whack before taking a long sip. "I'm...fine," he said, drinking more.

Convinced he had finally regained control over himself, he waited until Richard had reseated himself, then turned his attention to Priscilla. The best course of action to take, he thought, was to ignore the reference she'd just made to his being potential husband material to Gracie. "So you saw the show this morning? You didn't tell me at the club." He looked for his napkin, but it was no longer on his lap. It must have fallen to the floor while he was coughing.

Priscilla waved her hand. "There really wasn't time, was there? I mean with so many people waiting afterward to meet you...well, I figured there would be time enough to discuss that later."

"So what did you think?" he asked, looking on either side of his chair and not seeing the napkin.

Priscilla's smile was awfully attractive and familiar. Then

he realized it was because it was exactly like Gracie's. "I thought you did a marvelous job." Dylan looked at Gracie as if to say "See, she approves of you," when her mother continued. "You and the host seemed to get along famously, Dylan. The girls and I agreed that you were the definite winner."

Gracie sighed. "It wasn't a debate, Mother."

"It wasn't? Well, it certainly seemed that way to me." She straightened her jacket sleeves. "It was also clear that I'm not the only one who finds your thoughts on…reproductive science a little…out there, dear."

Since attention was no longer focused on him, Dylan leaned over to retrieve his napkin. He moved the tablecloth out of the way, and popped his head under the table. The first thing that caught his eye was the way Gracie was sitting with one leg tucked under her bottom, though from above she had perfect posture. He also noticed she was barefoot and bare legged, something that had escaped his attention before. Blindly groping around, he found his napkin, allowing his gaze to travel up the smooth, pale length of her long, long legs. God, but she had incredible legs.

He nearly swallowed his tongue. She also had an incredible vulva. A fact defined because she wasn't wearing any panties, either.

"The word is sex, Mother."

Heat rushing down to his own decently covered private area, Dylan couldn't help himself from staring at the red-gold thatch of fleecy curls edging the rim of her swollen flesh. He swallowed hard, filled with the overwhelming urge to reach out and claim the area with his palm, to seek out the pink bud even now peeking at him through the protective curtain.

All at once he was back at that hotel in New York gazing upon her in her shower in all her naked, lathered-up glory. And he'd never wanted her more.

He noticed that above him the table had gone silent. Then Gracie made a small sound and slapped her thighs together.

Dylan smacked his head against the table on his way back up.

"Oh, there you are, dear. Is everything all right?" Priscilla asked.

He waved the piece of linen in his hand, his words curiously gravelly. "I, um, must have dropped it earlier."

He didn't dare look at Gracie for fear of what he might see there in her face. Afraid of what his own face would give away.

Priscilla happily filled in the void. "Anyway, Dylan, after dinner I was hoping that you and I might have a talk. Privately. There's something Grace and I were discussing—"

Gracie's gasp brought all eyes to her, despite Dylan's vow not to look at her. But if she was thinking about the eyeful he'd just gotten of her under the table, her shocked expression wasn't revealing it. Rather, she seemed to be responding to what her mother had just said.

"What is it, Grace?" her father asked.

She hurriedly wiped her mouth on her own napkin. "Nothing. I just remembered I have clothes in the washer. In fact, I'd better go put them in the dryer now."

Richard frowned and Priscilla made a disapproving noise. "I'm sure it can wait until after we've finished," she said.

"I'm done."

"But we haven't had dessert yet. Consuela made your favorite. Cherry pie."

"I'll have some later." She catapulted from her chair, yanking on the hem of her skirt repeatedly. "If I don't get some clean clothes to put on soon, I'm going to freeze to death. Pardon me."

With that, she hurried from the room, taking tiny steps, presumably not to reveal more than she already had.

Dylan wanted to go after her, but he wasn't sure that was such a great idea.

"Richard!" Priscilla said, agitated.

Gracie's father sighed. "What would you have me do,

Cilla? She's a grown woman. I can't order her to sit because you want her to.''

She gestured toward Dylan. "But we have a guest."

Richard rested his forearms on the table. "Yes, that we do, dear. And don't you think it imperative that we not make him feel uncomfortable?''

Priscilla sat back, nonplussed. "She gets it from you, you know. That…that stubborn streak…."

Dylan slowly put his own napkin on the table and got up. "Excuse me. I seem to have gotten…something on my tie. I'm going to go see if Gracie has something to treat it with until I can take it to the cleaners."

He wasn't even certain the couple had heard him as they continued their lively debate on which of them, exactly, Gracie most resembled.

As he left the room, he resisted the urge to tell them she didn't resemble either one of them. As far as he was concerned, Gracie was a one-hundred-percent pure original.

And hotter than any one woman had a right to be.

GRACIE KNOCKED HER FOREHEAD several times against the laundry room door. Good Lord, had her mother really hinted that she was going to ask Dylan for sexual advice, just as she'd asked Gracie? She groaned. Wasn't it bad enough she'd asked her own daughter? Did she now have to go flinging the details of her personal life with her father—or lack thereof—at a total stranger?

She tugged at the hem of her dress in frustration and groaned again. The one and only time she forgoes underwear and Dylan has to lose his napkin. She clamped her eyelids closed. She could only imagine what he'd gotten an eyeful of down there. If the sound of his head banging against the table had been any indication, it was a whole precious lot.

A hot shiver ran over the surface of her cool skin. Okay, so her little peep show, no matter how unwitting, did seem a bit…risqué and excited her in retrospect. The thought of him skimming her exposed privates when she wasn't looking, right under the watchful, critical eye of her parents, held a certain naughty appeal.

What had he thought? she wondered. Really thought? That she'd done it on purpose? Did he find her hot and want to throw her onto the table right then and there?

She bit her lip. Not that his true feelings made any difference. He would never do anything. He'd also never admit that anything she did turned him on. At least not with words. His body, however, let her know exactly how it felt whenever it got the chance. Which wasn't often enough for her.

"God, what are you thinking, Grace?" she asked herself, adopting her mother's tone. She wrapped her fingers around the door handle. "That you want to be his beck-and-call girl?"

She grimaced. No, that's not what she wanted. That whole scenario had too much of a one-sided tone to it. And she wanted Dylan's side very much included, preferably squeezed between her thighs. For more than one night or two. She wanted him there until…well, until she no longer wanted him there.

There, she'd admitted it. She wanted Dr. Dylan Fairbanks for more than a one- or two-night stand. She wanted…more. A full-blown relationship. She wanted to debate their different viewpoints over dinner at a swanky French restaurant…or a rib joint. She wanted to crawl beneath the conservative veneer he wore like a suit—in fact it was a suit—and find out what really made him tick. She wanted to try out every single last impossible position outlined in the Kama Sutra, then when they finished, start all over again.

Was that too much to ask?

She nodded. Yep, it was.

She lifted the lid to the washing machine and sorted through the items that needed to drip dry from those that could go into the dryer, then she put a second load in.

"This place is larger than it looks."

At the sound of the familiar masculine voice Gracie nearly toppled straight into the wash basket. She swiveled around to stare at Dylan where he leaned on the doorjamb. And her mouth went dry at the teasing grin he wore.

He flicked his tie. "Do you have something to treat this with?"

"What did you do with my parents?" she asked.

He laughed. "I locked them in a closet. What do you think I did with them? They're in the dining room discussing the finer points of dinner etiquette. In fact, they probably haven't even realized I'm gone."

She turned toward the shelves behind the washer, fingering through the items there until she found a stick of stain pre-treater. "Here. This should do the trick."

It was only after she had taken the lid off and was dabbing at the quarter-sized stain on his tie that she realized the proper thing for a modern woman to do would have been to hand him the stick. If their roles were reversed, and she was at his place, he certainly wouldn't be applying a pretreater to a spot on her dress.

Then again, she recognized the move for the telling one it was. This was not succumbing to some hidden desire to mother Dylan; rather she was dabbing at his tie for the simple reason to be nearer to him.

She took a quiet breath. God, but he smelled good. He always smelled good. Like he had just come from a shower, his skin all squeaky clean and soap-scented.

And she was the naughty little girl responsible for soiling that image.

She reached for his hand and dropped the stick into it. "Here. I think I got it all, but you might want to double-check." She tugged on the silky material then released it. "Nice tie. That a gift, too?"

He applied more of the solution, his gaze on her rather than the spot. "No. Bought this myself."

Her attention drifted to his midsection. It was only when she got there that she realized she was looking to see if he had on his double-locking belt. He didn't.

She leaned her bottom against the washing machine and

crossed her arms, considering him. "Tell me, Dylan. What's the real reason you're here?"

He grimaced and handed her back the stick. She recapped it and put it on the shelf behind her, then resumed her position.

"Your mother is a very hard person to say no to."

She took a deep, steadying breath, trying to ignore how tempting it was right now to slam the door shut and take him right here, right now, in the laundry room. "I don't mean here as in the house. I mean in this room."

"Oh."

She dropped her gaze to stare at the fine hairs on her forearm. "Yeah, oh."

She stood there for a long, silent moment, listening to the sounds of the dryer whirling, the washer filling, and decided that now was as good a time as any to call a halt to whatever bizarre attraction pulled them together even when it was obvious his intentions lay elsewhere.

He cleared his throat. "You know, Gracie, I've been doing some thinking. Well, actually, it just occurred to me now, but that's besides the point. Considering what I have been thinking ever since we met...well, it's ridiculous it hasn't occurred to me before now."

She picked at her fingernails, thinking she needed a manicure. So long as she didn't look at him, ignored how damn good he looked and smelled and how much she wanted him, this could work. "Oh?"

"You're not going to make this easy on me, are you?"

She raised her brows but not her gaze. "Make what easy, Dylan?"

She heard him draw in a deep breath, then release it. "The fact that I'd like to stop fighting this...strange attraction I feel for you and just start going with the flow."

Heat swept low in her belly and, though she had vowed she wouldn't, she looked at him full in the face. "What?"

His half smile was both sexy and completely adorable, if

that were even possible. "Are you going to make me say it again?"

She continued staring at him, wondering if he had really said the words, or whether she had imagined them. "I think you're going to have to because right now I can't quite bring myself to believe you."

"Believe what?" His voice lowered to a dangerously seductive tenor. "That I've been a jerk?"

He moved closer and she laughed a little breathlessly. "No, that I already know."

"Okay, I suppose I deserved that." She felt his fingers on her bare knee before she saw him reach there. He slowly drew his fingertips up, bringing the hem with him. "So what is it you're having a tough time believing then, Gracie?" He was close enough that his breath heated her cheeks. His fingers continued their upward trek, circling to follow her inner thigh. "That I don't want to...fight whatever this thing is that's going on between us anymore? That I, Dr. Dylan, am willing to admit that not even I completely understand what's happening, but that it's time I stopped trying to control it and let nature take its course?"

His fingers reached the vee of her legs and pressed against the hair there. Hair that was already dripping with need for him. She fought to keep her knees from buckling. "Yes. I guess that would be the concept I'm having a hard time with."

She moved to kiss him, but he caught her chin in his other hand, holding her still, his gaze sliding to her lips. Under cover of her dress, he drew a finger the length of her opening, making her shudder from her head to her toes.

"Well, then," he murmured, his gaze lifting back to her eyes. His pupils were so dilated they threatened to take over the green of his irises. "I guess I'm just going to have to prove it to you then, aren't I?"

She nodded and quickly licked her lips, trembling at the prospect of him determined to prove anything to her. Using his thumb and forefinger, he parted her swollen, throbbing flesh, seeking and finding her sensitive core. Air gushed from her lungs and she collapsed back against the washing machine for much needed support.

He groaned and rested his temple against hers. "God, you are so hot...so wet."

Gracie turned her face into his, needing to kiss him, to thrust her tongue deep into the warm recesses of his mouth, swallow his breath. He pulled back, again holding her chin still.

"Uh-uh," he whispered, running the pad of his thumb across her upper lip then following the line of her lower. "I want to see you achieve orgasm. Watch the rapture on your face...hear your cry."

Under her skirt, he thrust a finger deep into her dripping wetness. Gracie went completely boneless. Who knew strait-laced Dr. Dylan could be oh, so deliciously wicked?

He slowly withdrew his finger but, before she could draw a breath, thrust back in, this time with two. Gracie's nipples under the coarse denim tightened to the point of pain as she fought not to close her eyes and surrender to the phenomenal pleasure rippling through her. She steadfastly held his gaze, pulling her bottom lip between her teeth and biting hard.

His thumb found her clit at the apex of her damp curls. She twitched involuntarily, moaning when he began rubbing the sensitive fold of flesh in small circles even as he withdrew his fingers again, this time twisting them so that her muscles clutched the digits even more tightly.

Then she was hurtling over some unseen precipice, roughly clutching his shoulders and riding out a wave of pleasure so incredible she was afraid her parents would hear her cry of release.

As her climax ebbed, Dylan slowly withdrew his fingers and pressed his lips against her damp temple. "God, do you know how beautiful you are?"

Then he finally kissed her.

Drawing his mouth along the length of hers, he dipped out his tongue and traced the edge of her lips. Gracie recognized the raw need in his eyes, but he appeared to be allowing her the time she needed to recover. Which happened sooner than she anticipated simply because the pleasure, while incredible, had been achieved without him.

Thrusting her hands into his hair, she pulled him closer, allowing for a more pronounced meeting of their mouths. She tugged hungrily on his lips, delved her tongue madly into his mouth, desperately wanting to unleash the animal she saw lurking in the depths of his eyes, in the heat coiling his muscles beneath his jacket. Impatiently she tugged his jacket down, his shirt open, then reached for his slacks. It wasn't until she held every glorious inch of him in her palms that she convinced herself that this was really happening. Dylan wasn't going to change his mind. Pull away. He wanted her as much as she wanted him, and the effects of that knowledge were dizzying.

Then she realized she didn't have any protection.

Oh, God, no....

She bit hard on her bottom lip, then hungrily kissed him again. "You're not going to believe this, but I don't have…anything."

He gazed from one of her eyes to the other, then held up a foil package between them.

The significance of him having a condom hit her full in the stomach.

He caught her earlobe between his teeth as he sheathed himself. "Even when I was too stupid to know what I wanted, my body always knew."

Behind her, the washer stopped its jerky movements, distracting her enough for her to be confused when he grasped her hips and gently turned her away from him toward the machine. Her breath caught as he pushed her dress up around her waist then directed her to lie chest first across the length of the surface. Cool air touched her bare bottom, leaving her feeling exposed…and oh so horny as she thought of him looking at her, exploring her bottom with both his gaze and his hands.

Beneath her, the machine began the spin cycle. She caught her breath, bracing her hands against the back to steady herself, the swollen flesh between her legs quivering as Dylan parted her thighs and placed the tip of his erection against her opening. Gracie closed her eyes tightly, wanting him, needing him to fill her so badly she could scream, but he just stood there, perched on the brink.

Restlessly she tried to push back against him, but his hands on her hips prevented the move.

Then slowly he breached the threshold.

Gracie cried out, arching her back as he sank into her inch by torturous inch, then just as slowly withdrew.

Her breasts throbbed, her stomach quaked, her hands itched to touch something other than the cold metal of the washing machine…but she was completely at his mercy. And loving every minute even as she fought against it.

Thrust by delicious thrust, he incrementally increased the pace, but was still very obviously in control of himself and, by extension, her.

Gracie thought she would die from the frustration of it all.

She felt his hands on her bottom, kneading, caressing, then he drew his thumbs along the length of her crevice, parting the flesh there and thrust into her to the hilt.

The speed of her second climax caught her completely unaware, snatching away her breath, swirling through her like a roaring tornado until it had touched every muscle, every inch, contracting her muscles around his erection, and robbing her of every bit of control she had.

A deep sound of need emanated from Dylan and suddenly he grasped her hips, holding her in place as he thrust deeply into her again…and again…and blessedly again, until she felt him go rigid, every inch of him filling her, his fingers digging into her soft flesh, her name on his lips…and toppling her right over the edge again with him.

The spin cycle ended with a quiet thunk. Dylan lay against her, his breathless pants matching hers as she lay against the cool surface. What they had just shared far surpassed anything she had thought herself capable of. It definitely left their first time far in the dust. And she thought that had been mind-blowing.

This…this….

Well, this was something that transcended even her professional ability and was outside her personal experience to even try to categorize.

"Grace?"

Gracie blinked, the fact that Dylan hadn't said her name slowly seeping through the warm, sated haze blanketing her along with Dylan's hard, damp body.

"Grace?"

More clearly now…closer. *Her mother,* she realized with an aftershock of terror.

Dylan seemed to catch on at the same instant she did. But it wasn't until the doorknob jiggled that the true gravity of the situation hit home.

Gracie shot her leg out from between Dylan's and slammed the door where it had begun to open. A surprised gasp sounded from the kitchen.

"Oh, God," Dylan said, quickly withdrawing from her.

Despite her awkward positioning, Gracie made a sound of disappointment. Not only because he'd left her, but because he'd still been erect while doing so.

Damn her mother and her awful sense of timing.

The door bucked under her foot. "Gracie…I insist you open the door this instant."

"Here," Dylan said, rumpled and sexy and fully dressed. "Let me."

Gracie saw where he had wedged his own shoe-clad foot at the bottom of the door and dropped her leg. She straightened and turned as her mother knocked insistently. Dylan jumped. Gracie had to stifle a laugh at the ridiculousness of the situation.

She felt as if she was sixteen again, when she'd sneaked an eighteen-year-old neighborhood boy up into her room where they stole a few kisses. As now, Priscilla had seemed to sense something amiss and had barged in on her.

It was after that episode that Gracie learned the value of door locks.

She grimaced. Of course, she and Dylan would have to pick probably the only door in the entire house that *didn't* have a lock. Think about it. Who really needed to lock themselves into the laundry room?

A pronounced sigh came from the other side of the wood. "Grace, I won't have you pouting in there like a child when we have a guest present. Where are your manners?"

Dylan met her gaze and she had to clamp her hand over her mouth to keep from laughing.

It took her a moment to realize that Dylan was about to move his foot and open the door. She grabbed his arm. "No...no, not yet."

She gathered the articles of her clothing she planned to hang in her bathroom and put them into the empty wicker basket, then carefully checked her hair. She looked up to find Dylan grinning at her in a way that made her stomach turn around as animatedly as the dryer basket.

"Are you ready?" he murmured.

She reached out and picked a piece of lint from his silky dark hair, then nodded. "Yep."

Priscilla was in the middle of another assault on the door when Dylan tugged it open. "Oh!" She quickly righted herself, then looked at the two of them. It took a few seconds, but she finally appeared to register that Gracie hadn't been neglecting their dinner guest at all. That in fact she had been providing her own naughty brand of entertainment behind that closed door.

Dylan jabbed a thumb over his shoulder. "We were, um...I was just...."

Gracie quietly cleared her throat. "Dylan was keeping me company while I waited for the, um, washer to finish." She smiled widely. "So where's that dessert? Suddenly cherry pie sounds mighty good."

10

San Francisco

THREE DAYS HAD PASSED since their tumble in the Mattias family laundry room during the spin cycle. Three days of plane trips, radio interviews, Internet chats, newspaper journalists…and white-hot sex with Gracie.

Dylan thought his lungs were going to explode as he lay naked across the San Francisco hotel room bed. He loosened his grip on Gracie's slender hips and cracked open his eyes. He nearly groaned at the sight of her sitting gloriously astride him, her breasts heaving as she fought to steady her own ragged breathing. Her head was thrown back, her long, artful neck arched, her silken red hair tickling his knees behind her, her nipples engorged and blushed from the attention he had just laved on them. His gaze dropped to where the red-gold fleece between her legs meshed with his darker hair and an aftershock that could have easily registered on the Richter scale quaked through him.

He swallowed hard, thinking it incredible that the sex between him and Gracie had only gotten better and better. In the past seventy-two hours he'd seen more bathrooms than he could count…and his muscles ached from the inventive positions they had to come up with in order to have sex in enclosed places. The airplane bathroom, especially, had proved a challenge, but one they'd risen to…twice.

Damn, but he just couldn't seem to get enough of her. Not when he sat across a table from her in a crowded restaurant and reached under the tablecloth to see whether or not she wore panties. Not during joint book signings where he swore he would bust if he couldn't touch her just once. And certainly not at night when they tumbled into whoever's room was the closest, half the time not even making it to the bed before they were going at it, hot and heavy.

Staring at the contrast of his darker hands against her pale skin, he budged his thumbs inward until he pressed against what he had come to call her magic button. Touch it and bam, he was given access to the slick, wet enclave just beyond and all the magical secrets that lurked there.

Gracie gasped and caught his wrists. He chuckled, watching as she lifted her head to stare down at him. He wondered if there was a sexier sight in the world than Gracie's face after they'd just had sex. She smiled. Absolutely not.

"You're going to be late for your lecture," she murmured, running her fingertips down his chest and to his lower abdomen, causing a quick intake of breath.

"Screw the lecture."

She laughed. "Hmm...that could be interesting."

She slowly lifted herself from the length of him, her eyes widening at his still-aroused state. "Why, Dr. Dylan, I'm beginning to think nothing's capable of satisfying your little friend."

He hiked a brow. "Little?"

She pinched off the end of the condom, then removed it. But rather than leave him in peace, she wrapped her fingers around his width. "Figuratively speaking...of course." She tightened her grip and moved her hand ever so slightly, causing his hips to buck into her touch.

This time he caught her wrist before he could throw her back down to the bed and thrust into her sweet hot flesh like nobody's business...as if he hadn't just spent the past three hours since breakfast with Tanja and Rick doing just that.

She laughed and got up, wrapping the spent prophylactic in tissue and throwing it into the garbage.

Dylan closed his eyes and swallowed. This was crazy. He couldn't even remember the guy he'd been just a short time ago. And he couldn't seem to get a handle on the new, bizarre, sex-hazed reality that was currently his life. Morning, noon and night, all he could think of was being between Gracie's tight thighs. The minute he'd finally decided to give in to his hunger for her, he'd fully expected the forbidden edge that was drawing him to her to abate. Instead, his stomach-tightening, penis-hardening reaction to her had only grown more acute.

He blindly finger-combed his hair back. He'd counseled a self-proclaimed sex addict once, years ago when he was first starting out. The patient had been a professor at the university where he was teaching at the time. It was rumored that he'd slept with at least five percent of his female students annually, and that percentage rate was rising. The professor's meeting with him hadn't been voluntarily, rather the board of trustees thought it would be a good idea if he sought some counseling. It seemed that one of the girls he'd been with claimed the sex hadn't been completely consensual.

It eventually came out that it had been, that the nineteen-year-old had been upset that the sex hadn't led to more than sex.

Of course, it didn't help matters any that the patient was married. To another faculty member at that.

Gracie sat down on the mattress next to him. "So what happened?"

Dylan blinked his eyes open, not realizing he had spoken his thoughts aloud until that moment. It took him a moment to adjust to the fact that Gracie had not only heard, she was responding to him. She had put on a robe and was watching him with weighty expectation. Dylan considered the string of events from her viewpoint, then answered, "I don't know."

She frowned. "Do you think you helped him?"

He fingered the hem of her robe, tugging on it just a tad so he could peek at her swollen womanhood. "It's just so hard to tell with these things, you know? Here I was, this greenhorn fresh from having written my doctorate thesis on human sexual behavior, when…this guy, old enough to be my father, completely chucked all of my beliefs out the window."

Just like you're doing now.

She lay her hand against his chest. "I'm sure you're exaggerating."

"Am I?" He absently caught her hand in his. "He transferred out the next semester. And all I kept thinking was 'Thank, God.' Our sessions...they were filled with my believing that his promiscuity was age related. You know, middle-age crisis, seven-year itch—though he and his wife had been married for twenty years, a daughter away at college. I'd convinced myself that he was no sooner a sex addict than I was. But all he kept telling me was that he couldn't help himself. An attractive girl smiled at him and it was a foregone conclusion that he would sleep with her." He grimaced. "He swore he didn't feel euphoric afterward, as though he'd carved a notch in his belt. But he would leave the room in which he had just bedded a coed, another student would smile at him, and the whole cycle would start over again.

"He was...*insatiable* is the word he used. If sex was there to be had, then he would have it."

Gracie's hand had stilled beneath his. "Any root problems that you could uncover? A childhood incident? Sexual or mental abuse? Religiously fanatical parents? Or the opposite, sexually liberated?"

He was surprised to find himself grinning at her. "This question from Dr. Hottie? I would have thought you'd say something along the lines of 'Maybe the guy just liked having sex.'"

She drew her hand away from his. "Very funny, Dr. Dylan. I guess I'm curious because I haven't come across an honest-to-God sex addict yet, that's all." She tightened the belt to her robe. "I've had patients profess to love it and label themselves as such, but no one truly addicted."

He curved his forearm under his head, propping himself up so he could look at her more closely. "What type of patients do you get?"

She twisted her lips. "I get all kinds. Frustrated house-wives, complaining husbands, the single career woman who thinks men can't handle a woman who's both successful and has a healthy sexual appetite, male professionals who are find-ing their sexual identities." She smiled. "You know, all the normal wackos who just really need to get laid properly by the right person. And by right, I'm not necessarily talking about the opposite sex, either."

He laughed. "Hmm…wackos. Is that a certified term?"

Her face went serious and her eyes took on a faraway look. "But I think the ones with histories of sexual abuse who are just trying to undo the damage done to them so they can enjoy a seminormal sex life are the most difficult."

The shrill ring of the phone seemed to jar them both out of their thoughtful clouds and they looked at each other.

Gracie laughed. "I can't remember whose room we're in. Yours or mine."

"Yours."

She twisted toward the nightstand and snatched up the re-ceiver. "Hello?"

Dylan turned his head away, ignoring the fact that by some sort of silent mutual agreement, they'd decided to keep their relationship a secret. Oh, yes, her mother might suspect, and they already knew Rick and Tanja did, but in public they acted like two professional, unpersonal colleagues.

He smiled. Well, at least when no one they knew was around, anyway.

Gracie hung up the phone. "That was Tanja. I told her you weren't here, but she said that on the off chance that I hap-pened to see you, to remind you that your lecture is in half an hour."

Dylan couldn't have gotten off the bed faster had he been shot from a gun. A quick shower and a fresh suit later, he came out of the bathroom to find Gracie still sitting on the bed wearing the hotel robe, her nose buried in a psychology journal, her laptop on and perched in front of her and a note-pad, filled with scribbling, on her leg.

"You sure you don't want to come?" he asked. "You might learn something."

She peeked at him without raising her head. "Ha-ha." She closed the journal. "No, you go on ahead. It's your alma mater and definitely your forum, and so not mine. There's something about ratty tweed jackets that makes me break out in hives."

He chuckled and tossed a towel she'd left lying on the side of the bed at her. "Those are my esteemed colleagues you're talking about."

"Better yours than mine."

He was coming to like these little verbal sparring matches with her. She kept him on his toes in a way that was energizing and amusing.

"Look, I'm driving out to my parents' place in the valley later this afternoon. Do you want to come?"

He wasn't sure who was more surprised by the impromptu invitation—him or her.

Earlier he'd told her that he'd be busy for the rest of the day, but hadn't explained why. It was one of the reasons they'd ended up in bed together so early, knowing they wouldn't be together that night. Now he'd not only revealed his true plans, he'd asked her to join him.

He never asked anyone to visit with his parents. Not even Diana.

It was the first time he'd thought of Diana's name in more than just passing since making the decision to put his life on hold. Now he cringed.

He hadn't tried to contact Diana, and she hadn't called him. But he knew he'd soon have to reach some sort of decision about her, about their relationship. The logical conclusion would be to break his plans to propose to her. To break off with her, period. But nothing much in his life seemed motivated by logic lately.

Gracie's gaze seemed to rake his face, apparently trying to read the myriad emotions he was probably displaying.

"Thanks, but no." She smiled, but he noticed there was

something decidedly…thoughtful about the response. "I think I've had enough of parents in general for at least a month." She picked up her notepad. "Besides, I have my weekly radio call-in show the day after tomorrow and I haven't even begun to think about what I'm going to say."

Dylan hadn't realized he was holding his breath until it came out in a loud rush. "Okay." He considered kissing her goodbye, then thought better of it. Aside from it making it tougher to leave her, the action would seem so…normal in what was a very abnormal relationship. At least for him. "I'll see you in the morning then."

She nodded, having already reopened the journal. "Bye."

SIX HOURS, a long lecture, a tedious luncheon and a cigar with his colleagues later, Dylan thought of how easy it would be to turn south back to the San Francisco hotel and Gracie.

He drove his late-model Jaguar through the winding roads of Napa Valley, the late-afternoon sun highlighting the different shades of verdant green. Despite the beauty of the area, he really didn't want to make this trek out to his parents' compound. But it had been a month since he'd last seen them, and he knew from experience that if he didn't make the effort, they would. And without a doubt at the most inappropriate time in his schedule.

He rubbed the back of his neck, marveling at the tension there. He recalled the first time Moonbeam and Frank had popped up on his doorstep. He'd been living away from home for the first time in his life in a frat house just off campus. A month into the semester, the senior frat brothers threw a bash to celebrate the end of hell week and to officially welcome the junior members into the group. In a word, he'd been sloshed, happily indulging in all the juvenile behavior he'd never gotten a chance to while growing up.

It was while he had his head positioned under the nozzle of a beer keg, a fellow frat brother next to him doing the same in a race to see who could down the most draft without puking, that the door opened and there stood his parents.

He hadn't been ashamed of his behavior. No, he knew Moonbeam and Frank would probably hail the event as part of his coming of age, let him sleep it off, then try to ply him with their holistic hangover remedies the following day. Rather he'd been ashamed of them.

Dylan shifted uncomfortably in the driver's seat, tapping down the sun visor to cut off the sun's reflection.

Absently he pondered if he would have felt as...out of place had his paternal grandfather not told him that he'd been born to a higher station in life. During that Sunday afternoon visit to his grandfather's wealthy, sprawling estate, his grandfather had detailed how his parents had given away his birthright to various charities, using the last of the money to start their own self-sufficient ranch—basically a modern-day commune—before he was even born.

Strange, he'd never considered why his grandfather had not given him more if he truly thought Dylan deserved it.

Not that it mattered anymore. Grandfather had died ten years ago ironically leaving the bulk of his estate to institutions that would carry his name. He remembered thinking at the time that in the end his grandfather's behavior hadn't been much different from his parents'. Except his parents had done it while they were still alive and had made no ironclad stipulations that their names be connected to the donations.

He grimaced and caught himself scratching his left arm through his suit jacket. He stopped himself, thinking of the mudlike concoction his mother would cake all over him if she noticed. Then thinking what Gracie might do to help alleviate the pain...

Ah, Gracie. He caught a glimpse of his smile in the rearview mirror and stared at his reflection, amazed. Why, he didn't know. He wanted to have sex with her all the time, so it only stood to reason that thinking of her would bring a smile to his face.

Still, it did amaze him.

What also bowled him over was how much he missed her, though they had only been apart a few hours.

He reached out and switched on the radio, thinking that it was already beginning to happen. He was questioning the validity of the relationship and its dubious future. How long had it been since he'd given up the fight? Three days? While the sex had only gotten better instead of worse, he was a little surprised at the rapidity of his probing of their...curious union. The instant he was away from her, he began absently noting their differences and calculating what they would add up to in the long run. Ignoring their philosophical differences for the time being, he thought of the others.

He was a morning person who jumped out of bed, liked to get in a jog and saw that he had a big, balanced breakfast before starting the day. She slept till ten, dragged herself out of bed, hated exercise of any kind, took at least an hour before she was coherent and coffee—lots of it—made up her breakfast.

He sent his things out to the laundry the instant after he'd taken them off while she allowed nearly every item she owned to pile up before she even thought of seeing to laundry. He tugged at his tie, remembering proof of that at her mother's house when she'd been minus one pair of panties.

Browsing through shops after a book signing in Seattle, he'd learned that her taste in decor was funky, trendy and contemporary, while he preferred heavy pieces with a history and dark, dramatic colors.

He planned out everything in advance down to the last detail, allowing for little surprise and budgeting everything down to the penny. She was a procrastinator who freely admitted she worked best under deadline, hated balancing her checkbook, and gave at least a fiver to every beggar she came across. Which, in San Francisco, was every street corner.

He caught a glimpse of himself in the mirror again, but rather than the frown he expected, he found a half smile still firmly in place.

"Yes, Dr. Fairbanks, you have officially joined the ranks of the lustfully insane."

Oh, he'd figured out sometime yesterday that that's what

he was suffering from. An extreme case of lust. An adult version of a really bad crush. And until he saw it through to its natural conclusion, he wouldn't be able to concentrate on anything else.

Of course, he didn't allow himself to think beyond that. Not now. There would be plenty of time for analyzing his behavior and how it impacted his own personal belief system later.

He realized that later was a time down the road when Gracie was no longer a part of his life and felt a leaden sensation in his stomach.

"You're just thinking of all that great sex you'll be missing out on," he told himself.

Up ahead was the turnoff for his parents' place. The words El Rancho had been branded into a large piece of redwood and nailed to a sign at the end of the road. He turned onto the gravel driveway, looking around as he drove at a speed that wouldn't put a million gravel dings in his Jag. To the right, between neatly tended fields, were tiny houses, cottages really, that served as quarters for the newer or transient residents, those on their way to other places or in need of a little help until they got back on their feet. A little farther in and to the left were larger places. Houses that had their own mailboxes, running water, and looked exactly like they had been taken from the pages of middle suburbia…except that they had all been built by ranch residents and there were no locks on any of the doors.

He continued on down the two miles leading to his parent's house, never before considering how much the land would bring should they decide to sell. In the heart of Napa Valley the considerable acreage would undoubtedly restore the entire inheritance they'd voluntarily given to charity.

The prospect was astounding.

It also made him feel guilty as hell just thinking about it.

No. He'd never ask his parents to sacrifice anything on his account. Not anymore. Even if the thought had occurred to him before now, he highly doubted he would have seriously considered it even then. Everywhere he looked, everything he smelled, from the rich soil, the cool damp air, the hearty vegetation was where his parents lived. What they were. They were as much a part of the earth as the crops they planted.

Unfortunately, he'd never thought much of getting his hands dirty.

He pulled up in front of the low-slung, Spanish-style hacienda he had grown up in and felt an interesting pang deep in his stomach. Somewhat like that of being home. Which was odd, because all he'd ever felt before when returning to the place was dread. Wariness over what his parents had planned this time. What bombshell they would drop. A few years ago it had been their announcement that they were putting aside a portion of their land to grow marijuana for distribution to the terminally ill. The year before last, hemp was all the rage. He still had a scratchy, hideous shirt tucked in a bottom drawer at home, a gift from his mother last Christmas.

Getting out of the car, he supposed he should be thankful that they'd never displayed any interest in the paranormal or any cultlike behavior.

A car was parked off the side of the driveway. A newer one, which immediately set it apart from any vehicles that might normally be on the property at any given time. Frank still drove an old Ford truck, justifying the gas expense by saying that none of his money had gone to the sky-choking, environment-destroying automobile industry in the past thirty years. Besides, he rarely drove it. Dylan didn't even want to speculate on the date on his father's driver's license.

He got out of his car, leaving his overnight bag in the back just in case the opportunity for a quick getaway arose and he could drive back into the city for the night. Entering the house, he knew better than to call out. No one would answer anyway. He'd tried it a few times when he was in the third grade, only to find his parents along with myriad other "family" members in the living room. He'd once asked his mother why no one had responded. She'd said that it was up to him to want to be part of the group. They'd decided the day they'd found out she was pregnant with him that they would never pressure him into doing anything. It was up to him to find his own path in life.

He still thought that was a little too much freedom to put on any one child's shoulders. By going out of their way to never pressure him, they had created a whole type of other pressure. The pressure to make the right decision.

He closed the door behind himself, his eyesight needing no adjustment because it was just as bright inside the house as outside. Painted in airy white, the entryway was as he always remembered. As was the living room with nary a chair leg in sight, but rather various-sized pillows that encouraged "sharing" as his mother said. The kitchen still smelled of cinnamon and various homegrown herbs. No preservatives allowed on this ranch.

He drummed his hands on the hand-painted ceramic countertop and frowned. Where was everyone? He couldn't remember a time when it had been so quiet here. What he wouldn't have done for a little quiet while growing up.

But right now he'd prefer a little noise.

It wasn't as though they didn't know he was coming. He'd called the other day to tell them of his visit. His mother had dismissed the entire notion of calling ahead, as she always did. The house was always open to him, she said. To live, to visit, to do with as he wished.

He preferred to call.

The sound of laughter came from beyond the open back door. Okay, there it was. The familiar sound. He'd probably go back there and find the pond his father had personally dug out years ago teeming with ranch residents.

But when he opened the door he saw only three people and a dog.

His mother. Completely nude.

His father. Completely nude.

Gracie. Who, shock of shockers, was wearing a bathing suit.

And his dog, Killer, who was in the pond and swimming his way.

He winced.

What were his parents doing naked? They had never been nudists. At least not in front of strangers. Was nudism this year's surprise?

His father's jackknife dive into the water told him that, yes, it undoubtedly was.

Then there was Gracie.

Damn if his libido didn't blaze to life at the mere sight of her sitting swinging her legs off the edge of the handmade pier at the west end of the fifty-yard pond. He knew she looked delectable naked, but in a swimsuit she was an out-and-out knockout. Just looking at the way her breasts pressed against the red-and-white striped bikini top, her nipples plainly erect, and thinking of the way the springy vee of hair cushioned the decadently brief bottoms, made him go rock hard. And forget the way the sinking sun set her red hair ablaze, making her look like Circe, the ultimate of Greek witches, and just as impossible to resist.

"Just call me Odysseus," he said under his breath.

At that moment, Killer climbed from the side of the pond and bolted for him, stopping only a foot away and giving a mighty shake that soaked Dylan from head to toe. He had the sneaking suspicion the mutt had done it on purpose.

"Dylan!" his mother called out from where she was getting into the pond nearer Gracie. He looked at her. And wished he hadn't. He didn't want to see that the years of healthy eating and countless hours spent working in the fields had gifted her with an attractive body. He didn't want to notice his mother's body at all. She *was* his mother, for God's sake.

"Maid's day off?" he commented, stopping where he was and crossing his arms over his chest.

His father's chuckle reached him where he was scooping water from his face. "Just trying to go back to nature, and improve our way of life."

"Well, you could improve my chances of not having a

heart attack by putting something on. A fig leaf, I don't care. Just so long as I don't have to see your...family jewels flapping in the wind."

Gracie's bark of laughter drew his gaze to her. Funnily enough, he felt like laughing right along with her.

If only he could figure out what she was doing here.

His father swam to the side of the pond nearest Dylan and hauled himself out of the water, letting it stream down him unhindered. Dylan cringed. "Geez, Dad, did you really have to do that?"

"Yes, I did." He smiled. "You've always been a little too stodgy for your own good. Gives me nightmares some nights thinking about how much you resemble my old man."

"Yeah, well, you're *my* old man, and I could go for you resembling someone who is a little less wacko."

He caught the amusement in Gracie's eyes at the mention of the term she'd used earlier that morning.

Was it only six hours ago when that had happened? It seemed a lifetime ago.

He shifted his gaze back to his parents. Thankfully his mother was a little less...free. She wrapped a towel around herself when she came out of the water to give him a hug and a sloppy kiss. He was surprised how genuine his own hug and kiss back was.

"So," he said, clearing his throat. He tried not to watch his father walk across the grass to where a pitcher of what was likely herb tea waited, but failed. It wasn't every day you saw your own father walking around naked as the day he was born. "What gives with the nudist bit? Not thinking of changing the format of the ranch?"

His mother laughed and walked toward the pier. "No, we're not. Just something your father and I like to do when we're alone together. There are other nicer places we go when we want to hang out with other closet nudists."

He followed her. "Um, Mom, I hate to point this out but...you and dad? You're not alone."

"Are you talking about Gracie? Because if you are, she said she didn't mind when she got here about an hour ago."

An hour? His mind swam with the things his parents could have told her about him. "I was talking about me."

"Dylan, it's not like we don't have anything you haven't seen before."

She was right there. His parents weren't really big on closing the bathroom door during showers or other...events. "Yes, but if it's all the same, I prefer if life has some mysteries. Especially when it comes to my own parents."

They finally reached the pier where Gracie was sitting. In deference to the warmness of the afternoon, and the soaking he'd taken from Killer, Dylan shrugged out of his suit jacket and loosened his tie as he looked down at her.

"Hi," she said simply, Killer taking a possessive seat next to her.

"Hi, yourself." He hung his jacket on top of a piling. "I thought you said you had work to do."

"I finished."

"Oh."

A shadow of something swam through her eyes, then was gone. She patted the wet, smelly dog. "Anyway, I thought after you got the inside scoop on my family life, it was only fair I get a gander at yours."

"Got more of an eyeful than you bargained for, didn't you?" He crouched down next to her, clamping his hands together between his knees instead of reaching out to tug on the strings at the back of her bikini. See how much she really approved of this nudity thing.

Only he was half-afraid she'd leave the top off.

"So what's the verdict?" he asked, interested in her thoughts on his parents.

She tucked her hair behind her ear. "I'm curious to know why you don't mention your parents in either of your books." She motioned to where his mother had entered the pond again on the other side. "Why you let the reader assume you're from a conservative background when...well, you're so obviously not.''

''So you managed to get your hands on a copy of my first book, huh?'' He grinned. ''That must have taken some doing. I personally bought all two hundred copies.''

She smiled. ''You didn't answer my question.''

''I know.'' He reached out and twirled a curl around his index finger. ''I could ask the same of you. While you never come out and say it, you lead the reader to believe that your parents are a by-product of the seventies disco era.''

''I do not.''

His grin widened and he tugged on the hair, nearly groaning when it forced her head back, exposing her delectable neck to his line of vision. ''Not in so many words, but that's the impression I came away with.''

''Then I'm disappointed that you didn't read the entire book.''

He lifted his brows. ''Oh?''

''In Chapter Eight I talk about the strong patriarchal roles that are apparent in even my own family.''

''Do you give examples?''

''Of course.''

''Are you going to tell me what they are?''

''Nope.''

He caught himself laughing. ''I knew you were going to say that.''

She rubbed Killer playfully behind the ears. ''I didn't know you were a dog kind of guy, Dylan.''

He grimaced. ''I'm not.'' He rose to a standing position, wondering just how much his parents had told Gracie about him. And at what point she would use the information as ammunition.

''All right, everybody,'' his father called out. ''It's dinnertime. Any special requests?''

Dylan cupped his hands over his mouth. ''Clothes.''

Gracie's sexy laugh made him smile.

11

SHIRTSLEEVES ROLLED UP, Dylan stood side by side with his mother at the sink washing and drying the dishes.

He slanted her a covert look, glad she had decided to dress for the event. He'd never much cared for her long, flowing dresses, but he'd take them over her nudity any day.

"I like her."

He handed her a clean plate for drying, pretending he didn't know who she was talking about. "Who?"

She nudged his arm. "You know who."

Yeah, he knew who all right. She was talking about Gracie.

All throughout dinner he'd felt awkward somehow. He figured it was because this was the first time since his ex-wife that he'd brought a woman to his parents' house. Well, he hadn't exactly brought Gracie, but that was neither here nor there at this point. Still, that explanation hadn't seemed to pan out. As he'd watched the three of them laugh and joke over what seemed like a lifetime of his misdeeds and growing pains, he'd finally hit on it. She was more at home with his parents than he had ever been.

"I like her, too," he murmured to himself.

He grimaced, afraid of what he'd just revealed, and said almost defensively, "Of course you like her. She's just like you two."

"Oh, I didn't say Frank liked her. He can speak for himself. I said I did."

"Point made."

She smiled at him and he found himself smiling back. "So

whatever happened to the other woman you said you were dating? Diana, wasn't it?''

Sometimes he wished his mother couldn't read him so well. Especially since he couldn't figure either of his parents out to save his life. He was sure she'd seen his wince. "What do you mean what happened to her?''

"Why did you stop seeing her?''

He cleared his throat. "I haven't.''

Few were the times he'd been capable of shocking his mother. But her slack-jawed response meant he had. "What do you mean you haven't?''

He shrugged. "Exactly what it sounds like.''

She lowered her voice. Another characteristic that went against her nature. She was always free about her opinions, seemingly uncaring of who heard what. "Do you mean you're...dating both of them?''

He shifted uncomfortably from foot to foot. "In a manner of speaking...yes. I suppose you could say that.''

Dylan handed her another plate. She put it down on the counter without drying it. "Well, either you are or you aren't, Dylan. Which is it?''

He plunged his hands into the dishwater, searching for the silverware hiding out somewhere in there. "It's more complicated than that.'' Fork prongs stabbed him. He withdrew his hand and stared at it to make sure no serious scarring would occur. "Let's just say that Diana and I were very much a couple when I began the tour. Then I met Gracie. And she and I also became a couple....''

"Dylan, I'm shocked.''

He grimaced. "Trust me, so am I.''

The kitchen fell silent. After a few moments, she resumed drying the plates, and he finished washing. From the living room drifted the sound of Frank's hearty chuckle. He could only imagine what Gracie was telling his father. Why did the prospect make him...well, not so upset?

"What are you going to do?'' his mother finally asked.

He shrugged. "I really don't know, Mom.''

"So you're just going to leave both women hanging until you do know?"

"I wouldn't call what I'm doing letting them hang, but…yes."

She narrowed her gaze on his face. For the first time he saw disapproval in her eyes and it was a powerful thing. She'd never disapproved of anything he'd done before. He found it strange—and unsettling—that she'd chosen now to start.

"Do they know about each other?" she asked.

"What does that have—"

"Do they?"

"Gracie does."

"But Diana doesn't."

"Right."

She put the clean plates in the cupboard then smoothed the damp towel out on the counter to dry next to a bowl of granola. "No wonder."

"No wonder what?"

She looked at him full in the face. "No wonder that girl in there doesn't know if she should stay or go."

He laughed. "Gracie? Trust me, she doesn't have a hesitant bone in her body. You could put a sign around your neck that says she's not welcome here and she'd probably set out to change your mind."

His mother shook her head. "Is that what you really think?"

"Yes, it is. Why?"

"Because you have it all wrong, that's why."

He looked at her for a long moment, trying to put together what she was saying with Gracie's behavior tonight. Could his mother be right? It seemed incredible, but after the 180-degree turn his own life had taken recently, he wasn't quite so ready to rule anything out, as he might have done before. At least not yet.

It was then he realized that Gracie had been a little…distant from him during dinner. Oh, she smiled. She joked. But most of it had been directed at his parents, not him.

Could it be that she was also questioning exactly where they stood? That she needed something beyond the great sex they shared?

He leaned against the counter, the prospect mind-boggling. He'd been so wrapped up in his own thoughts, trying to sort out his own feelings, or rather purposely blocking them, he hadn't stopped to factor in Gracie's.

Of course, she'd never given him cause to, either.

His mother touched his shoulder, making him jump. "Are you ever wound up. When we go into the other room, I'll light a eucalyptus candle to help calm you."

"Just what I need," he said dryly.

She laughed. "You know, if you stopped being such a smart-ass all the time, determined to find differences between us, I think you'd discover that we have a lot more in common than you believe."

"Tough sell."

"Oh, I don't think so." She tilted her head. "There's something…different about you this visit. You don't seem so anal. Oh, you say the words you always say. Make cracks at Frank and me. But the bite's missing somehow."

Dylan began rolling his shirtsleeves down. He'd noticed the same thing. Though what had brought about the changes was anyone's guess. And what impact the change would have on his relationship with his parents…well, that remained to be seen.

"You know, I was just remembering when you first brought Julie to meet us."

Dylan grimaced at the mention of his ex-wife. "Talk about someone you didn't like."

"What makes you think that?"

He shrugged. "Oh, I don't know. Maybe the way you went out of your way to shock her. Point out what life on the ranch meant. And underscored that you fully expected me to move back here, and oh, wouldn't it be nice if it were soon, so that Julie and I could raise our kids here."

His mother laughed. "You have to admit, it was effective."

"Did you ever stop to think that I just might have wanted to spend the rest of my life with her?"

"Yes, despite what you believe, I did. Unfortunately, I had a feeling Julie didn't feel quite the same way. I got the impression that no matter what you did, she would eventually end up leaving you. I guess I thought the sooner the better for both of you." She sighed. "How is she doing lately, anyway?"

He rubbed the back of his neck. "In the middle of divorce number three."

"I'm not surprised."

He grinned. "No, I guess I'm not, either."

The twang of guitar strings sounded from the direction of the living room. Dylan grimaced, suspecting Frank was now going through his collection of original albums.

This was going to be a long night.

Then something occurred to him. "Is that why you and Frank decided to indulge in a little exhibitionism? For Gracie's sake? To test her?"

She looked at him. "I wish I was as devious as that, but no." She smiled. "But if we had, I'd have to say she passed with flying colors. Barely even blinked an eye."

"That's probably because they were ready to fall out of her head." He crossed his arms, sorting through everything that had just passed between his mother and him. Funny, he'd never really thought of their relationship in the typical mother-son way. But considering things now, wasn't the time they had just shared exactly what a normal family would do? Her gently prodding. Him responding. Their comments giving them both things to think about?

"I don't suppose you'd care to give me any advice on my current situation, would you?" he asked.

Moonbeam adamantly shook her head. "Nope." She grasped his shirtfront. "This is something you're going to have to figure out all on your lonesome."

"Now there's a concept."

She tugged him in the direction of the living room. "Better

to have you curse me for giving you too much freedom, than have you blame me for bad decisions that may or may not have come as a result of my advice. Come on. Let's go join the kids. They're playing my song." She hesitated. "However…if I were to decide to offer advice or anything, it would be that I think Gracie's perfect for you." She smiled. "But, of course, I wouldn't do that."

"Of course not." He caught her hand for a moment. "Mom?"

She looked at him automatically.

"Have you ever done anything conventional in your entire life?"

"Sure. I had you."

OH, THIS WAS SO VERY, very good…and so very, very bad.

Gracie lazily ran her fingers across Dylan's sweat-coated chest, finding something surreal about the thick hemp-stuffed tick they lay on top of in the middle of the bare wooden floor of his old bedroom, the fiery light from dozens of flickering candles dimming the thousands of stars visible beyond the balcony doors.

"I can't believe I had sex under my parents' roof," he murmured, twirling a strand of her hair around his finger in that way that made something in her chest go thunk. "And that I enjoyed it."

She halfheartedly thwapped him. "Very funny."

He chuckled quietly. "I didn't mean it that way."

"I know."

She stretched her leg along the length of his, shivering at the crisp hair against her smooth skin. "Actually, I've come to an interesting conclusion. Promise you won't laugh."

He raised his free hand and swore.

"I'm convinced we were switched at birth."

His chuckle vibrated his chest beneath her hand. She smiled and rubbed her nose against his bare shoulder.

"I like your parents."

He tugged on her hair. "Then we have something in common." She looked at him. "I like your parents."

She smiled. "What's the matter with yours?"

"Aside from the fact that they're in a suspended state of childhood and like to parade around in front of visitors completely nude?" He shrugged. "Absolutely nothing."

"I think they're refreshing."

"I think they're demented."

She slid her foot down to the top of his. "Is that your professional diagnosis?"

"Nope. Completely personal. Besides, Frank agrees with my assessment."

"He used to be a child psychologist," she said rather than asked. She'd found out a lot of surprising information about the modern-day flower children over dinner, then afterward as they listened to what she suspected was Frank's entire record collection over a couple of bottles of homemade wine.

"Shocker, isn't it, considering they raised such a screwed-up kid."

"You're not screwed-up," she disagreed, wondering if he really felt that way. "Just a little...uptight."

"Oh, you think so, do you?"

"Uh-huh."

"And what do you prescribe to...treat this illness of mine?"

She made a U-turn with her hand and sloped down to his erection. Incredible as it seemed, he was hard again. She wrapped her fingers around the silken width then rubbed the pad of her thumb over the bead of moisture at the tip. "Hmm...I don't know. But give me a minute. I'm sure I'll come up with something."

For long, quiet minutes they lay like that. Him rubbing his hand down her back and caressing her bottom, her lazily stroking him. Gracie determined that she should have been exhausted. But oddly enough, she wasn't, even though it was four in the morning and she'd been up since six the previous morning.

She supposed that part of the reason was because her mind refused her peace. Though she told herself she was happy with things just the way they were, she was beginning to suspect that wasn't entirely true.

Oh, the sex was spectacular. That wasn't the problem. In fact, if anything, the heights Dylan took her to every time he slipped between her thighs grew more and more dizzying.

But, somewhere over the past couple of days the dynamics of her relationship with him had begun to transform. Which wasn't surprising in and of itself, since it was only natural that the more time they spent together, the more intimate they would become.

It became more obvious that while she willingly gave herself over to the burgeoning emotions, he was holding back. Oh, not in obvious ways. He was too smart for that. It was the little details that began to add up that gave her pause.

Like the fact that she knew his apartment was in San Francisco and he hadn't said word one about going there. She had begun to suspect he hadn't even gone himself until she saw the Jaguar parked in the driveway. While it wasn't beyond the realm of possibility that he'd rented it, chances were pretty slim, meaning he had gone to his place and purposely not mentioned it to her.

Another bit of information he hadn't revealed—and she hadn't asked about—was the woman he had supposedly been on the verge of proposing to. Was that why he hadn't taken her to his place? Was he living a double life, and going to extraordinary measures to make sure they didn't overlap?

Then there was this morning when he'd accidentally invited her to his parents' house. He looked like someone had dumped the contents of an ice bucket down the front of his pants when he'd realized what he'd done.

Of course, she'd turned him down. But over a late lunch with Rick and Tanja, she must have come off as a little too needy, asking them what they had planned for the day when it was obvious they wanted to be left alone. That's when

Tanja had passed her the address to Dylan's parents' and suggested the drive would be the perfect way to see the area.

What was a woman to do? Go to a show by herself? Walk the piers? Go to Chinatown? Or go see exactly what Dylan was trying to hide from her?

She thought his attitude toward his parents was quaint. But also she saw that there was more behind his behavior than probably even he realized. Rather than the shame he hinted at, she suspected he was actually trying to protect his parents and their way of life from others.

"You got awfully quiet all of the sudden," Dylan said, breaking into her thoughts.

"Yeah."

"Is that all you have to say?"

"For now? Yeah."

"Well, that's illuminating."

At this point, Gracie didn't particularly like the direction of her thoughts. And since the only time she could shut off her mind was when she was having sex with Dylan, she raised herself up on her elbows and smiled down at him suggestively.

He chuckled. "Uh-oh. What's going on in that beautiful head of yours?"

"I've just come up with a prescription plan."

"Uh-huh."

She drew her tongue along one flat nipple, then moved over and did the same to the other. He threaded his fingers through her hair and gently tried to tug her to his mouth.

She caught his hands. "Oh, no. Not part of the game plan." She moved his wrists until his arms lay at his sides.

As she ran her tongue along the middle of his stomach, dipped lower, then came back up again, she relished his quick intake of breath.

"Do you, um, mind telling me what is?"

She laughed against his skin. "Are you always this bossy?"

"Always."

"Then remind me to invest in a gag tomorrow."

She dipped lower again, flicking her tongue along the edge of the crisp, curly hair between his legs. "Does a gag normally play a role in your treatments?"

"Depends on the patient." She caught the head of his erection between her lips and sucked deeply. His answering groan and the bucking of his hips from the tick set fire to her own limbs. She released him. "Now be quiet. The doctor is in session."

Curving her hand around the base of his erection, she drew the very tip of her tongue down one side, then back up the other, repeating the movement until nearly her entire tongue made contact with him.

She'd positioned herself so that she was straddling his left leg. When the rough hair of his knee began rubbing against her swollen womanhood, she shuddered. Gripping him more tightly, she slowly slid her mouth down over the rigid shaft, applying light suction and curving her tongue around him so she could pull him deeper. Then she withdrew, following her lips with the upward thrust of her hand.

He groaned and reached for her hair. She looked up to find his half-lidded, passion-filled eyes watching her. She tilted her head and placed tiny little flicks down the length of his erection while holding his gaze, then fastened her mouth from the side, beginning a slow torturous rhythm with her hand.

"Good Lord, you're going to be the death of me, woman."

She pulled the tip of his arousal into her mouth, then released it. "Maybe. But you're proving to be the life of me."

Then she gave her full attention to the task at hand, her own desire rising with his, rubbing her pelvis against his leg as she increased the tempo of her mouth and hand.

She sensed his climax in the sudden stiffening of his legs, the straining of his pelvis against her hand, the locking of his jaw. He tightened his fingers in her hair to give her warning, to pull her away, but she merely took more of him in her mouth, knowing that what she was about to do was possible but having never tried it before.

"Gracie…please."

She grasped his closest hand in her free one and held him still as she continued her up and downward motion, then positioned the head of his erection against the back of her throat. Unable to hold back any longer, his hips bucked up off the mattress and she felt the hot stream of his sweetly bitter seed in the back of her mouth.

Finally he lay back against the makeshift mattress, out of breath and spent. She slowly took her mouth from him, thoroughly licking the remaining dampness from his skin.

"I've never…no one's…God, I didn't even know…" He gazed down at where she had rested her cheek against his lower abdomen. "That was incredible."

She smiled at him. "So I take it you're happy with my prescription?"

"Oh, baby, I'm more than happy. You've just earned a patient for life."

12

Miami

"GREETINGS AND SALUTATIONS, listeners. This is Dr. Gracie Mattias. Thank you for joining me tonight for a very special edition of 'Sex Talk Live.'" Gracie leaned into the mic at the affiliate radio station in Miami, Florida, one hand re adjusting her headphones as she gave the toll-free number listeners could call nationwide with their questions or comments. She said all this by rote, having hosted the weekly two-hour program for the past year and a half and comfortable with the format and protocol, only needing an update on who the sponsors were of the show before she went on.

Normally she used her local Baltimore radio station to handle the broadcast, along with their engineers and producers But since she was on the road, Rick had made the necessary arrangements to have a sister station and its staff host the show. Last week they'd run a series of clips of some of he more interesting conversations with listeners to cover her ab sence.

"Now, I don't know how closely you've been following my schedule over the past two weeks but if you haven' caught one of my appearances coast to coast, then you've likely heard of them. If neither applies, well, then, I want to know what rock you've been hiding under and whether or no there's room there for me.

"For those who are familiar with my goings-on, then you've probably also become familiar with another docto who specializes in the same area I practice...and that, of course, is sex.'' She purposely drew the word out, then smiled at Dylan while he grimaced next to her at a small round table usually used for guests. "The dashing and delectable Dr. Dylan Fairbanks is who I'm talking about, and he's generously agreed to join me for tonight's show, so you'll actually be getting two heads for the price of one." Under the table she slipped out of one of her heels then slid her toe up the back of Dylan's pant leg. "So I'm sure you'll join me in welcoming Dr. Dylan to our lively forum."

Dylan cleared his throat. "Thank you for having me, Dr. Mattias."

Thank you for having me, indeed, she thought, the tension that had begun to plague her in recent days rearing its ugly little head.

That day in San Francisco, the visit to his parents' ranch, had thrust her onto an emotional roller coaster she was searching for the end to. When they were alone together, she could no sooner deny him or her own needs than she could the earth's gravitational pull. When they had sex, her body sang with exquisite pleasure, reassuring her that there could be nothing intrinsically wrong or bad in being with Dylan in this elemental way.

Afterward, she caught herself examining his comments, looking for the true meaning behind them, or worse reading a significance into them that probably wasn't there.

She didn't like not having control over her careening thoughts...or her body.

The strange thing was, she sensed Dylan was thinking along the same lines. She'd catch him staring off into space with a grim look on his face that said he was mentally pulling something apart. And she knew that that something was her.

Forcing herself to focus on the matter at hand, she glanced down at the touch-sensitive computer screen set up between them that outlined callers and briefly described the nature of

their questions. She looked at Dylan and indicated she wanted
to go with Wendy from Wichita who had a question on feminine suppositories. Dylan shook his head and pointed to Don
from Denver who wanted to talk about being an eighteen-year-old virgin.

Gracie made a face then touched a selection somewhere in
the middle. "In honor of our host state, the first caller is Fran
from Fort Lauderdale. Hi, Fran. What's on your mind tonight?"

"Um, hi, Gracie. Am I on the air?"

"Yes, Fran, if you're talking to me then you're on the air."

"Oh! Okay, um, I just wanted to say how much I enjoyed
watching you on TV last week. I mean I've been a fan of
your radio show for like six months now, and it was great
finally seeing what you look like."

"Thank you, Fran. I'm glad I got the chance to put a face
to the name for you. I take it you haven't visited the home
station's Web site, then? Because there's more information up
here than you've ever wanted to know about me."

"No, I'm sorry, I haven't seen the site. I don't have a
computer yet. But I'm hoping Santa will think I've been a
good little girl and buy me one for Christmas."

Gracie laughed. "I'll bet someone's a happy camper right
now."

Fran's sigh came across the line loud and clear. "Well,
that's just it. *One* of us is happy."

Dylan cleared his throat again, obviously awkward as he
positioned the microphone closer to his mouth. "Are we talking about your husband, Fran?"

Gracie rolled her eyes. He would ask that question. Before
she'd given herself over to her attraction for Dr. Dylan, she
would have found his question amusing, perhaps even offered
to indulge in a playful debate on the subject. But now that
their own behind-closed-doors activities proved you didn't

have to be married to enjoy mind-blowing sex, his conservative attitude pricked at her patience.

Thankfully the topic was moot. Fran answered yes, that she and her husband had been married for eight years.

"The problem is this," Fran said. "While I'm happy to, you know, give him blow jobs—"

Gracie hit the delay button, cutting the words "blow job" from the broadcast and replacing them with a prerecorded "oops, I said a bad word" then interrupted Fran.

She smiled at Dylan. "I think the description the censors prefer is that you don't mind performing oral sex on him, Fran."

"Oh. Sorry."

"No apologies necessary. So, we've established that you're happy to perform oral sex on your husband. Sounds good so far. What's the problem?"

"Yes, well, you see…he's not into returning the favor. In other words, he won't go down on me."

Gracie glanced at the on-site producer on the other side of the glass divider to see if the expression would send up any censor flags. He shrugged and she let it slide.

"I see. And obviously you're a little upset by his oversight."

Oversight? Dylan mouthed. She smiled.

"Yes, I am."

"And have you told him of your feelings, Fran?"

"Oh, yes. I mean, no, not in the beginning, but a couple years ago I commented on it."

"And what was his response?"

"That he didn't like it."

Dylan cleared his throat in that way that signaled Gracie that he was about to speak. She wrote a brief note, telling him to give her another signal, like touch her on the arm, or just jump right in lest listeners get the impression he was hesitant. Either that, or ill.

"I think you'll be happy to know that your husband's response is not all that unusual, Fran. Statistics show that a good percentage of men are uncomfortable performing oral sex on their wives."

A brief silence. Gracie bit her lip to keep from filling the dead air, deciding to give Dylan the benefit of the doubt.

Finally Fran said, "Yes, but how do I change that?"

Gracie hiked a brow at Dylan, curious to hear what he had to say.

"Well, my advice," he said slowly, "is that you don't."

"Pardon me?" Gracie couldn't help putting in, trumping her own decision to let him run with the caller.

"I said that I don't think she should try to change his behavior. I mean, if the guy's uncomfortable, then he shouldn't force himself to do it. And neither should his wife."

Fran's tinny voice came back. "And do you think it's comfortable for me to give him…er, perform oral sex on him? If you ask me, he has it much easier."

Gracie gave a quiet laugh. "You touch on an interesting point, Fran. So let me ask Dr. Dylan this. What's the sole purpose of performing oral sex?"

"Well I think 'sole' is a little too constricting."

"You're right. I'll amend that to overriding reason. What is the overriding reason for performing fellatio on your mate?"

He cleared his throat again, but this time she recognized that it was because he was uncomfortable. "To give your partner pleasure."

"Uh-huh. That being the case, do you think it's fair that Fran's husband is denying *her* that pleasure?"

"To the contrary, I believe Fran's being unfair by suggesting her husband force himself to do it. Look, let's set up the scenario. Her husband, giving in to her demands, decides to give it a shot. He's uncomfortable, awkward, and doesn't have a clue what he's doing to begin with. Tell me, what are the odds that she'll end up getting any pleasure out of the exercise?''

"None," she agreed. "Because you've basically just suggested he give it a shot. As in one time. Implying that hey, if it doesn't work out, well, he'll never have to do it again." She smiled. "Of course it's not going to work out. Because the guy will just be going through the motions. In fact, he may set out with the intention of failing."

"Which just emphasizes my advice that he not be asked to do it."

"Okay, Dr. Dylan, answer me this. Do you believe giving good…fellatio is an inherent skill, or is it something that has to be learned?"

"What are you getting at?"

"The quality of oral sex you give depends on the amount of time and attention you put into it. It's an art, if you will. Like the old saying, 'How do you get to Carnegie Hall? Practice, practice, practice.' Well, in this case, how do you give exquisite pleasure to your partner? Do it again…and again…and again. Sooner or later you're bound to get it right."

"So you're saying that Fran should make him do it not only once, she should insist on him doing it several times."

"I'm saying that Fran's husband needs to try to approach all this from a different angle. His wife is not asking him for this because she wants to make his life hell. She simply wants to be pleasured. Desires equal time. Something that as her husband, he should be interested in doing."

"I disagree."

"Obviously." She laughed. "Okay, Fran, you've heard Dr. Dylan's advice. Mine is this—tell him to get down there or else you're cutting him off. He won't go down on you, you're not going down on him. Got it?"

Fran's voice was much happier. "Got it. Thanks, Gracie."

"Oh, and you might want to think about saving up for your

own computer, because I don't think Santa's going to be very happy this Christmas. Good luck.''

From the looks of it, Fran's ''Santa'' wasn't the only unhappy one. She glanced at Dylan to find him gaping at her. She squinted at him. He'd known going into this that their perspectives on human sexual behavior were polar opposites. She couldn't understand what would surprise him at her response.

She gestured toward the monitor. ''Why don't you decide which call we take next, Dr. Dylan?''

On went the eighteen-year-old virgin from Denver, and out faded Gracie's attention.

Not that what the caller had to say wasn't interesting or comment-worthy. She suspected that had he come on with a comment like ''I'm a virgin—at least I think I am. Do space aliens count?'' she still would have zoned out. No, her distraction had to do with the similarities that emerged between their conversation with Fran, and the blocks she was currently stumbling over in her sizzling, definition-bucking relationship with Dylan.

At that moment five days ago, in her mother's laundry room, had Dylan felt he'd been forced to do something he'd rather not do? A prisoner of his hormones, so to speak? Like Fran's husband and his dislike of performing oral sex on his wife, did Dylan view their relationship as a one-shot deal? A case of temporary insanity that a little—okay, a lot—of sex would help him get over?

Had he gone into all this expecting that it would fail?

She absently bit her bottom lip, at once knowing that what she feared was true. He hadn't had any intention of truly cutting loose and seeing where things went. He'd only partially done so, all the while holding on tightly to his belief that there was no future for them. By doing so, he was essentially guaranteeing that there wouldn't be.

''Thanks for calling, Don.'' The significance of Dylan's

words sank through the thoughtful cloud threatening to explode in her head. "And good luck controlling that libido. Remember, it's just a matter of mind over matter."

Gracie picked up on her cue to say something, anything. The only problem was, she hadn't heard a single thing the caller had said.

Dylan thankfully took up the slack. "You were awfully quiet during that call, Gracie. What, no bones to pick about my advice?"

She shook her head. "Not right now, Dr. Dylan. After all, virginity is your specialty, not mine." She repositioned her headphones and said, "Okay, who should we go with next?"

She glanced down at the monitor to find it ablaze with callers. She couldn't help her surprise. While she always had a steady stream of calls, she'd never garnered this type of a response.

Touching a button without prejudice, she sat back, settling in for the next hour of nonstop call-ins, nearly all of them weighing in on where they stood on the contrary advice they'd given Fran. Which was usually the way Gracie liked to have things work. Start off with a controversial topic or caller, and bam, the show was off and running. She'd had some shows that dragged nearly the whole two hours and it had been trying just to get through them. But tonight she didn't have to worry about coming up with items to fill the gaps, or reword advice she'd basically given the caller before.

The only problem was, she'd never realized how much of her listening base had been silent up until now. But, oh boy, were they making their opinions known tonight. Dylan and his conservative take on affairs had been the one to wake them up.

She twisted her lips, listening as Dylan wished a twenty-year-old who wanted to wait for her wedding night good luck, then she disconnected the caller. She didn't think this new slant was such a good thing. Especially since she suspected that the root of her concerns about her relationship with Dylan lay in the advice he gave consistently, straightforwardly and without a tinge of remorse.

"Wow, you guys are really hot tonight," Gracie said, having to page down in order to see the entire caller queue. "Tell you what. For those of you just wanting to put your vote in on the Fran fellatio issue, I'm going to have my home station's Web master put up a poll on our Web site so you can add your two cents. But for the second hour of the show, I'd like to continue on to other issues."

Dylan leaned over and budged her right earphone aside. "What's the matter, Gracie? Can't handle the heat?"

She turned away from her mic. "Just trying to remind you whose show this is." She flashed him a bright smile, then pushed the button for the next caller. "Hello, Josh from Jasper. What's your question tonight?"

There was a long pause.

"Josh?" she repeated, dead air a four-letter word in the radio world.

"Uh, yeah, hi."

"Hi, Josh. You're going to have to speak into the receiver a little louder so we can hear your question." Talk-show tactics to get the caller to talk, period.

"Okay. First, I just want to say that I agree with Dr. Dylan on the oral sex issue."

Gracie frowned and Dylan grinned.

Refusing to rise to the bait, and resigned that the majority of callers would continue to weigh in despite her request they not, she said, "My screen says here that we've spoken before, Josh?"

"Oh." Obviously he'd been hoping to restart the Fran debate. "Yes. We have. I've spoken to both of you, in fact."

"You mean you called earlier tonight?" Dylan looked at her and she shrugged, not recalling a Josh from Jasper, although the engineer changed names and cities when callers indicated they preferred anonymity.

"No. A couple of weeks ago. When you were on that New York morning radio show."

"You caught that, did you, Josh?" Gracie motioned to Dylan, who thoughtfully rubbed his brows. "Gotta tell you, that was a new experience for me and one I'm not anxious to repeat again anytime soon, if you know what I mean."

"Do you remember me?" Josh asked.

Dylan's eyes brightened and he touched her arm. "Of course we remember you, Josh. Although I think the name you were going by then was John, right?"

"Right."

Gracie nodded. Okay, now she remembered. "For the listeners who may not have heard that conversation, John was having some problems interesting his wife in having sex more often. Is that right, Josh?"

"Right."

"So," Gracie said, stretching back and taking her mic with her. "Did you take my advice? Talk to your wife about her secret fantasy then turn your house into a replica of it?"

A pause, then. "She told me she doesn't have a secret fantasy."

"I see," Gracie said slowly. "So did you improvise, then?"

"Yes," he said with relief. "I wasn't sure if I should have done that, you know, until you just said something. I'm glad you approve."

Gracie smiled. "Just so long as it worked."

The pauses between the caller's responses caused dread to begin building up in her stomach. Normal hesitancy she'd come to expect. After all, it usually hit the caller during the actual call that they were on national radio in front of God and everyone.

But there was something more at work here. And Gracie wasn't sure she wanted to find out what.

After another moment, Dylan asked, "What did you do, Josh?"

"Well, since she'd told me that she didn't really have any secret fantasies, I decided to try to guess what she might like. I arranged for all that romantic stuff—you know, that you see in the movies—to be sent to our house, then I set it all up before she got home from work. You know, flowers, wine, candles, soft music. And since I can't cook, and I didn't want her to have anything to clean up anyway, I ordered in from our favorite restaurant."

"Sounds good so far," Gracie said. "Was she surprised?"

"Oh, yes. She was surprised all right."

Dylan looked at her. "Doesn't sound like it was a nice surprise, though, was it?"

"No. She accused me of putting too much pressure on her. Then she told me she'd eaten at the office and went to bed. Without me."

Gracie leaned forward. "Sounds to me like you two might lead pretty stressful lives, is that right, Josh?"

"You could say that."

She thought she just had. She'd been hoping he would say a little more. "Let me know if this hits home. You both work full-time jobs. Money's a little tight. You're still relatively young and would like to have more than you have right now and are pretty much working for the future. Does that sound about right?"

"Yes."

"So on this particular night your wife was probably pretty tired, wasn't she? Sometimes stress and exhaustion can make people do or say some things they really don't mean. Have you thought about trying this again, say on the weekend? On a night when neither of you haven't worked during the day, and don't have to go to work the next? Say a Saturday?"

"That was a Saturday."

"I see. And your wife worked that day?"

"She works every day."

Not good.

Dylan touched her arm, sending tiny little shivers dancing along her skin. "Josh, sometimes grand gestures aren't really what's needed. You know the saying. Sometimes the best things in life are free. So I'm going to suggest this. Next time your wife comes home, have dinner ready and the kitchen cleaned. Nothing fancy. No candles that indicate you're interested in anything more than doing your part. Then when you're just sitting around say the television, or reading the newspaper, offer to give her a back massage. Better yet, a foot massage. Make it look like sex is the last thing on your mind."

Gracie cleared her throat, then cringed as she recognized herself making Dylan's mistake. "Actually, Josh, I think, on that night, sex really should be the last thing on your mind. You should tell yourself from the beginning that it's not in the cards so there are no underlying intentions she might pick up on that may set her off. It also guarantees that you won't be upset if nothing does happen." She warmed to her topic. "In fact, if she indicates she wants to get intimate, you should refuse her. Tell her that's not what you're after and just offer to hold her."

"But how does that solve my problem?"

"It doesn't. Not that night. But it's a step in the right direction that will hopefully lead you down the full path to renewed sexual intimacy between you and your wife."

"Nicely said." Dylan's voice sounded in her ears.

"Why thank you, Dr. Dylan. I think that's the first time we've agreed tonight. On that note, I think it's time we took a brief commercial break." She glanced at the monitor. "Make sure you don't touch that dial, because Monica from Missoula is on the line and wants to talk about bondage. Per-

sonally, I can't wait to hear where Dr. Dylan stands on thi
issue.''

DYLAN STOOD on the marble-tiled balcony outside one of th
best hotel suites Miami had to offer and stared out at the sun
sparkling surface of the Atlantic Ocean. He drew in a dee
breath of the thick salt air, allowing the sea breeze to tug a
his unbuttoned white shirt and shoot through his hair. I
seemed odd that a thousand miles north, one of the first snow
storms of the season was battering New England.

He shook his head. Surreal.

As was just about everything else in his life right now.

He remembered last night's showdown with Gracie on na
tionwide radio and couldn't help a grin. It wasn't so long ag
that he would have choked on any response he'd made to hi
professional and sexual counterpart's words of wisdom. Bi
over the past few days he'd learned to give just as good a
he got. And it felt damn good.

Of course, he admitted that wasn't the only reason he fe
good. He'd come to some sort of decision last night on th
way back to the hotel after torturous days of indecision sinc
they left San Francisco. That determination had gelled int
reality this morning when he'd woken to find her still sleer
ing, her rounded little bottom and slender back curled agains
his side, the smell of her sex, their sex, filling his nose.

His mother was right. Gracie was perfect for him.

He stood still for long moments, waiting for objections t
present themselves, for fear to begin gnawing away at the ne
roots, for lifelong convictions to quickly erect a wall agains
what he'd come to see was inevitable from the instant he firs
laid eyes on savvy, sexy Gracie Mattias in the shower on tha
fateful autumn day in New York.

Nothing.

Nothing but a sense of rightness so profound that for a
instant it was easy to imagine himself one with the sea an

sand sprinkled out like precious jewels just beyond the balcony railing.

He grinned again and slid his hands into his pants pockets. He supposed the suddenness of the realization should be cause for some concern. Told himself that caution might be the better part of valor. That time was the ultimate test of any relationship's durability. Especially given his history. One failed marriage. An almost-engagement derailed. But much in the same way urgency filled him whenever he was in the same room with Gracie, so was the desire to claim her as his, completely, the next time he saw her.

He absently rubbed his stubble-covered chin. Of course, he was overlooking the little detail that she might not want to be claimed. By him or anyone else. During the past few days, she'd seemed to grow more and more distant from him. Her contagious laughter was slower in coming. Her lovemaking more intense, serious even, as though she were searching for an elusive something she couldn't find and he didn't know how to give her. He'd been so wrapped up in himself, he hadn't even considered how she felt about all of this beyond Moonbeam pointing out that she felt something more.

What if he and his mother had it wrong and Gracie didn't want anything beyond fantastic sex?

The thought numbed him. Was it possible that she didn't want anything beyond today? This moment? Was she still living out her own personal extended sexual safari and he was the prey she would cast aside when lust waned?

He slowly finger-combed his hair, the breeze instantly undoing his efforts though he couldn't bring himself to care. He tried looking at the situation from her side, tried to gain insight into her point of view, but found it difficult without tainting it with his own. He could come up with at least a half-dozen reasons why she shouldn't want him for the long haul. Hell, that part was easy for him because he'd hung on to the same reasons for so long himself.

He withdrew his hand from his pants pocket, taking out the antique engagement ring along with it. Clicking the velvet box open, he looked down at it and frowned. The platinum band with three large diamonds shone dully in the bright light. Not Gracie at all. She needed something that was her. Something that took the light in the room then reflected it, increasing its strength tenfold.

He needed to find a way to break down any final barriers that she might have erected between them. And he was sure there were a shitload that he'd only given her the freedom to fortify over the past few days. While he sensed a somewhat desperate longing in her lovemaking lately, he also sensed that she had yet to give him everything. And it was exactly that everything that he needed. Not only to appease his ego. But to prove that what they shared was more than just great sex. That his philosophy that great sex came as a result of a deeper connection, a greater understanding still held true for him. The reason why they were so good together was that they were made for each other. Complete opposites in every way. She was the yin to his yang. Well, if you went in for that kind of thing, anyway. He normally didn't, but right now, standing on that beachfront balcony, staring out over the vast Atlantic as if he was gazing out upon the uncertainty of the future, he couldn't come up with anything better.

And he couldn't help thinking that the key to convincing her of the same lay in what had brought them together: sex.

He shoved the ring box back into his pocket. But first he needed to arm himself....

13

JUGGLING WHAT ADDED UP TO a month's budget in shopping bags, Gracie stepped into the slot that opened up in the hotel's automatic revolving door. Comfort buying, she thought, though for some reason she didn't feel all that comforted. As if to prove her point, she nearly toppled right off her high heels, a virtual death sentence in the enclosed space. She was forced to choose: her dignity or the bags. Dignity won hands down and she released at least three of the half-dozen bags in order to steady herself against the revolving glass. Before she could regain her equilibrium, the contraption spit her out into the lobby. She swung around, watching her lost bags make another go-around.

Dropping the remainder of her bags to the floor, she sighed. Well, better the bags be stuck in the apparatus being propelled in circles than her, right? Although she really didn't need a revolving door to accomplish that for her. She was doing quite all right by herself in that department.

"Ma'am, can I help you?"

Ma'am? Gracie scowled at the bellboy in a hat similar to those worn by minstrel monkeys and motioned to where her bags were coming up in the revolving door.

She didn't think it possible, but her day was rapidly going from bad to worse. She squinted against the late-afternoon sunlight reflecting off a chrome bumper of an approaching limo, then hurried to rescue her other belongings, nearly colliding with the bellboy who had the same thing in mind. She stumbled back, motioning for him to go ahead. He presented her with his rear end. She fought the temptation to give him a propelling push, sending him sprawling along with her bags. She figured it was no less than he deserved for calling her "ma'am."

She caught herself smiling. Well, as close to smiling as she'd been all day. She'd take it. Even if it meant her amusement had come as a result of maiming someone else.

The small smile vanished completely when he reached out and punched a button that stopped the revolving door from…well, revolving.

A moment later, the world was set back on its axis and he stood in front of her holding all of her packages, the door moving on to terrorize its next unwitting victim.

"Why don't I see to these for you. What room are you in?"

She told him, then fished a tip out of her purse and gave it to him. She bit her tongue to keep from asking if he'd be around later when she inevitably decided she didn't need a lick of the clothing she had just bought and wanted to return the items. Instead, she smiled.

The bags and the bellboy gone, she slid off her shoes, then sighed as her bare feet cooled against the smooth marble floor. An older couple, reminding her just a little too much of her parents, walked by, frowning at her. Ignoring them, she padded toward the house phones. She plucked up one of the receivers and dialed the number for Rick's room. After seven rings, the line automatically switched over to voice mail. She pressed disconnect then tried Tanja's room. Nothing there, either.

Earlier, Rick was supposed to meet her for a late lunch with reps from the regional distribution center. He'd been a no-show. She and the three Floridians had waited two hours, then headed on over for a tour of the warehouse, after which she signed five hundred copies of her book. Her feet ached, her fingers had permanent pen indentations, and she just wanted this tour done and over with.

She realized the significance of what she'd just thought as she left a message for Rick on Tanja's voice mail then slowly replaced the receiver. It went without saying that once the tour was over with, so was her fun little tryst with Dylan. She didn't want to use the word *affair*. Despite her modern take on life and sexuality, she hated to think of herself as "the other woman."

But no matter how much she argued the point, that's what she was, wasn't it? While Dylan wasn't married, she had no reason to believe he didn't still plan on becoming engaged. And at least until the tour ended tomorrow and they inevitably went their separate ways, she was openly cheating with a guy who planned to spend the rest of his life with someone else.

That was a bitter pill to swallow.

Making a beeline for the concierge's station, she stood in the line three people deep, peering over shoulders to try to gauge how long the wait would be. It might just be more convenient if she went on up to her room and checked her voice mail. If she had been thinking, she might have scribbled down the code to remotely access the system. Then again, she hadn't expected Rick to disappear off the face of the earth.

The line shortened by one as a tall blond woman stepped up to the desk. Good, maybe—

"Dr. Dylan Fairbanks…"

Gracie's stomach plunged to her feet as she overheard the name. She leaned to the other side of the guy in front of her, trying to listen in.

"Tell him Diana Evans is waiting for him in the lounge, please. I'll be there for the next hour."

The guy in front of her shrugged his shoulder. It wasn't until that moment that Gracie realized she'd had her cheek smashed against his back in her effort to eavesdrop. She mumbled an apology, then moved completely next to him, moving up when he did as one Miss Diana Evans finally turned and stepped away from the desk. She hesitated, looking around the spacious lobby, then began walking toward the small lounge.

Gracie felt as if someone had wrapped their hands around her lungs, denying her air as she watched the woman walk away. There was no doubt in her mind the woman was, in fact, Dylan's Diana. And she was here to see Dylan.

Neat, short, honey-blond hair. Pretty blue eyes. A body to kill for. A stylish suit and low heels. Even the guy next to her nearly pulled a neck muscle trying to get a look. Gracie irrationally felt like thwapping him in the arm from where she still stood in her bare feet on the other side of him, her hair frizzy and mussed from the past two hours hoofing it through trendy little shops in the humid air, her impractical high-heeled shoes, nearly touching the floor, dangling from her fingers.

She swallowed hard, watching as the striking woman disappeared into the dim interior of the lounge. Well, it wasn't difficult to figure out what Dylan saw in her. Diana Evans was the quintessential woman that all men looked for. In fact, if she weren't happily heterosexual, she might just have wanted to marry her herself.

"Ma'am?"

As if in slow motion, she turned to find the guy in front of her had left and that she was standing a desk away from the concierge.

"May I help you, ma'am?"

She fought the urge to bean him with one of her shoes. Bet he hadn't called Diana Evans "ma'am."

"Um, yes. Are there any messages for Gracie Mattias?"

She caught the flash of impatience on his face.

"*Dr.* Grace Mattias?"

He made a show of looking around his counter space. "And you might be?"

"Dr. Grace Mattias," she repeated evenly, thinking she might just have to bean him with both shoes.

Impatience turning to flirtation, he smiled at her. "Sorry, ma'am, but I don't see anything here."

"It's *miss,* you nimrod. Oh, and thanks."

She stepped away from the counter, her gaze drifting again to the lounge, then scanned the nearby area. A grouping of couches and chairs was positioned not too far away from the lounge entrance, as were a couple of leafy plants. If she could pull one of the plants over to the chair...

She caught herself. What was she thinking? Was she seriously considering hiding behind a palm and staking out Dylan? If he went into that lounge, hugged the pretty, blond Diana and proposed to her on the spot, what would she do then? Congratulate him?

"Excuse me, ma'—"

Gracie whipped around to face the concierge again. Her glare must have told him not to dare call her ma'am again. Instead, he said, "Dr. Mattias, I'm sorry, but I do have a message for you."

She sighed in relief and leaned again the counter. Thank God. She really needed to talk to someone, and it looked like Rick was going to be her man.

She accepted the brief, handwritten note, realizing immediately that it wasn't from Rick. "Meet me in Suite 1001. Six o'clock." Signed, simply "D."

Glancing back toward the lounge in case he had somehow gotten by her, she turned the note over, thinking that maybe he'd made a mistake. That the note was for Diana, not for her. After all, they already had rooms. Separate, of course. It didn't occur to her until now that Dylan's motivation for keeping separate quarters might not be the secrecy he proclaimed, but was more likely because of the woman waiting for him just off the lobby.

No. The note was for her. Her name was written on the outside in the same, sprawling handwriting.

She murmured a thank-you to the concierge and began walking toward the elevators. Well, if this was going to be the kiss-off meeting, damned if she was going to look like something the cat threw up during it. She punched the elevator button, then shoved the crumpled note into her skirt pocket. She wouldn't think of standing him up. To do so would be to make herself out as a spineless coward. And she wasn't about to be a coward now. Spineless or otherwise.

Besides, given Dylan's anal tendencies, he'd probably track

her down. To make sure that she knew exactly where things stood between them.

And where did they stand?

After spending so many days not standing, she supposed that standing itself would be a first.

The elevator finally dinged and she stepped inside the empty claustrophobia-attack-waiting-to-happen and pressed the button for her floor.

She toyed with the face of her watch. She'd find out in just a little under an hour, so why give herself a headache now?

She sighed and gave in to the urge to lean against the wall. What did one wear to such an event?

DYLAN CHECKED HIS WATCH for the third time, but it didn't read much later than the last time he'd looked at it. It was a quarter past six. And still no Gracie.

He paced the length of the suite, past the four-poster bed with its filmy white curtains, the champagne chilling in a shiny silver bucket, the half-dozen flower arrangements, all roses in varying vivid colors, then stopped in front of the special table set for two, complete with food that was delivered at promptly two minutes till six. The lighted candles were already dripping wax. He glanced at his watch again, sighed and considering dousing the flames.

He'd called the concierge the instant he'd returned to the room a half hour ago. Yes, he was told, Dr. Grace Mattias had picked up the note. And no, it wouldn't be a problem to have a privacy block placed on the phone for the remainder of the evening.

So where was she?

A low knock sounded at the door. Swallowing thickly, he began to rush toward it, then told himself to slow down. Pausing briefly to erase any panic that might show on his face, he curved his fingers around the doorknob and pulled the door open.

Only to find Tanja standing there.

"Can I come in?"

He didn't have a chance to answer that no, she couldn't, before she was breezing on by him.

Dylan grimaced and peeked out the door into the hallway. Empty.

He closed the door and turned to see Tanja sitting on the edge of one of the armchairs, completely oblivious to the seduction scene laid out in the suite.

"Rick left me."

His brows shot up on his forehead. He amended his guess to distracted.

For a long moment he stood rooted to the spot near the door, not knowing what he should do. To say he and Tanja had never been…personal with each other was a major understatement. The confident PR rep was always in control of herself and his agenda, even when she manipulated that agenda to serve her own needs.

He cleared his throat. "How did you know I was here?"

She rolled her eyes then looked at him, but said nothing.

He didn't have to ask again. She'd probably threatened the concierge with bodily harm to get the room number. He had no doubt wiry Tanja could best anyone twice her weight just with sheer determination.

He glanced at his watch again. Twenty after. Stepping to the table, he blew out the candles, then went to sit on the sofa opposite Tanja.

She made a low, mewling type of sound. "Oh, God, how was I supposed to know that his surprise was for us to get married at the county courthouse?"

For the second time, Dylan's brows shot up. "Married?"

Sure, after the incident in the Houston bookstore stockroom, he'd guessed that Tanja and Rick were…intimate. But, married?

She nodded and sniffed, producing a wadded-up tissue from the side pocket of her cargo pants. "Yeah. Married. Can you believe it?"

Given the changes wrought in his own life over the past week or so, he was ready to believe just about anything.

"I take it you turned him down?"

She looked at him for the first time, her dark eyes red-rimmed. "Of course I turned him down. What do I look like, some sort of idiot?" She blew her nose loudly then sighed heavily. "Sorry. You didn't deserve that." She waved the hand holding the tissue. "It's just...why can't he accept that I can't even think about getting married right now? I've just gotten promoted. Moved into my own apartment in New York after rooming forever with two other girls. Then there's the little problem of his living in Baltimore, over two hundred miles away."

Dylan was still trying to work out the scene at the courthouse. "He had a ring?"

"Yeah." She held her left hand out, flashing him a modest-size pearl engagement ring. Even as he looked at it, he noticed she didn't. "Isn't it the greatest thing you ever saw?"

He nodded, thinking it was the appropriate thing to do.

She dropped her hand back into her lap. "Do you want to know why I know exactly how far Baltimore is from New York? I'll tell you. Because that's where I used to live. Where I grew up. In fact, it's where Rick and I first met. In high school. But we were both going out with others at the time. After high school we dated a bit. Then I moved to New York and...well, we just kind of drifted apart." She frowned. "At least until we bumped into each other again on this godforsaken tour."

"You're from Baltimore?" So this thing between Tanja and Rick had been going on for a lot longer than he and Gracie had ever suspected.

She didn't hear him. Or at least she acted as if she didn't. "When I asked him how we'd go about solving the little distance problem, do you know what he said? He told me that he'd automatically assumed that I would return to Baltimore. That I'd...proved whatever I set out to in New York and that it was time to come home." She stared at him. "I love New York." Her eyes teared up all over again. "And I love Rick."

Uncomfortable and not at all sure what he should say, he asked, "So...what happened when you told him no?"

She rolled her eyes, as if running out of patience with a slow child. "We argued. Of course. Right in front of a jury pool. Then he...left." Her voice broke. "And I haven't been able to find him since." Tears streamed down her face and she tried unsuccessfully to mop them up. "He's not answering his cell phone...he hasn't been back to his room. I...just don't know what to do."

Dylan didn't know what to do, either. Worse yet, he couldn't come up with another question to ask her.

What was standing out clearly in his mind was that Rick and Tanja's situation wasn't all that different from his and Gracie's. His gaze snapped to the intimate little table for two, the provocative bed and the flowers everywhere, and he felt panic rise in his throat.

If Tanja was currently career-minded, with any thought of marriage or kids far on the back burner, then Gracie was doubly so.

And he may have been about to make one of the biggest mistakes of his life.

Tanja suddenly appeared uncomfortable, as if the act of unloading had cleared her mind, allowing her to understand exactly what she had just done. Which was share a huge hunk of her personal life with him.

Her gaze darted around, then retraced the path more slowly. When she looked back at him, her eyes wide, her purple-tinted hair sticking up at odd angles from where she'd been running her hands through it, Dylan had to look away.

"Oh...I'm like totally interrupting something, aren't I?" She shot from the chair. "I'm so sorry."

Dylan got up after her. "There's no reason to apologize."

She tried for a shaky smile. "God, I can't believe I just said all that to you."

Dylan grimaced. "Why?"

"Well, because, like you're my boss. Well, not my boss, really, but you know what I mean. And besides, even though

I don't know what's going on with you and Gracie, I know you don't approve of...well, promiscuous behavior.'' She stuffed her tissue back into her pocket. "You probably think I should have married him, huh?''

Dylan followed her to the door. "I think you need to do whatever you feel you have to, Tanja.''

She turned back toward him and he cringed, because she looked on the verge of tears again. "Thanks," she said, throwing her slender arms around him.

Dylan stood awkwardly, nearly knocked backward by the surprise onslaught. He held his arms out, not quite knowing what to do with them. Then he managed to clumsily pat her on the back a couple times before dropping his hands to his sides.

"Thank you," she said again, then gave him a peck on the cheek.

"Um, don't mention it.''

She opened the door...to find Gracie standing, hand in the air poised to knock.

"Oh!" she said, clearly startled.

Dylan was so glad to see her, it was all he could do not to yank her in, shove Tanja out and then slam the door. Especially given the hopeful expression on Tanja's face, as if again forgetting the scene of seduction mapped out behind him and assuming Gracie was there for her and not him. Either that, or she was so wrung out she was desperate for another ear. A fresh ear. A woman's ear to hear her story of woe.

Afraid she was about to latch on to Gracie like some long-lost relative, he cleared his throat. "Tanja was just leaving," he said.

His gaze slid back to Gracie. He finally registered exactly how she looked. And felt the bottom drop out of his stomach.

Where he had dressed down for the evening in a pair of white string-drawn cotton pants and matching shirt, she had dressed up. He'd never seen her look so damn good. The black dress she had on stretched down to her freckled little feet, the neckline dipping enticingly, as if the edge of the fabric itself wanted to touch the delectable mounds of flesh, and the stringiest of straps disappeared over her sculpted shoulders, left bare by the upswept style of her hair. She could have easily have gone to a museum event, the opera, or been at home in one of those jazz joints Tanja had gone to in Chicago. All that he could think about was how damn much he wanted her.

At the thought of Tanja, he turned to find her beginning to open her mouth, her gaze seeking Gracie's, her expression hopeful.

Dylan none too gently guided her out into the hall. "I'm sure it will be all right, Tanja. Why don't you just go back to your room and get some rest. Things of this nature have a way of working themselves out."

He cringed at the obvious lie and at the fresh welling of tears in her dark eyes.

"Wait," Gracie said, fishing through a tiny black, beaded purse. Dylan wanted to groan, thinking that if she were about to hand Tanja a tissue, he wouldn't be alone with Gracie for at least another hour. Instead, she held out a room key. "Rick came by my room about a half hour ago." She smiled. "I'm guessing for the same reason you came to Dylan's." When Tanja merely stared at the hole-punched piece of white plastic, Gracie pressed it into her hand and told her the room number. "You decide what you want to do."

Tanja nodded almost imperceptibly and began to turn away. Then once again she was launching herself into someone's arms. This time Gracie's.

Dylan stared at his shoes, deciding not to watch the display of feminine bonding, not looking up again until Tanja had murmured her last thank-you. Gracie stood speechless as the waiflike PR rep hurried down the hall toward the elevators.

"So that's why you were late," he said in relief.

She looked at him with a blank look on her fascinating face, apparently taking her a minute to make the mental transition. "Oh! Yes."

She came inside and he closed the door and locked it, then

checked the locks again. "You could have called." He thought he detected a hint of tension around her lips.

"I tried. Someone put a privacy block on the phone."

"Oh. Yes." He grinned. "That, um, would have been me."

He stood back as she slowly wandered around, touching a rose petal here, caressing the gauzy curtains on the canopy bed there. As she explored the room, he allowed his gaze to openly explore her.

She looked absolutely...beautiful. Exquisite. And as she moved, he saw that the dress wasn't entirely conservative. He caught his breath at the sight of the nearly hip-high slit up the left side of the black material that revealed not only a decadent amount of leg, but the fact that she wore thigh-high black stockings and a lacy black garter.

He instantly grew rock hard, prepared to abandon all his carefully laid-out plans, forget about dinner getting cold on the table and just throw her to the bed and plunge into her wet, hot flesh, dress and all.

Even as she examined the romantic trappings, he sensed that she was ultra aware of him. His impression was confirmed when her gaze swept him from eyes to feet, then lingered at the thick ridge he was sure stood out cleanly under his white cotton pants. Her knuckles turned white where she grasped one of the iron bed posts, then her pink, pink tongue darted out to lick her lips.

She laughed quietly. "Looks like I'm not the only one who did some, um, shopping today."

While she played for normalcy, he noticed the sudden shallowness of her breathing, and the way her nipples pressed tantalizingly against the black fabric. He swore he could make out her heartbeat there. At the base of her graceful neck, just beneath her pale skin.

Dylan swallowed hard and silently counted to ten, afraid that if he didn't rein himself in, his slow, night-long seduction would be over in less than fifteen minutes.

"I...ordered dinner." He motioned toward the table, then forced himself to step to it where he relighted the candles.

She came to stand on the other side, her brown eyes black in the flickering light. "I'm not…hungry."

His hand froze where he was about to uncover the warming tray. He chuckled. "Funny…suddenly, neither am I."

At least not for food. Gracie, on the other hand, he wanted to devour from the tip of her curly head to the arch of her high-heeled-clad feet.

Her gaze darted away from his in a way that was uncharacteristic for Gracie. She'd never played coy with him before, so it was inconceivable that she would start now. He noticed the way she practically mangled her evening purse and knew something was up. Something other than an insatiable body part of his.

"Uh-oh. What's the matter?" he asked.

Her surprise was evident as she looked at him. Still she said nothing.

He started to slowly round the table to stand nearer to her. She rounded it the other way, making sure distance was maintained. Dylan wanted to groan, feeling like a starving man having prime rib dangled just out of his range.

"Well, gee, if I was unsure something was wrong before, I'm sure now," he said. The absence of any playfulness in her movements told him that tenfold.

She seemed to realize what she was doing to her purse and stuck it under her arm. She didn't put it down. Didn't make a move to sit. And everything that was Dylan began to worry. "Tell me," he continued.

Her small smile gave him cause for hope. "God, this is just so damned awkward."

He slipped his hands into his pants pockets, trying to ignore how much her words sounded like she was on the verge of giving him the brush-off.

"You know I've always been honest with you, Dylan. And I'm not going to stop now. All I ask is that you…be honest with me." She tucked a curly strand of hair that teased her right shoulder behind her ear. "I saw Diana."

At first he didn't understand the significance behind the

words. Then it finally began to seep through his concern. *She'd seen Diana.* This is what all this was about. Her choice of attire. Her distance. Still, despite everything, there was no denying that she was just as drawn to him as ever. He could tell by the way she stood rigidly still, the high color in her cheeks and her moist eyes unable to disguise her feelings for him.

He prowled around the table, this time without her making a move. God, but she smelled good. And her skin radiated a heat that reached him the mere inches he stood away from her.

He slowly circled her, then came to stand just behind her. He caught her quick intake of breath. Her shallow swallow. With the lightest of touches, he drew the tip of his index finger along the fine column of her neck down to where her pulse pounded out an erratic rhythm.

He knew at that moment that he could tell her anything. Play it off, pretend he didn't know what she was talking about. Or admit that yes, Diana was there at the hotel but offer no more. Whatever he told her, he knew one thing for sure: she was his.

He only had to make her admit it.

"Where?" he murmured against her neck, absorbing her shiver though he still stood away from her.

He felt her pulse leap beneath his fingertip. "In the lobby. An hour and a half ago."

"I see." He nodded, moving his finger along her beautifully defined collarbone then dipped it down to rest between her breasts. It was damp and warm there, not unlike other, more inviting parts of her body. "That probably would have been right before I met her there then."

He felt her stiffen and immediately curved his other hand around her rib cage, drawing her back along his hard length. She didn't fight. Didn't argue. She merely stood stiffly, her ragged breathing telling him that despite what his words implied, he could still have her. The prospect fascinated him.

He pressed his lips against that same pulse point at the base of her neck, feeling it leap for an altogether different reason. "Along with her new boyfriend."

"What?" her voice was barely above a whisper.

He moved his head to the other side of her neck, pressing another kiss to her sweet-smelling skin. "Funny, but while I was away having my world turned upside down by a certain redhead, Diana met someone else, as well. A colleague, as irony would have it. A man who swept her off her feet. Much as someone else swept me off mine."

A small sound escaped her throat and she collapsed against him, all the tension leaving her body like a sigh. He tightened his arm under her breasts to keep her from crumpling to the floor.

He brushed his nose against her hair, wondering how many pins were in there, and how much fun he was going to have taking every one of them out. "So, tell me, Gracie. If you thought Diana and I were still a couple…what are you doing here?"

He cupped one of her breasts through the thin fabric, relishing her strangled sigh. "To show you what you'd be missing." She slid her hand over his, then shifted until his skin lay against hers just inside the neckline of her dress. She wore nothing underneath, the hot sphere of flesh fitting perfectly in his palm. Then she moved his fingers so that he was pinching her distended nipple.

Her shiver made him want to groan.

He traced a wet trail down the length of her neck, then back again. "Well, then it's a good thing I don't plan on missing anything, isn't it?"

She wantonly pressed her lush bottom against his arousal then sought his other hand. "Uh-huh."

Somewhere in the back of his mind he realized this wasn't going at all as planned. He was the one who was supposed to be in control. To seduce her senseless, until nothing remained but the love that he knew she felt for him. But he was helpless to do anything, fascinated by her own unfolding plan for seduction.

Her hand on top of his, she pulled it across the fabric around her waist, then bent slightly forward, sliding it inside the slit at her side. His fingers hit silky stocking, then they were moved beyond that to the creamy bit of flesh that was softer still. Then his fingers were being burrowed under the soaked crotch of her panties and he felt how much she really wanted him when her body shook in an undeniable series of shudders. Enthralled with the rapturous display, he pressed his hand against her engorged flesh, feeling her juices drip down through her curls and around his fingers.

His own pulse hammered out a need so intense it took every ounce of restraint he had not to take her right now.

Had he ever wanted a woman so desperately? Had he ever had a woman want him so much that she should come at the faintest touch?

Her shudders subsided and she leaned even more heavily against him, relying solely on him to hold her upright. Support he was only too willing to provide as he parted the swollen folds of her womanhood and delved his fingers into the hot wetness awaiting him inside.

Her hands remained on his, both at her breasts, and between her legs, encouraging him…guiding him.

God, but she felt so damn good. So ready for him. He rubbed the pad of his thumb against her enlarged hood, absorbing her shudder, then slowly slid two fingers into her dripping flesh. Instantly, she rocked against his hand, her hips jolting forward then back again, betraying a need that went beyond that of conscious want, transcended inhibition, reducing her to one hundred percent hot-blooded female to his one hundred percent willing male.

Feeling her on the verge of another climax, he groaned and withdrew his fingers, knowing that this time she wouldn't come alone. She uttered a protest and he turned her so he could pick her up. She grasped his shoulders to steady herself, then all too soon he was laying her across the soft white bed then following her up. His gaze slammed into hers, seeing in the depths of her eyes a desire so consuming, he nearly shoved her dress up right then. Instead, he lowered his mouth to hers, finally claiming her lips.

She pulled him against her length, his erection fitting perfectly between her spread thighs, her hands ripping at his shirt, tugging at the drawstring to his pants. He caught the marauding limbs and held them still at her sides, plundering her mouth with his tongue, drinking in her low whimpers, nipping at her swollen lips until she sighed against the mattress, giving in to his demands to be in control.

Continuing his assault on her mouth, he reached behind her and slowly unzipped the dress, restraining himself from the overwhelming desire to rip it off. Soon enough, he tugged his mouth away from hers so he could draw the thin straps down the length of her arms, then drag the fabric down over distended nipples. Nipples that he immediately pulled deep into his mouth, one by one, leaving them pink and wet. She arched her back and he grabbed the opportunity to haul the dress the rest of the way down then tossed it to the floor beside the bed.

This time when she reached to undress him, he let her, too distracted by all the wondrous curves and shadows and valleys of her body. All too soon his pants and shirt rested next to her dress and she was sliding down the mattress to position herself under his hard arousal, jutting her hips up until her soaked panties were all that separated them. When she reached down to do away with even that barrier, he caught her gently by the wrists again. His pulse pounded in his ears, blood roared through his straining erection, and he knew he was one second away from breaking every last detail of the plan he'd so carefully laid out since this morning.

"Uh-uh," he said, twining his fingers with hers, then bringing her hands to his mouth where he languidly kissed them, fighting to regain some of the precious ground he had lost in the past few minutes. "Please...indulge me."

The width of her pupils had nearly obliterated the brown of her eyes as she watched him. A long minute later, she swallowed, then nodded ever so slightly. He smiled and slowly began lifting her arms above her head where he'd fastened two gauzy ties around the bedposts. Keeping his gaze locked with hers, he loosely circled the fabric around each of her wrists, then closed her fingers over the leads. Without telling her, he communicated that her bondage was completely voluntary. All she need to do was let go, and she'd be free.

The sight of her stretched out beneath him, voluntarily, completely at his mercy, did crazy things to his libido. He slid down until he was crouched between her thighs, then hooked both his index fingers under the waist of her red and black lace panties. Slowly, torturously, he drew them down…lower, and lower, until the top of her red-gold curls sprang from their imprisonment. Groaning, he fastened his mouth around the wet spot in the silk and softly blew. She gasped and her hips bucked from the mattress. He smiled, realizing she'd put her panties on over the garters, guaranteeing that he wouldn't have to unfasten them in order to bare her. He continued the downward movement until she'd lifted her legs, allowing him to toss the indecent scrap of silk aside along with the rest of their clothing.

Spreading her legs out on either side of him, he gazed down at her engorged womanhood longingly. Oh, how he wanted to bend down there, lave her, drink from her, until she screamed out his name in orgasm. But what he was working toward…well, it was more important than any one climax. When she reached climax again, he wanted to be there right with her. He wanted to coax her to look into his eyes. And he couldn't do that if he was lost in the soft, damp curls between her legs.

Sitting back on his haunches, he curved his hands between her legs and under her hips then tugged her until her bottom was elevated off the mattress, her swollen flesh resting against his hard, throbbing length.

Go slow, he ordered himself, resisting the overpowering urge to plunge into her hot flesh, thrust into her, his plan be damned. But there was too much riding on this. Too much at stake to risk for a quick release.

Instead, still clutching her bottom, he drew his hips so that the inflamed tip of his arousal rested between her swollen folds. But rather than thrusting in, he thrust up, through her flesh, not stopping until his head rested against her engorged hood, all the while holding her gaze captive with his. Her white teeth flashed as she bit on her bottom lip and he slowly drew his erection back through the silken valley, only to quickly thrust upward again.

Her eyelids fluttered closed and she arched her neck. "Please…oh, God, please."

He swallowed past the thick need his throat. "Tell me, Gracie. Tell me what you're feeling."

Her eyes cracked open, the dark passion in them setting him on fire as he repeated the move.

She cried out. "I want you to take me, Dylan. I'm so hot I feel like I'm burning up."

Good. Good. That's where he wanted her to be at this point. Where he needed her to be.

He drew his hips back, preparing her for another almost penetrating thrust, but rather than move upward, he propelled downward, burying himself in her to the hilt. She gasped and arched clean off the bed, her hands grasping the ties loosely binding her wrists, her breasts quivering from the unexpected move.

Everything that was hot and wet and wonderful and Gracie surrounded him, squeezed him, pulled at him, tempting to give himself over to release. He fought against it, gritting his teeth in determination. He ignored her soft pleas, battling to regain some of his all too precious control.

Finally he slowly withdrew from her.

"Look at me, Gracie," he softly commanded.

Her eyelids fluttered open and she restlessly wet her lips.

"That's it. No matter what, I want you to keep looking at me. Okay?"

After a long pause, she nodded.

And he plunged into her hot flesh again. This time halfway. Then pulled out again, her soft protest and upward thrust of her hips telling of her disappointment. Moving one of his hands from her bottom, he grasped her hip, holding her in place as he slowly entered her again, again halfway, then withdrew. He didn't know how long he could go on. Didn't know how long she would let him. But he needed to see this through to the last of his endurance. Needed to coax her toward a destination they had merely glimpsed before. Wanted to show her that great sex was great sex but making love…well, that was the ultimate utopia. And the only way he could do that was by making her admit that she loved him.

Again he thrust into her, this time a little farther, his gaze holding hers, his skin coated with sweat from the effort. Nearly his entire body shook from the price he was paying. But still he fought on. Thrusting and withdrawing, slowing when she appeared too close to climax, plunging when she least expected it. Purposely taking her breath away. And in the process losing just a little bit more of himself to her.

He leaned forward, resting his damp temple against hers. He tried to slow the pounding of his heart, his jaw clenched tight. "God," he whispered. "I love you, Gracie."

Beneath him, she stilled.

He tightly closed his eyes, praying she wouldn't pull away. She didn't.

He plunged into her deeply. Only when she was once again panting for release did he pull back to his knees.

Then he plunged again, entering her just a little more shallowly.

"Dylan!" she cried.

He thrust into her until he could thrust no more. "Tell me, Gracie."

He withdrew.

She closed her eyes and began restlessly moving her head back and forth. He caught her chin in his free hand and captured her mouth with his. "Tell me."

Every inch of him inside every inch of her, he began rubbing against her swollen bud, the friction caused by their mingling eliciting even more heat.

"Tell me, baby."

Her breath caught, her eyes held an intensity he'd never seen before, telling him that she knew exactly what he wanted from her. And that he would get it. Although not without some cost.

Still, he thrust hard again, bringing her legs up off the mattress. He grasped her knees, trapping them between them.

"Tell me," he ground out.

Holding his gaze, she freed her hands from the makeshift ties and thrust her fingers through the hair at either side of his face. "I..." She bit her lower lip and cried out as he thrust again. "I...love...you."

The world crashed around him, then under him, lifting him to a place he hadn't even dared imagine existed before, and pulling her right along with him.

14

SOMEWHERE BETWEEN dusk and dawn, Gracie awakened with a start, her breathing raggedly painful, her skin coated with sweat. In her dream, she'd been skillfully, unwittingly stripped of her most fundamental defenses. Laid bare, her greatest fear held out for her like a bullfighter tempting a bull with his red cape. Daring her to tell him she wasn't a fraud.

It took her long, quiet moments filled with only the irregular sound of her breathing to figure out where she was. Sense Dylan's heat reaching out from where he slept next to her.

She lay silently, the night before drifting back to her much like the song of the early birds floated in on the pungent sea air. She turned her head away from where Dylan slept, tucking her chin against her shoulder and swallowing hard. Her body was blissfully sore, every muscle aching and raw. It seemed as if her very soul was foreign to her somehow…as if Dylan had expertly, cunningly reached inside her and claimed it as his own.

Worse, she didn't know how she felt about it. Had she willingly given Dylan what he'd asked for…or had he stolen it from her?

She closed her eyes, the sweet smell of their mingled sex calming her in a way a thousand breaths couldn't, and, between her thighs, rekindling the fire she was beginning to fear would never go out. A fire that burned for Dylan and Dylan alone. Almost of its own accord, her body shifted to the side and sought a more direct contact with his heat. She shivered in renewed awareness as he unconsciously hummed and turned into her, pressing his growing arousal against her bottom, his hand sliding down her quivering belly and pressing against her sex.

Then the white, gauzy mist of sleep reached out wispy fingers and claimed her once again.

She couldn't be sure how long she'd slept. It could have been an hour. It may have been ten. But this time when she awakened, it was to the sound of the surf through the balcony doors, and the warmth of what could only be the sun streaming across her sheet-covered body. She smiled and stretched her arms out languidly above her, blindly reaching for the makeshift bonds that had effectively held her captive the night before.

God, talk about your fantasies. She'd certainly indulged in her share from the instant she'd hit puberty and grew aware that she wasn't one of the guys. But this…a delicious shiver rippled over her skin and she arched her back.

"Good morning."

Dylan's voice was low and very, very near. Keeping her eyes closed, she smiled. "Is it morning already?"

The feel of something on her chest drew her brows together. It wasn't Dylan's hand. It wasn't the sheet. The object was slightly heavier. But small.

Thinking it might be food, she hummed and slowly cracked open her eyelids.

"Marry me, Gracie."

Her breath balling in her throat, she stared at the ring box resting between her breasts and watched as Dylan clicked it open then lay it against her skin again. The marquise-cut diamond, flanked on either side by two other diamonds, embedded in the dark blue velvet, caught the morning light…and sent her heart racing from zero to sixty in a nanosecond flat.

She bolted to an upright position, catapulting the box and the object within across the bed where it landed upside down. She dragged her gaze from it to Dylan, where he sat on the side of the bed in his white drawstring pants. He smiled at her and smoothed her red hair back from her face.

"What…what did you just say?" she asked, resisting the

urge to bat his arms away from her. She felt the urgent need to think. And she couldn't do that when he was touching her. A fact she suspected he knew all too well.

He dipped his finger into his mouth, then drew the damp tip along her collarbone to her right breast, where he circled the nipple. She shivered, everything that was her responding to him.

She swallowed hard and caught his wrist. Not...entirely...everything. Her brain was still working. And it wanted answers.

His chuckle was low and slid along her spine like a touch. "I said, marry me, Gracie."

He leaned over and kissed her. But she could do little more than stare at him in shock, her lips frozen, her eyes wide. He ran his tongue along the rim of her bottom lip, then her top, dipping inside to coax a more welcoming response.

She shot from the bed, dragging the top sheet along with her and shakily pulling it against her bare chest. She stared at him, convinced he'd gone insane.

His grin never wavered. "Not exactly the response I was looking for."

"No? Well, that makes two of us. Because you couldn't have shocked me more had you told me you were a twin and I slept with both of you last night." The sheet refused to cooperate and she realized she was standing on it. Stepping to the side, she jerkily circled the silky material around herself twice then tried three times to fasten it at the top. It wasn't until she tried to move that she discovered she'd wrapped herself as tight as a mummy. She kicked at the bottom until she'd earned enough room to walk.

"God, Dylan, have you completely lost it?" She paced frantically one way, then the next, not knowing where she was going, or if she should be going anywhere. "Marry you?" She stumbled over one of her shoes from last night, then kicked it out of the way, her heart beating a million miles a minute. "I...can't...marry you!"

She was vaguely aware of him getting up from the opposite side of the bed, then rounding it. "Why not?"

His steadfast grin only made her...more confused. And just a little angry. "Because...because just last night I thought you were going to break things off, that's why not." She stopped in front of him, holding on to the front of the sheet for dear life. "Because not even ten days ago, you had planned...were convinced you wanted to marry somebody else, that's why not."

She resumed pacing, needing to put some distance between them and make some sort of sense out of her thoughts. Near the table, she swung back around. "Is that...the same ring?"

The grin finally vanished.

She groaned. "Oh, my God! It is, isn't it? You were going to propose to me using the same stinkin' ring."

"Correction. I did propose to you."

"With the same ring!" she shouted. She resumed pacing, this time in a different direction. "What am I talking about? Who cares about the damn ring? I still can't figure out why in the hell you would even offer it to me."

"Because I love you."

She winced, her heart giving such a tremendous squeeze she had to stop pacing. She clamped her eyes shut and swallowed hard.

"Listen to me, Gracie," he said, his voice sounding just over her shoulder, his hot breath caressing her bare shoulder. "That ring was the one my grandfather used to propose to my grandmother. It holds a special significance for me."

When she spoke, her voice came out a whisper. "Did you give it to your first wife, too?"

The telltale anxious clearing of his throat told her that he, indeed, had.

She shot off again, in yet another direction, nearly covering every square foot of the large suite. The sheet caught on the coffee table and she gave it a yank, ignoring the ominous tearing sound.

"Look, Gracie...I knew the ring wasn't...hell, it just

wasn't you. But when it comes down to it, it's just a piece of
metal and rock, isn't it? Isn't it a little ridiculous that you're
making such a big deal about it?"

She glared at him and kept pacing.

He heaved a sigh. "If it makes any difference, I placed an
order for another ring, a different ring, one that had your name
written all over it, yesterday while I was shopping. It…it just
wasn't ready in time, that's all."

She tripped over something that toppled her onto the bed.
Making a sound of frustration, she righted herself and glared
at the offending object. It was her new dress. The one she'd
purposely worn last night to show Dylan what he would be
missing out on. Way back when she'd convinced herself he'd
meant to end things between them.

Instead, he'd asked her to marry him.

He came to stand at the foot of the bed, leaning against the
iron post. She busied herself picking up the dress and trying
hopelessly to smooth the wrinkles out.

"What's really the matter, Gracie? Both you and I know
it's not the ring."

She plucked up her shoes, tempted to throw one of them
at him—heel first. "Though we both know that offering me
the same one is in extremely bad taste."

His grin made a comeback. She did lob the shoe at him.
He easily caught it, staring at it as if it were her foot, then
running his long, tapered thumb along the arch of it.
"Granted."

She rearranged the sheet across her breasts, then held her
arms stiffly at her sides to prevent it from falling down. "God,
you're serious, aren't you?"

She discerned his nod from the corner of her eye but refused to look at him.

She didn't say anything for long moments, couldn't think
of a single thing that would accurately describe the panic she
felt bunched up in her chest. She was so wrapped up in her
own thoughts, or lack of them—that she jumped when he sat

down next to her. She automatically shifted to put some much needed distance between them.

"Listen, Gracie...I know all of this is sudden."

She made a sound of agreement.

He reached for her hand. She pulled it away. "But I've been doing a lot of thinking over the past couple of days and...well, I came to the conclusion that this is the next step in the natural progression of things."

She jerked to stare at him. "Maybe in your book, Dylan," she cringed, realizing it *was* in his book. Literally. "In mine...well, there are lots of things that come before the 'M' word. Like career. Financial success. An understanding of self."

He chuckled quietly. "I've never known a woman more comfortable in her own skin than you."

She restlessly ran her hands through her hair, trying to undo the bedroom tangles, then gave up. "Well, that's just a perfect example of how little you do know about me, then, isn't it?"

She moved the dress in her lap to the bed between them, absently smoothing the cool, dark material. "Don't you see? You've...screwed everything up. You've screwed me up. It was bad enough that I didn't have the puzzle in my head quite put together when I met you. Then you had to go and mess the pieces all up again." She caught herself balling the dress in her hands and forced herself to stop. "And the damnable thing about it is that none of them fit anymore."

He slowly placed his hand over hers. "That's only natural."

A gargled sound of irritation escaped her throat and she got up from the bed again, no easy feat while wrapped in the sheet. "Don't you dare try to psychoanalyze me, Dylan."

"I'm no—"

She pointed a finger at him, stopping him in his tracks. "It's my turn."

He grimaced. "I wasn't aware that I'd had mine yet."

"Tough."

She picked up the dress, then tried to find the corner of the sheet she had tucked against her chest. "So you're interested in psychoanalyzing me, are you, Dylan? Well, then, why don't you try this one on for size?" She finally found the corner, then after several struggles, determined that the only way she could get out of the damn sheet was to turn out of it. She did, catching herself when she would have fallen over. "I...don't...want to...be...my mother."

She threw the sheet over him, preventing him from looking at her in that heated way she knew would set her blood to boiling with desire instead of anger. He pulled it down, his gaze strictly limited to her face even as she tugged on her panties. "Explain yourself."

She picked up the garter and silk stockings then threw them across the bed, abandoning them. "If you had read my book, I wouldn't have to."

He winced. She almost felt sorry for him. Almost. If only his reaction and his behavior up until that point didn't emphasize every last belief, or lack of belief, she had about the institution of marriage and man-woman relationships.

"Okay," she began. "Marriage, as a whole, is supposed to be based on mutual respect, trust, and one hundred percent effort from each partner, right?"

"Right," he said slowly, obviously trying to follow her argument.

"It doesn't exist."

"What doesn't? Marriage?"

She picked up her dress, turned it front to back, then tugged the zipper the rest of the way down. "The ideal of marriage. Of course marriage exists. So does a fifty percent divorce rate." She raised a finger, almost ignoring the fact that she was lecturing him in nothing more than her panties. "Do you know why those marriages fail, Dylan? Because those couples act strictly on emotion, not respect, not trust."

His smile made her heart trip in her chest. "Sounds like something out of my book."

"No way. Because in my book I go on to say that even when couples think they have it, many don't. Not really. The fact remains that to this day, ninety-nine percent of the marriages succeed or fail solely based upon the actions of the female.'' She shimmied into her dress, pulling up the spaghetti straps over her shoulders one by one. ''She's the one who's expected, no, must, put her own interests aside, all her career ambitions, anything and everything that was important to her before the marriage in order to make it work. Oh, she may still work. Appear to go about her life in the same way she did before. But she really isn't. She's the one who has to make all the sacrifices, while the man makes none. In fact, he's the one who reaps all the benefits. Tell me, Dylan, what do statistics prove when it comes to the running of the shared household? Don't know? Let me tell you. In one hundred percent of the cases, the woman is mostly in charge. And why not? Because somebody has to be, right? So where she might have just let the laundry go until, say—'' she waved her hand, reaching for an example, then a perfect one occurred to her ''—until she didn't even have a clean pair of panties left, now she not only has to see to her own, she has to take care of the man's.''

His grin nearly derailed her. ''I think we've already established that I don't have a problem with you going without panties, Gracie.'' She glared at him and he held up his hands. ''And I'm certainly not asking you to wash my underwear.''

She had to do the equivalent of a Harry Houdini trick to get up the dress's zipper, but she did it. ''Aren't you? Then tell me, Dylan. Why is it that I've read both your books, not once, but twice. And you...you haven't even read my book once?''

She bent over, searching under the bed for her shoes. She found one. Then realized she had thrown the other at him earlier. Leaning over him, she lifted it from the mattress. Then her gaze snagged on another object, very near to where the second shoe was. The ring box.

He cleared his throat. ''I simply haven't had the time to read it yet.''

She drew back and sighed. ''Wrong answer. You haven't

read my book yet simply because you don't respect my opinion enough to even learn it. And that lack of respect will ultimately lead to the infringement upon everything I feel is important. Your lack of interest in understanding me, the way my mind works, learning what moves me beyond sex…well, that disinterest will inevitably turn into you discarding what's important to me. And that leads to divorce." She laughed humorlessly and slipped on her shoes. "Because hey, let's face it, one day you both wake up and you find you're not the same people. Instead you're the people you've made each other and guess what? You just don't like each other very much anymore."

Leaving her hair a massive tangle around her face, she planted her hands on her hips and stared at him. He looked as if she had just jerked the sheet he was sitting on right out from under him, his eyes round and somewhat unseeing. "So?" she said.

He seemed to shake himself out of his reverie. "Well…that was certainly an interesting little scenario you just painted, wasn't it?"

She swallowed hard. "And one I'm not interesting in living." She pretended to smooth the wrinkles out of the waist of her dress. "You know, you could have just let things continue on the way they were. Had you considered that?"

He blinked several times. "That would have been better?"

She nodded. "Yes, because when a couple is dating, neither partner is in a position to put the other out. The scales, if the woman is determined enough, can remain balanced."

He nodded, as if still in shock. Then his eyes cleared and he shook his head. "Then you're not sharing, either. Not really. Not where it counts." He ran his hands through his sleep-tousled hair several times in anxious jerks, looking more handsome than he had a right to at that moment. "The fact remains that I…" He searched her eyes. "That I believe in marriage, Gracie. It's what I'm about. Who I am. And I can't continue a relationship without knowing the end result. Or at least predicting it." She watched his throat contract around a swallow. "I love you. I want to marry you. I want to have kids with you. Is that so bad?"

Emotion welled up in her chest, threatening to choke off air. She nodded nearly imperceptibly, her voice coming out in a raspy whisper. "Yes...it is."

She stood there for long moments, almost wishing he would say something to try to change her mind. Or change his own. Throw his hands up in the air and say "Okay, we'll do it your way."

But he didn't. He sat there as stubborn as ever. And, she realized, she was also too stubborn to give an inch.

She slowly reached around him, grasping the ring box. Popping it open again, she took one long, last look at the bit of metal and rock, as he had called it, then snapped it back closed. Taking his hand, she carefully placed it in the middle of his palm. "Thanks, but...no."

Sliding her hands from contact with his, she turned and gathered her hair clasps from the bedside table, then her purse from the untouched dinner table, and headed for the door.

It was only when she realized that he wasn't coming after her, wouldn't be coming after her, that she felt the first big, fat, sloppy tear splash from her eye and onto her cheek. She told herself she wasn't crying because she'd just turned down Dylan's heartfelt proposal. No. She was mourning a relationship that had been the best thing she'd ever had in her life.

She bit determinedly on her bottom lip then quickly pulled the door open and bolted through it.

IT SEEMED TO TAKE an eternity for Gracie to get back to her room. She ended up riding the elevator up and down twice before finally getting off on her floor, completely immune to the curious looks she received from fellow guests. They were in tennis whites and casual day wear; she was still dressed to the nines and feeling more exposed than ever in her life. Not just physically. Emotionally she felt as if she wore her throbbing heart on her sleeve. That is if she'd had a sleeve.

Even when she finally reached her floor, it took her three

complete circuits around the triangular hall to figure out which room was hers. Mostly because the number refused to emerge from her pain-clogged mind and the damn thing wasn't written on her card key for security purposes.

Security purposes. She tearfully wondered if there was some sort of security one could purchase to guard the most precious of objects…her heart.

Not that it mattered now. It was far too late for any of that.

She slid her card key in several times before the little green light finally flashed. Not taking any chances that the mechanism would change its mind, she quickly opened the door and rushed inside.

And became instantly aware that she wasn't alone in the room.

Gracie went very still. She wasn't sure how she knew there was someone else there, but she did. Call it human instinct, the basic desire to survive. The tiny hairs on the back of her neck stood straight out and an ominous shiver swept across her exposed skin.

Before her, the room was cloaked in shadows, the heavy curtains blotting out even a sliver of light. Her first thought was that Dylan had changed his mind. That he had decided to accept her on her terms and had come to tell her that. But she was sure that she would have sensed his presence rather than feel threatened.

She turned and immediately tried to leave the room.

"Don't."

Her leaden fingers hesitated over the door handle at the one-word command. Definitely not Dylan. Not even a voice she recognized. She supposed it was too much to hope that the man behind her was a male maid upset she was going to get fingerprints on the freshly cleaned door.

She slowly turned to face the intruder, her heart thump thumping in her chest. She rubbed the heels of her hands against her damp cheeks then looked at him. She was pretty sure she'd never seen him before. But he was looking at her as if they knew each other very well.

"Pardon me," she said, "but I, um, think one of us has the wrong room."

He moved his hand, revealing the gun he held. "You don't know who I am, do you?"

She looked at him again, her heart rate accelerating beyond normal range. She fought to hold on to reason and battled to be calm, when she felt anything but. "No. I'm sorry...I don't know who you are. Have we—"

There was a light pounding on the door behind her back, making her realize that she'd unconsciously leaned against it for support. "Gracie? Gracie, are you there? Open up please...we are nowhere near finished with this conversation."

Dylan.

Gracie felt dizzy, her gaze darting from the gun to the man's face, then back again. She swallowed against the bile rising in her throat.

"Is that Dr. Dylan?" the man asked quietly, the gun wavering then righting again.

Gracie nodded almost absently, wondering how he knew her...knew Dylan...and wishing she could remember him.

"Invite him in. He needs to take responsibility for his actions as much as you do."

Responsibility for his actions? As much as she did? What was he talking about? She knew for a fact that she'd never counseled the man. She never forgot a face. And she knew for certain that the odds were stacked against her and Dylan having shared a patient, seeing as they were located on opposite coasts.

"I said invite him in!" the man shouted.

Gracie jumped, then turned around to do as he ordered. Her hands shook as she turned the handle. The door opened, but only a scant couple of inches. She met Dylan's confused gaze through the opening and tried to shake her head.

A cold, hard hand encircled her arm then she found herself being yanked back from the door, helpless as the man opened it and aimed his gun at Dylan's chest. "Come in, Dr. Dylan."

Gracie stumbled backward, the back of her knees hitting the bed. The way the man kept saying Dr. Dylan began to zoom through her brain cells, but she couldn't seem to find the information she sought.

"What's going on here?" Dylan asked darkly, looking from her to the man.

The intruder fastened all the locks, then motioned for Dylan to step farther into the room. He did, coming to stand stiffly next to Gracie.

"Good, it's better this way. With you both here."

Dylan's eyes narrowed. "I'm sorry, sir, but do I know you?"

"We," Gracie corrected, clearing her throat. "Do we know you."

Dylan frowned at her and Gracie shrugged, indicating she had no idea who the man was, either.

The man smirked. "Oh, I think you should know me. Considering that you both ruined my life."

Gracie's stomach dropped to somewhere in the vicinity of her feet. She'd heard of stalkers, and had learned early on the necessity of having an answering service field calls from the general public, but she'd never actually met one up close and personal before.

After what had just gone on between her and Dylan, she could have gone without this experience.

"I'm John from New York," he said. "Or Josh from Jasper. Whichever you prefer. But my real name is Jerry Presser and I'm from Orlando."

Realization dawned on Gracie. The guy who had called them during the radio show in New York, then again the day before yesterday, seeking advice on how to put his and his wife's sex life back together.

"My wife left me. I…did what you said. Twice. And she packed up all our stuff, our three kids and slapped a restraining order on me."

Gracie stared at him. The rims of his eyes were red, he looked like he hadn't shaved recently, and his clothes smelled as if he hadn't changed them in days. He was somewhere in his late twenties or early thirties, and it struck her how close in age they all were.

She glanced at Dylan for guidance and found him looking at the stranger in deep contemplation.

"Sir...Jerry...I'm sorry to hear that. But if that's the case, then it's my guess there was much more wrong with you and your wife's relationship than lack of sex."

Gracie glanced from the shaken man, to Dylan, then back again, unable to believe that they were so similar, yet so apart. Jerry used the back of the hand that held the gun to wipe away beads of sweat collecting on his brow.

Her mind whirled. The terrifying situation, on top of everything else that had just happened, threatened to overwhelm her. She bit hard on her bottom lip, feeling hot tears prick the backs of her eyelids anew. Air. She needed air. She turned, rushing for the balcony door.

"Stop!" Jerry ordered.

She did so immediately, her fingers still clutching the curtains, her lungs refusing to pull in the oxygen she needed as she tried to gain control over her emotions. The light cast an eye-blinking glare on the man holding them hostage, giving his skin a greenish tint. She glanced back at the doors and her breathing stopped altogether as she remembered another set of balcony doors at another hotel room in another city. Her mind began to race. The Miami hotel was owned by the same chain as the Houston one had been. And this time her room was located on the second floor. Easily accessible from the ground level. Did she dare hope...?

She snatched her hands from the curtains, trying to feign nonchalance. "I...I just thought we could all use some air, you know? I can't seem to catch a breath."

"Leave it closed."

Gracie looked to Dylan, who frowned again. She licked her lips. "You're sweating. Maybe it will help cool the temperature in here."

She cringed the moment she said the words. They were in

Miami, for God's sake. It was always hotter outside than it was in.

"Oh, for crying out loud, let her open the door," Dylan said, clearly exasperated. "What do you think she's going to do, jump?"

The man named Jerry looked from him to Gracie then at the gun in his hand.

"May I?" she asked hopefully, her heart beating a thunderous rhythm against her rib cage.

Jerry finally waved the gun. "But then I want—"

Gracie grasped the balcony door with both hands, sending up a silent prayer as she yanked the door open.

Instantly the room filled with the piercing sound of the same siren she'd encountered in Houston.

Of course, she hadn't worked out what to do from here....

Jerry swung around, staring at the wall speaker in the corner, his hands clamped over his ears.

"Do something!" Gracie said to Dylan, grabbing for the phone as the prerecorded voice spoke over the speaker, apologizing for the interruption.

Dylan finally sprang into action, grabbing Jerry's gun arm as she dialed 911. Jerry fought for control and an elbow to his midsection sent both men barreling into Gracie. As the 911 operator's voice came on the line, Gracie pulled the receiver from her ear and brought the plastic receiver down hard on Jerry's head.

A HALF HOUR LATER, after Miami police officers had led Jerry Presser from the room in handcuffs, and after Gracie and Dylan had both given their statements, Gracie closed her hotel room door against the last of the officers. She shuddered at the locks there, not feeling reassured that the police suspected Presser had likely gained access while housekeeping had been cleaning her room.

Hugging herself, she turned to face Dylan where he stood in the open balcony doorway.

As it always did when she saw him, her heart dipped low in her stomach than bounced back up again, filling her throat.

As if sensing her attention, he turned from the view outside, his face drawn into long lines, his eyes watchful and...full of determination somehow.

"Are you okay?" he asked.

She nodded. "I'm fine. Or at least I will be when my rattled nerves realize the threat has been removed." She rubbed her arms, cold despite the blast of thick, steamy air flooding through the open balcony door. "And you? How are you doing?"

He shrugged, as if his condition was of no concern to him. "I'm okay."

Considering they both had had a gun pulled on them and had been held hostage—even if it was for only a few minutes—she supposed that they had fared far better than they might have. Gracie told herself she should be grateful. If not for Dylan's somber, significant stance, she might have.

She managed to summon up a halfhearted smile. "So...you, um, wanted to talk to me?"

Confusion flicked over his features then he frowned, looking down at his shoes. "Yeah. I guess I did."

"Did?" she said, finding her voice little more than a whisper.

He nodded then curved his hand around the back of his neck. "After what happened I...well, I don't know what to say."

Gracie caught herself wringing her hands in front of her and forced herself to stop. "I know what you mean."

He glanced at her as if to ask if she truly did understand. "Something like that, someone like Jerry...well, they have a way of making you wonder about yourself, don't they? Compel you to rethink your profession and the impact you have on others' lives."

"We're not to blame for his problems, Dylan."

"Yeah, I know...but still." He sighed. "Look, Gracie. I'm

not really sure why I did come to your room. Clearly you're not going to change your mind...."

His words trailed off and she realized he was asking her if she had rather than stating it. She shook her head. "No...I'm not."

He dropped his hand to his side. "That's what I figured." He glanced toward the open balcony door then back at her. "And I'm not going to change mine. So that brings me back to what I'm doing here."

Gracie bit hard on her bottom lip. "Um...maybe you wanted to say goodbye?"

He stood there for a long moment, saying nothing.

"Yeah," he finally murmured. "Maybe that's it. I came to say goodbye."

He moved toward the door, then hesitated a moment when he drew even with her. Then he bent to place a soft, torturously sweet kiss against her temple. "Goodbye, Gracie."

She closed her eyes and moved to lean into him, but he had already moved away. Moments later, she heard the door clap shut behind him, leaving her completely, utterly, totally alone with her broken heart.

15

THE DRAPES WERE DRAWN TIGHT, the air in the room was stale, and the television silently flickered images across where Gracie lay on the bed, the bedspread half on, half off a portion of her bare legs. Two days had passed since she'd left Dylan behind in that sumptuous suite, balked at his proposal, but it could very well have been two years, the way she felt.

She aimed the remote in the general direction of the TV and absently surfed through the channels, the untouched lunch tray she'd forced herself to order not tempting her from where it sat on the nearby ottoman, beside the ignored tray from the day before.

She distantly knew she should eat something. Then she reminded herself that she had. She had choked down half a muffin that very morning. And the tasteless sucker still sat like a rock in the middle of her stomach.

She rolled over onto her back to stare at the ceiling, the sound of crinkling paper barely catching her attention. Lethargically, she dislodged the offending piece of literature, holding it above her and staring at it. Chapter eight of her book. A book from which she'd torn each and every page the previous morning, grouping each into chapters, the empty hardcover sporting her picture on the back sitting spine up near the door.

She moved each page behind the last as she scanned the words, the once familiar text and ideas now reading like a foreign language.

Sighing, she put the chapter down right where she'd found it, then lay back against it. She'd come up with a reason for the placement of each small stack of papers, but was now unable to remember what it was.

She stuck her thumbnail between her teeth and glanced at the silent phone. Everyone was gone. She was the only one who remained in steamy Miami. Not that the temperature mattered to her. She kept the unit in her room at the same level and hadn't stepped foot outside for two days.

Rick had called her the morning of her...breakup with Dylan, telling her he was heading back to Baltimore if she didn't need anything more. She told him to go ahead, and while he was at it, take a few days off. Both because he deserved it and she needed some major time alone to work her way through her thoughts and feelings.

Then there was Dylan.

She hadn't tried to contact him. What she had done was call the concierge, threatening him with a personal visit if he didn't tell her what she wanted to know. And he had. Dylan had left the fateful suite only a short time after she had and a hotel limo had taken him to the airport where he presumably caught the next flight out to San Fran. On the complete opposite coast.

She absently wondered why she hadn't gone home. Oh, yeah. Because she temporarily didn't have a home to go back to. Good reason. Her condo was still being renovated, the contractor having left a message with her answering service saying he needed another week. That meant that if she went back to Baltimore, she'd either have to stay with her parents or check into a hotel. Since she was already in a hotel, she'd decided to stay put, placing a standing request with the same concierge to tell housecleaning she'd call if she needed anything, but until then they were to stay away. He began to tell her it was hotel policy that the maid at least check the room, but her torrent of curse words had stopped him in his tracks and he agreed to see to her request.

She turned her head and stared at the piles of paper laid out purposefully all over the floor, chair, desk and even the bathroom counter and the side of the tub, some covered with notes, others hardly touched, then rolled over again, kicking at the covers that held her captive. Despite her stationary state, she'd gotten very little sleep. Every time she closed her eyes, snippets from her last showdown with Dylan mingled with Jerry Presser's phone-ins, oftentimes rewinding like a video-tape and replaying again, freeze-framing on certain images. Dylan opening the ring box and laying it against her chest, his grin devastating. Jerry Presser emerging from the shadows of her room, holding a gun on her and looking like a man on the edge, beaten and desperate. Then there was the vivid memory of Dylan sitting on the edge of that decadent bed looking at her as if she'd just snatched away his last dream and stomped all over it in her high-heeled shoes.

She groaned. God, she didn't even have to close her eyes anymore for the images and words to haunt her.

She picked up the remote again, staring sightlessly at the screen. It took a full five chirps of the phone for her to realize it was actually ringing. Changing the channel again, she blindly reached for the receiver. Probably the concierge calling to tell her her credit card limit had been reached.

"Yeah…hello?"

"Grace? Is that you?" Her mother's voice. Definitely her mother's voice. "Are you sure you got the right room number, Consuela?"

Gracie cleared her throat. "Yes, Mom, she got the right room number."

There was a sigh that she almost interpreted as relief. "Thank God. Where are you, Grace? I expected you home the day before yesterday. I can't even reach your assistant, what's his name—"

"Rick."

"Yes, that's it. I couldn't even get him on the line. Is everything all right? You're not sick or anything are you?"

Just in the head, she thought.

"Pardon me?"

Gracie realized she'd said the words aloud and fought to get her act together. She could barely handle Priscilla Mattias when she was at her sharpest. Pushing herself up from the bed, she sat and gathered her tangled hair on the side of her head. She grimaced at the white camisole and cotton panties she wore and fought to straighten them. "I'm fine, Mom. I just needed a couple days to myself." She tried to inject some enthusiasm into her voice. "Where better to do that in November than sunny Miami, right?"

She cringed. Even *she* didn't believe her tone. Fat chance her mother would buy it.

"Grace...would you like me to come down there?"

Wrapping her free hand around her midsection, she closed her watering eyes, finding it hard to believe that she had any tears left to shed. The day she'd walked out on Dylan and his proposal, she'd spent five straight hours soaking every pillow in her room. But now...well, now she could have done without the reminder that while she needled and teased and basically ran from her mother, Priscilla was always there for her when it counted. When she had her first period during seventh-grade gym glass, there her mother was, taking her out of school for the day and making all right with the world by taking her shopping in the women's department of every store they came across. When she was sick during her first year at university, her mother was on the next flight out, pouring chicken soup down her throat and sleeping on a cot in her dorm room until the bug finally fled. After a boyfriend had broken her heart, Priscilla had helped her make a dartboard out of his picture and had thrown darts at it right alongside her.

She had no doubt her mother would also be at her hotel room door faster than she could blink if she only said the word.

Yes. "No," she murmured instead, not sure what she hated more—her inability to snap out of her current state, or the desire to run into her mother's arms, tuck her head against her chest and pretend the world didn't exist. She bit hard on her bottom lip. "It's...nice of you to offer, but I'll be fine. Really, I will. I just need a little time, that's all."

Silence. "Is this about that nice Dr. Dylan?"

She nodded. "No."

"Grace, you don't have to hide anything from me. Even though we like to pretend that we don't, you and I...well, we know each other better than anyone else on earth."

"I know," she whispered, grabbing for the last roll of toilet paper she'd taken from the bathroom after she'd run out of tissue. She tore off a section and blew her nose, not caring that her mother would hear. "I'm telling you the truth. It's not about Dr....Dylan. It's about me."

"Okay," Priscilla said slowly.

Gracie ran the heel of her hand against her nose. "Anyway, I'm sick of thinking about my own problems," she said, meaning it. "Tell me...how are you doing. And Dad?"

"We're fine."

She moved the phone to her other ear. "Fine? Define fine, Mom. Did you talk to him?"

Priscilla's voice lowered, making Gracie realize that Consuela was probably still in the same room. "As a matter of fact, I did."

Shock pushed through her malaise. "You did?"

"Yes."

Her heart skipped a beat, dread mixing with hope in her belly. What if she'd been wrong? What if she'd been way off base in advising Priscilla to confront her father? What if two minutes of hastily voiced advice meant the end of her parents' marriage, much as it had Jerry Presser's?

She hardly dared ask. But she couldn't not ask, either. "And?"

"Grace, this is hardly a discussion to have over the phone."

"Right now it's the only place we can have it." Her knuckles hurt from where she was gripping the receiver too tightly. "What happened? Tell me, or else I'm going to ask that you put Consuela on the phone. I'm sure she'll tell me."

Her mother's gasp told her she'd made her point. "Okay, just wait a minute. I'm going to switch phones."

Gracie pushed from the bed and began pacing, mindless of the papers she stepped on, uncaring if she pulled the body of the phone from the bedside table. All she could think about was how readily she had dished out advice, even to her own mother, pretending that a degree in psychology qualified her to interfere in others' lives. Tell them what to do, when she didn't have a clue what to do with her own life.

Some expert she was. If she ever wrote another book, she would title it *How to Royally Mess up Your Life and Everyone's Around You.*

She didn't realize she was holding her breath until her mother finally told Consuela to hang up the extension. "All right. I'm back."

Gracie froze on the top of Chapter Four. "So?"

Priscilla laughed. "I'm in the bedroom. Appropriate place for this conversation, don't you think?"

"Mom," Gracie said.

"Are you sure you're all right, Grace? You sound… stressed."

"Don't change the subject."

"All right then…" she said slowly. "I don't know how to say this but to, well, just say it. Your father and I…we're back to normal."

Gracie's legs gave out from underneath her and she plopped down in the middle of the floor, relief flowing through her so profoundly she could have cried for a reason that had nothing to do with Dylan. "Really?"

"Actually, no," Priscilla said. "I wasn't entirely truthful with you. Things are better than normal. They're…great."

"Oh God, Mom, you don't know how happy I am to hear that." She crossed her legs under her, ignoring that she'd just mangled another chapter of her book. "So tell me…what did he say? What did you say? I want you to share everything."

Priscilla's laugh made her blood surge through her veins in a way it hadn't for days. "I'm not so sure I should be sharing this with you."

Gracie rolled her eyes toward the ceiling. "Oh, fine. Tell

me the problem but don't tell me the solution." She caught a shadow of a smile pulling at her mouth and offered up a silent prayer of thanksgiving to whomever might be listening. "Spill it."

And her mother did.

It turned out that three months ago during a normal checkup, her father had been diagnosed with a prostate problem. A blockage of some sort that his physician was concerned may or may not have been cancer. Of course with some outdated, gallant notion, or perhaps out of sheer fear, he hadn't shared the news with his own wife. Rather, he'd sweated out the three months of tests and examinations until Priscilla confronted him with his distance. As luck would have it, the latest prescription had cleared up the problem and he'd just been given a medical thumbs-up. Which also turned out to be all he needed to try to make up for lost time with his wife.

Priscilla wound down her story and the line finally went silent for the first time in fifteen minutes. Gracie leaned back against the bed, her eyes closed.

Her mother cleared her throat. "So I guess I have you to thank, Gracie. If you hadn't…told me to confront him, I might never have known what happened. He probably just would have come home one day and taken up right where he'd left off and that three months would have been between us forever."

She smiled into the phone, thinking for the first time in days that maybe, just maybe, she wasn't a fraud. Perhaps there was still some good she could do. "I'll send you the bill in the morning."

"You wouldn't dare," her mother exclaimed.

"Don't bet on it."

She got to her feet again, sitting on the edge of the bed. Not lying across it, not listing to the side, but sitting, as if on the verge of doing something else. And it felt good. She began wrapping up the call, telling her mom she didn't know when she would be home, but that it would probably be soon, and that she'd call her the instant she arrived.

She was just about to hang up when her mother said, "Oh, by the way. I read your book."

Gracie nearly dropped the telephone receiver. "What?"

"You heard me, Grace. I read your book."

She glanced around the room where her copy was scattered about the floor in bits and pieces. "And...?"

"And I can't tell you how proud I am of you."

Her heart filled to almost bursting. "Thanks," she whispered. "You have no idea how much I needed to hear that right now."

"Oh, I don't know. Mother's intuition told me it's exactly what you needed to hear. Now come home so we can discuss those areas I disagree with."

Gracie smiled. "Soon, Mom. Very soon."

She slowly replaced the receiver then got up, standing still for a long moment, contemplating the room around her. She knew she still had a long way to go before the world started making complete sense, if it ever did again. And she suspected the ache in her heart for Dylan would never go away. But at least she felt capable of breathing again. Truly breathing.

She picked up the phone again, putting a call in to Rick's answering service for him to contact her as soon as he was able, then placing another order with room service. Suddenly she was starving. Then she hung up, yanked open the curtains and the balcony door beyond. When it didn't emit a loud screeching alarm, she smiled, took a shower and started putting back together the pieces of her book. This time in a different order. And minus a couple of chapters. And as she did so, she couldn't help feeling as if she was reconfiguring the puzzle that she had told Dylan about. That one she had accused him of screwing up.

She paused, holding the papers tightly to her chest as she stared at the phone. For the briefest of moments, she thought about calling him. Letting him know that she'd been wrong.

He hadn't screwed up her life at all. He had merely forced her to take a better, closer look at it. It wasn't his fault that she hadn't liked what she saw.

Her throat grew tight, her heart pounded an erratic rhythm in her chest, and she felt that almost overwhelming physical need for him surge through her veins.

She picked up the phone. But rather than calling San Francisco, she pushed the button for the concierge. "This is Gracie Mattias. Send housekeeping up, please."

Then she turned from the nightstand and the telephone, knowing it wouldn't be fair to call Dylan now. Not to herself, or to him. Because facts were facts, and the overriding fact was she wasn't anywhere near the place she needed to be before she started figuring out more than the immediate future for her personal life.

As for her professional life…well, it was time to start putting the pieces back together. And she would begin that process by having Rick track down Jerry Presser in Orlando and get him some professional counseling. On her dime.

Next, she planned to come up with a proposal for her next book. A book that would nearly completely go against the advice she had given in her last….

16

New York City

THIS WAS JUST TOO WEIRD for words. Six weeks had passed
since Gracie's last visit to the Big Apple, but the snow-
covered streets and bitter cold made it seem like months. She
had changed just as much as the weather since that time she'd
stumbled on those high heels into that radio station where she
officially met Dylan for the first time. Now, dressed in more
casual flat-soled boots, ankle-length black leather skirt and
warm black turtleneck, she felt…older somehow. Correction,
much more mature. And much, much wiser.

Her publisher had gone for her new book proposal with a
considerable increase in advance monies. But that wasn't the
reason she was in New York. She climbed the steep steps to
the midtown church. No. Visiting her publisher and signing
her new contract was something her being there allowed her
to do. She was really there to stand up for her now ex-assistant
Rick Mahoney in his wedding to one spunky PR rep Tanja
Berry. She opened the door to the church and stepped inside,
shivering as she shrugged out of her black leather coat. She
told herself she really wasn't losing an assistant in Rick, she
was gaining a new friend in the shape of Tanja. But she knew
how much she would miss him when he moved to New York
to be with his new wife right after their honeymoon.

She had begun to move down the long aisle, her footsteps
sounding against the smooth marble, when she caught sight
of a familiar someone standing in front of the altar. Her steps
slowed.

Dylan.

Rick had told her he'd be there. That just as she was going to be Rick's best woman, Dylan had agreed to be Tanja's man of honor. Still, no amount of preappearance pep talk could have prepared her for her immediate physical response to him. Despite what had happened in Miami and the time that had passed, she felt desire for him so swift and sure she nearly tripped over her own feet.

He turned, spotting her, and the grin he'd been giving Rick froze.

Oh, God, but he looked better than even her memory of him.

She forced herself to walk the remainder of the way, giving first Rick a hug, then Tanja. Finally she faced Dylan. "Hi," she said, unable to help a smile she feared might swallow her face.

"Hi, yourself." His grin was just as wide. And made her throat go dry.

She forced herself to look at Tanja. "What, no long walk down the aisle? No flower girl? No long, lacy white dress?"

Tanja made a face, nervously smoothing down her trendy champagne-colored suit and shiny vinyl jacket. "It's called compromise."

Rick slid his arms around his wife-to-be's waist. "It's the price I had to pay to get her to agree to marry me in a church."

Tanja playfully elbowed him in the ribs and he feigned injury. "Just wait until you see the price tag on that doozy." She leaned back into him and tilted her dark head back for his kiss.

"Oh, no! Where are the purple spikes?" Gracie asked, staring at the other woman.

Tanja fingered her stylishly short, black hair. "I let them grow out." Her dark eyes twinkled. "Don't tell me you miss them?"

Gracie smiled. "As a matter of fact, I do."

Rick withdrew his arms. "I do, too. But she insists that if

she's going to get this new promotion she's up for, the purple streaks had to go." His grin took on a decidedly wicked quality. "So I had to settle for coloring other areas purple."

Gracie stared at him, mouth agape. "Um, Rick, that comment definitely falls into the 'a little too much information' category."

His chuckle was familiar, reminding her how much she was going to miss hearing it on a daily basis. "What? This from the preeminent Dr. Hottie? I'm disappointed."

Gracie stuck her finger into his chest. "Well, don't be. You never really did catch on that the only one allowed to tell off-color jokes was me."

She realized that during her conversation with the couple, Dylan had taken a noticeable step back. But it didn't stop her from being aware of him with every cell of her body. Or wanting him more than she ever had.

He cleared his throat. "Um, guys?"

They turned around to find the priest had joined them.

They immediately quieted down and settled into position Gracie next to Rick, Dylan next to Tanja.

While the couple exchanged vows, Gracie couldn't help but feel thankful that at least one of the relationships started during the PR tour had withstood the test of time. She looked at the bride and the groom, smiling at the love in their eyes, the passion evident in the way they touched. Her gaze moved past them to Dylan, and an inexplicable lump bunched up in her throat. Too bad another relationship couldn't have weathered the storm.

DYLAN CAUGHT GRACIE STARING at him, her heart so fully in her eyes that he nearly groaned.

There was little consolation in knowing that he'd been right. Knowing that what he'd felt for Gracie then, he still felt for her now. Nor did suspecting she still loved him help matters any, either. The fact remained that she was too stubborn too scared to take it to the next logical step.

And he was too much of a coward to give her the room she needed to grow into the relationship.

He stopped himself from tugging at his tie, the only one of the foursome dressed properly for a wedding. Then again, it depended on your idea of a wedding. While the vows were as binding as any he'd ever witnessed, he didn't think he'd been to a ceremony where neither the bride nor groom's family were present. And Tanja's casual attire, and Rick's tweed sports jacket and jeans, made them look more ready for a day at the mall. Then there was the fact that immediately following the ceremony there was to be no reception, no celebratory meal. No. The couple planned to lock themselves into a suite at Trump Plaza for the weekend, for what basically would constitute their honeymoon.

Dylan rubbed the back of his neck, thinking that Moonbeam and Frank would approve of the unconventional marriage ceremony. The complete opposite of the disapproval he'd suffered through when he'd returned to San Francisco alone and refused to talk about what had happened with Gracie. Not that it mattered. His mother had figured everything out, anyway. She called him one hundred kinds of stupid for being such a slave to convention. And for always needing the type of control over life that no one could ever get.

Not for the first time, he wondered if she was right, if he had been stupid. He'd caught himself pondering that very issue often over the past few weeks. Then he'd remembered the way Gracie had placed the engagement ring back in his hand and told him no and to banish any such thoughts from his mind.

He straightened his suit jacket. Of course, that was easy to do when he was three thousand miles away from her. Standing so close now he could smell her perfume, it was impossible.

Lord, how he wanted her. She looked different, somehow. More sober, composed, and even more unbearably beautiful. He allowed his gaze to devour her from head to flat heel. Despite the obvious external changes, he sensed that under all that clothing, and pulled-back hairstyle, she was still the same passionate, responsive woman who had once driven him nuts between the sheets. And probably would still be doing so had he not essentially given her the ultimatum of marriage or nothing.

Maybe his mother was right. He was a fool.

The priest pronounced the couple husband and wife. But it wasn't that which caught his attention so much as Gracie's burst of clapping, followed by a loud, rafters-echoing whistle as Rick and Tanja kissed. He couldn't help a chuckle.

They all thanked the priest, then hugged, and finally he and Gracie were standing on the front steps of the church alone, watching after the limo he'd hired as part of his wedding gift to the couple.

Gracie tucked her chin into the front of her leather jacket. "Nice touch, the limo."

"Thanks."

After six weeks and countless nights lying wide awake imagining what he might say to her if he had the chance, was that the best he could do? Thanks?

He cleared his throat. "Would you like to get some coffee?"

Her expression told of her surprise as her white breath filled the distance separating them. "Coffee?"

He grinned, gesturing to his right. "There's a place just down the street. Tanja says they have great pastry."

Her smile made him feel like someone had just sucker-punched him in the stomach. "I'd love to…but I can't."

"Oh."

"No. It's not what you're thinking. I have an appointment to meet with my publisher this afternoon."

He should have felt relieved, but he didn't. "That's okay."

"How about later?" she said. "I'm at the Marriott Marquis again. Are you?"

"No. I'm not staying. I'm on the red-eye back to San Francisco."

"Oh."

A taxi pulled up to the curb to let someone out. Dylan looked at Gracie. "Go ahead. I can get the next."

"Are you sure?"

No. He wasn't sure about anything except the almost overwhelming desire to yank her into his arms and find out if she tasted as good as he remembered. To see if she would still melt under one carefully placed touch. To discover if she still wanted him as much as he wanted her.

The taxi driver pressed on the horn, then cracked his window open. "You guys coming, or what?"

Gracie held up a hand to indicate he wait then turned back toward Dylan. "It was...um, great seeing you again."

He nodded, shoving his hands deep into his coat pockets. "You, too."

She began to walk toward the taxi, then moved back to him, giving him a quick kiss on the cheek. She drew back and gave him a more lingering kiss on the cheek. "See you," she said, walking backward and smiling.

He nodded and watched her get into the back of the taxi, standing stiff as a pole as the car pulled away from the curb.

He couldn't be sure how long he stood there, wondering if he would relive this moment for the rest of his life. Pondering what might have happened had he canceled that flight. Told her he still wanted her. Turned his head into her kiss.

Cursing under his breath, he turned in the other direction and began walking away.

GRACIE BLEW INTO THE LOBBY of the Marriott Marquis in Times Square along with a fiendish gust of winter wind. She should be feeling pretty pleased with herself right now. The meeting with her publisher and agent had far surpassed her expectations, the bonuses built into her contract enough to keep her in Victoria's Secret for the rest of her natural life. But throughout the meeting, and the drinks afterward at a swanky restaurant, all she could think about was how Dylan had looked standing outside the church. And how good it had felt to press her lips to his flesh. Even if it was just his cheek.

She looked around the lobby, questioning her decision to stay in the same hotel she'd been at last time merely because she was familiar with it. That was the problem. It was *too* familiar. Everywhere she looked, everywhere she stepped, another memory of Dylan sprang forth to claim her mind and play havoc with her senses.

Shivering off the chill that remained from outside and heading for the elevators, she wondered if it was too late to catch a flight out to Baltimore. She'd stayed overnight so she could shop in the city for the coming holidays, but right now the thought didn't appeal to her in the least.

An elevator dinged open and she stepped into it, smiling at a young couple that hurried in behind her. As she pressed the button for her floor, she couldn't help remembering the time when she and Dylan had been standing in this very elevator. And another young couple, not unlike the one that had entered, had indulged in some very risqué behavior behind them. She recalled the way he had looked, his eyes about ready to pop out of his head. The thought made her smile. As did the memory of telling him he needed a wild turn in the sack.

The smile faded away. She realized now that she'd been playing a wicked game of seduction even then, before she'd made the conscious decision to sleep with him in Chicago. A game that had seriously backfired on her. She'd be well served to remember that.

The elevator opened on her floor and she got out, her leather coat billowing behind her as she made her way down the hallway to her room. She thought about ordering room service, then grimaced, suddenly regretting having turned her agent down for dinner. But all she could think about was escaping any sort of company that would detract from her thoughts of the past. The mistakes she had made. And how seeing Dylan again had moved her to the bottom of her soul.

She fished her card key out from her handbag, wondering how much finagling it would take for Rick to get her on that flight to San Francisco tonight. What was she thinking? Rick was no longer her assistant. Right now he and his new wife were doing all those wonderful things that couples do on their honeymoon.

She worried her bottom lip between her teeth, surprised by how quickly the idea was taking root and how eagerly her mind raced forward with the details. She could pack up her stuff in no time flat, make it out to the airport, and do what she had to do to get on that flight with Dylan.

And after that? What would she do if he rejected her company?

Well, she'd have to do whatever it took to win him over. Because if one thing was becoming abundantly clear, it was that life was oh so much better with him in it.

She fit the card key into the door slot and tried the knob. Nothing. She stared at the little red blinking light and sighed. She would not take this as a sign that she wasn't meant to go to San Francisco. She wouldn't.

And if, when Dylan finally caved in, he asked her to marry him again? What would she do then?

Her palms went instantly sweaty as she tried the card again. This time it worked and she pushed the door inward.

And became instantly aware that she wasn't alone in the room.

Clouds of steam billowed out from the open bathroom doorway directly to her left. Her heart giving a hard triple beat, she stepped a little farther into the room while still managing to hold the door open. It hadn't been so long ago that she didn't remember the fear she'd felt when Jerry Presser had held a gun on her in her room in Miami. It also hadn't been so long ago that she didn't recall how concerned she'd been when Dylan had walked into her room while she was taking a shower on that fateful day. She wasn't about to impede any possible quick escape she needed to make.

But as she peeked around the corner into the misty bathroom, her grip slipped on the door and it slowly slapped shut behind her. Not that she noticed. She was too busy gaping at the man standing buck naked and grinning at her from her shower.

Dylan.

She blinked. Then blinked again, her gaze shifting from his marvelously defined abs, back to his face, then dipped lower again to where lather slid down his stomach, over the soft vee of hair leading to other, more interesting, and completely aroused places.

"Hi," he said, running the soap over his upper arm.

"Hi, yourself," she virtually croaked.

It was then she realized that there were worse things than coming home every night to find this fine, super-sexy specimen hanging out in your shower. To wearing his ring, and occasionally picking up his socks, and perhaps buying him extra pairs of underwear so he wouldn't have to worry about running out.

To hell with underwear...she wanted to keep him exactly like this.

She swallowed hard and allowed her purse to slide from her arm to the floor, her coat following after it. Hopping on first one foot, then the next, she yanked off her boots, and only had her leather skirt half off when she climbed into that tub and launched a full-scale assault on his mouth and body, hungrily trying to make up for the past six weeks in two minutes flat.

His telltale groan merely fed the flames licking at her. She lifted her arms, helping him take off her soaked sweater and grasping his head when he lowered his mouth to her nipples, pulling at each like they were the answer to world hunger.

"God, I've missed you," he whispered huskily, grinding his erection against her soft flesh.

"Have you?" she murmured between openmouthed kisses and insatiable flicks of her tongue.

He slid his hand to her bare bottom and pressed her farther against his steel-hard arousal. "Can't you tell?"

She moaned, wanting him, needing to feel him inside her this instant. Now. Her every muscle crying for a release she now knew only he could give her. She reached for his erection, intent on driving it home in her tight, wet and waiting flesh. He gently caught her wrist, holding her there, his other hand sliding up the line of her jaw and into her damp hair. She blinked to stare at him through the droplets falling from the showerhead. The weighty shadow in his eyes made her catch her breath. She braced herself. Ready for him to propose again. Ready for him to make at least a token argument so she could tell him yes.

"Gracie...I've been a fool. An idiot. So utterly stupid I don't know how I lived with myself without you."

She eagerly licked the moisture from her lips. She needed to hear the words. But right now she needed to make love to him more.

He tightened his grip, holding her in place.

"We don't have to get married in order for us to be together. I'll accept any conditions you lay down...just so long as you agree to reenter my life...my bed."

She squinted at him, surprised at the smile tugging at her lips. "Really?"

He kissed her deeply. "Really." He ran his thumb over her bottom lip. "I do have to warn you, however, that I probably will never give up trying to talk you into marrying me. It's just something I have to do—"

She clamped her free hand over his mouth. "I know. It's who you are." She slowly slid her fingers over his jaw, down the side of his neck, then entangled them in the wet hair sprinkling his chest. How easy it would be to leave things at that. Her body was screaming for release. Her heart was pumping an erratic rhythm in her chest. But as desperately as she wanted him physically, she needed to set things straight between them. Needed to tell him of the decision she'd come to.

When she wasn't looking, he'd dropped his hands to her thighs and begun parting her. She caught her breath...and his wrists. "Wait."

He looked at her, confusion clearly written across his striking face.

She briefly bit her bottom lip, then said softly, "I, um, just wanted to tell you that I've been just as big a fool as you've been. Bigger, even.'' She kissed him, then forced herself to pull away again. "That speech I gave in Miami...I was wrong.''

She felt his heartbeat speed up beneath her hand.

"I...blamed you for screwing up my life. When the truth is...you gave me life. You opened my eyes, challenged my beliefs, made me see that just because you don't know the outcome, what will happen years, perhaps decades down the road, that you can't rule out doing something now.''

His brows drew together, as if trying to work out what she was saying but not trusting himself to believe it.

She laughed nervously, focusing her gaze on his chest and the water that streamed down the tantalizing muscles outlined there.

"So...you know that question that you asked...and that I answered?'' Her breath hitched. "Well, if the question still stands, I'm changing my answer. To yes.''

His groan and ardent kisses was all the answer she needed. She finally gave herself over to the torrent of emotion and need whipping through her, allowing him to back her against the wall of the shower, not relaxing until he thrust into her to the hilt. Then a whole different type of tension began to spiral within her. She grasped his face in her hands and kissed him, and kissed him, and kissed him again.

He met her kiss for kiss, the passion on his face undeniable, the love in his eyes overwhelming. "Say it. Say 'I love you,' Gracie.''

She smiled against his mouth. "I love you...Gracie.'' She laughed at his surprised expression. Then she opened herself to the power surging through her, and willingly and wholeheartedly whispered, "I love you, Dr. Dylan Fairbanks. I love you...I love you...I love you.''

Epilogue

Chicago Suburbs
Six months later

"YOU CAN'T TELL HER to do that!"

Gracie snapped upright from where she had the back of Dylan's head cradled between her unfortunately clothed thighs in their shared home office. But neither one of them were at their desks. Instead, her contemporary corner of the room with its yellow walls and purple furniture stood abandoned, as did his corner with its dark green walls and heavy antique desk and bookcases. An hour before, they'd both wandered to the neutral territory carefully mapped out between the two spaces, Gracie sitting on the couch, Dylan on the floor in front of her with his laptop open on the coffee table.

He stopped typing in the middle of his weekly column. This week's question came from a woman in Oklahoma who was "seriously attracted"—her words—to a guy who worked at the same company she did, but in a different department, and wanted advice on how to approach him.

Dylan had just told her to seek out Dr. Gracie Mattias-Fairbanks's first book and check out Chapter Five on sexual safaris.

"Why can't I tell her to do that?" he asked, rubbing his head against where her right thigh was left bare by her cargo shorts.

"Because in my second book, I tell readers to disregard that advice."

He frowned up at her. "You do?"

She thwapped his shoulder. "You know I do."

His grin touched her in places his hands could not. And that was saying a whole hell of a lot, because he touched her everywhere. All the time. Even with both sets of their parents in the house.

Realizing she'd forgotten about Priscilla and Richard and Moonbeam and Frank, she glanced toward the double balcony doors overlooking the garden of their suburban Chicago ranch-style home, the location a compromise that put them more or less equally apart from their families. Besides, there was something…right about ending up in the place where they had first made love.

Gracie bit her lip, wondering how the two couples were faring. It was the first time in five days that they'd left them alone together. This morning she and Dylan had come to the mutual conclusion that they couldn't just go on playing mediators forever. And secretly shared their regret at having invited the couples to stay at their place for a full two weeks. Next time, they agreed, no longer than three days. Aside from their constantly having to be inventive in order to find a few important, hot moments alone together, they were afraid that if the couples didn't kill each other, they would give in and kill them all.

Dylan looked up at her. "What's the matter?"

She slowly shook her head. "I don't know. It's…too quiet out there." She ran her fingers through his hair. "You don't think they've drowned each other in the pool, do you?"

He ran his tongue along her upper thigh and dipped it under her cargo pants, causing her to gasp. She pulled his head away with a shaky jerk. "I'm serious."

He grinned wickedly up at her. "So am I."

Removing her hands from his hair, she got up from the couch and stepped toward the balcony doors. And nearly fell on her bottom from the shock of what she saw. "Oh, God, no!"

Dylan grimaced at her from where he'd resumed typing. "What is it?"

She urgently motioned for him to get over there. "Oh, Dylan, you've got to stop them before my parents go into cardiac arrest."

He was at her side in a blink. They stared out, wide-eyed, at Moonbeam and Frank, who had decided that their nice, modest neighborhood needed to be instructed in the finer points of nudism.

Gracie moved to yank open the balcony door, but Dylan caught her hand.

"What are you doing? I've got to stop them before somebody calls the cops."

"That's what the privacy fence is for, Gracie." He placed her hand against his growing erection. "Remember?"

"But my parents—"

"Are fine," he interrupted, groaning when she curved her fingers as far as she could around his hardening shaft. "Look."

Gracie did and thought she was the one at risk of having a heart attack. While her father sat at the patio table reading the *Wall Street Journal,* her mother was...oh my God, she wasn't!

A few hard blinks and a swallow later told her she was.

Priscilla Mattias had just dropped her robe, indulging in a bit of "when in Rome" behavior.

Gracie cringed and turned to press her face into the front of Dylan's oxford shirt. "Please tell me she just didn't—"

"Get naked? Sorry, I can't."

His chuckle vibrated her face.

"You know what this means, don't you?" he murmured, running his hands down her back to her bottom and pressing her boldly against him.

"That we'll probably have to have all our parents committed?"

"No. It means we have the house to ourselves for a few precious minutes."

She jerked to look up at him, flashing him a wicked smile. "How stupid of me...."

He swept her up into her arms and threw her to the couch, then followed after her. Pushing her shirt up and claiming a straining nipple through her bra, he asked huskily, "So...where, exactly, were we on that debate on children?"

She hummed, absently making sure they couldn't be seen over the side of the couch from outside, then undoing his zipper. "Let's see...one child, I think. In five years."

He sank deeply into her hungry flesh. She caught her breath and grasped his tight rear end, pulling him closer. When she felt him hesitate, she blinked up at him. "What?"

He grinned and thrust again. "Oh, I don't know. I was just—" he slowly pulled out and thrust again, sending her senses spiraling "—wondering what it would take to change that to two kids in three years."

She wrapped her legs around his hips, arching her back when he blessedly thrust into her again. "A miracle," she said.

He worked a hand between them and pressed his thumb against her hypersensitive bud, nearly toppling her over the edge even as he thrust again. "Let's see what I can do...."

*H*ugh Blake,
soon to become stepfather to
the Maitland clan, has produced three
high-performing offspring of his own. But
at the rate they're going, they're never going to
make him a grandpa!

There's *Suzanne*, a work-obsessed CEO whose Christmas spirit
could use a little topping up....

And *Thomas*, a lawyer whose ability to hold on to the woman
he loves is evaporating by the minute....

And *Diane*, a teacher so dedicated to her teenage students she
hasn't noticed she's put her own life on hold.

But there's a Christmas wake-up call in store
for the Blake siblings. Love *and* Christmas miracles
are in store for all three!

Maitland Maternity Christmas

A collection from three of Harlequin's favorite authors

Muriel Jensen
Judy Christenberry
&Tina Leonard

Look for it in November 2001.

Celebrate the season with

Midnight Clear

A holiday anthology featuring
a classic Christmas story from
New York Times bestselling author

Debbie Macomber

Plus a brand-new *Morgan's Mercenaries* story
from *USA Today* bestselling author

Lindsay McKenna

And a brand-new *Twins on the Doorstep* story
from national bestselling author

Stella Bagwell

Available at your favorite retail outlets in November 2001!

Silhouette®

Where love comes alive™

*Together for the first time
in one Collector's Edition!*

New York Times bestselling authors

Barbara Delinsky

Catherine Coulter

Linda Howard

Forever Yours

**A special trade-size volume containing three
complete novels that showcase the passion,
imagination and stunning power that these
talented authors are famous for.**

Coming to your favorite retail outlet in December 2001.

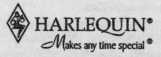

HARLEQUIN®
Makes any time special ®

CALL THE ONES YOU LOVE OVER THE HOLIDAYS!

Save $25 off future book purchases when you buy any four Harlequin® or Silhouette® books in October, November and December 2001,

PLUS

receive a phone card good for 15 minutes of long-distance calls to anyone you want in North America!

WHAT AN INCREDIBLE DEAL!

Just fill out this form and attach 4 proofs of purchase (cash register receipts) from October, November and December 2001 books, and Harlequin Books will send you a coupon booklet worth a total savings of $25 off future purchases of Harlequin® and Silhouette® books, AND a 15-minute phone card to call the ones you love, anywhere in North America.

Please send this form, along with your cash register receipts as proofs of purchase, to:
In the USA: Harlequin Books, P.O. Box 9057, Buffalo, NY 14269-9057
In Canada: Harlequin Books, P.O. Box 622, Fort Erie, Ontario L2A 5X3
Cash register receipts must be dated no later than December 31, 2001.
Limit of 1 coupon booklet and phone card per household.
Please allow 4-6 weeks for delivery.

I accept your offer! Please send me my coupon booklet and a 15-minute phone card:

Name: _____

Address: _____ City: _____

State/Prov.: _____ Zip/Postal Code: _____

Account Number (if available): _____

---

097 KJB DAGL
PHQ4012

Harlequin Romance®
Love affairs that last a lifetime.

HARLEQUIN *Presents*
Seduction and passion guaranteed.

Harlequin® Historical
Historical Romantic Adventure.

HARLEQUIN® *Temptation.*
Sassy, sexy, seductive!

HARLEQUIN *SuperRomance*
Emotional, exciting, unexpected.

HARLEQUIN® *American Romance®*
Heart, home & happiness.

HARLEQUIN® *Duets™*
Romantic comedy.

HARLEQUIN® INTRIGUE®
Breathtaking romantic suspense.

HARLEQUIN® *Blaze™*
Red-Hot Reads.

HARLEQUIN®
Makes any time special®

Visit us at www.eHarlequin.com   HSERIES01

Look to the stars
for love and romance
with bestselling authors

JUDITH ARNOLD
KATE HOFFMANN
and GINA WILKINS
in

WRITTEN
IN THE
STARS

Experience the joy of
three women who dare to
make their wishes for love
and happiness come true in
this *brand-new* collection
from Harlequin!

Available in December 2001
at your favorite retail outlet.

HARLEQUIN®
Makes any time special®

ADDED BONUS:
As a special gift to our readers, a 30-page 2002
Love Guide will be included in this collection!

Visit us at www.eHarlequin.com

PHWS